"The chemistry between L...
The end left me dying for more!"

—L. Wilder, Author of *Combust*

UNTO OBLIVION

Nurse Leila Matthews has seen it all, or so she thought until this morning. Into the chaos of her trauma ward walked a man more intense than anything she has ever known. His smile tore away all her defenses, and his kiss ignited flames damped for far too long—and a knowledge that such dangerous ripples are only the beginning.

Brody Davis is anything but safe. Wealthy, handsome, and unrepentantly single, the billionaire's first priority is himself...and the pleasure of every woman he's sure to leave. Yet his best friend's baby sister is temptation itself. If any female could make him stay, it would be Leila, whose sweet lips and sweeter flesh push him to be better than he believes he can. He desires a quick conquest. The battle for Leila's heart is yet to be fought. And he is not the only combatant.

PUSHED

A. F. Crowell

BOOK ONE IN THE TORN SERIES

www.BOROUGHSPUBLISHINGGROUP.com

PUSHED

ISBN 978-1-942886-73-0

To Mark, James & Chase

Thank you for supporting this crazy dream of mine. Love y'all!

ACKNOWLEDGMENTS

Wow, where do I begin?

First I need to thank my husband Mark and my boys. Thanks for being patient while I hid in the bedroom, stole the couch in the living room, and worked countless hours on this book. I hope that all of the quick dinners will be worth it. I love y'all to the moon and back!!!!

To Barb and Lois, the two best friends a girl could ask for. Thank you both for reading the first few chapters and encouraging me to keep writing. Lois, girl, I don't know how I would have gotten through this without bouncing ideas off of you and using you as my sounding board.

And to my Momma... Are there even words?! Probably not, but I'm going to try. Thank you for the countless emails and Facebook posts about writing your own books. Thank you for being my Beta reader. I appreciate you asking about the progress without pushing. Thank you for believing in me and supporting this dream, a dream I never knew I had or even wanted. Oh, and for reading *50* first. LOL!

Thank you to Boroughs Publishing Group for taking a chance on me. And to poor Michelle, my amazing editor. I swear I will get better as I go.

And to anyone who may read this, thank you, too. I never thought in a million years that I would write a book, but throughout the creative process I discovered that I really enjoy it—even if the characters don't listen and hijack the story!

Thank you!

CONTENTS

PUSHED

Chapter One

Leila

The ER was relatively quiet for a Friday at 4:45 a.m., especially since it had been raining for the better part of the humid summer night. I was a four-year veteran of the Shock Trauma Center at the Medical University of South Carolina in Charleston. Over the years I have seen it all, so nothing surprised or rattled me anymore.

Well, nothing until this Friday morning.

I was changing my scrub top for the first time that shift when a call came in from paramedics in route. I caught only the last few words, *"GSW to the chest with massive blood loss, five minutes out."*

Adrenaline started to pump through my veins, as it did every time they had a ballistics trauma in route. In the back of my mind, I cursed myself for being excited at someone else's horrible misfortune. *But this is my job and I'm damn good at it.* My best friend, partner in crime and fellow trauma RN, Barb Kelly, walked up to me as I was entering the locker room.

"Hey Lei, did you hear there is a GSW in route?" she asked with a little too much enthusiasm.

"Yeah, I was just gonna change really quick, it's still five minutes out. My last case was this huge biker with a superficial laceration and damn if he wasn't a big baby. The guy jumped at the sight of the lidocaine and knocked over the Betadine, which of course spilled all over me." Pulling the wet scrub top over my head, I tossed it in my locker.

Barb glanced over her shoulder, heading to the bathroom. "See ya in there. Oh hey, did they announce which trauma room they are putting him in?"

Talking through fabric as I pulled on a clean ceil blue scrub top, I told her, "Nah, I wasn't really paying too much attention. All I heard was GSW and I knew I had to change quickly so I could be the first one in there and beat you. I haven't had my adrenaline fix tonight. And before you ask, no, the big biker baby does *not* count." I stuck my tongue out at her with a giggle.

Barb chuckled and rolled her eyes as she closed the door to the bathroom. "Well, let me know which room. There is enough to go around."

I shook my head and started out the locker room door back to the pit to see where the charge nurse had assigned the incoming trauma. On the way down the hall, the call came overhead, *"Incoming GSW two minutes out trauma three."*

Damn, that was on the other side of the ER.

"Well, there is no way in hell I am running down the hall in my Danskos," I muttered under my breath. The last thing I needed to do was the Dansko roll on the way to the only really good trauma of the night. They are great shoes if you're on your feet for twelve hours at a time, but definitely not for running. I picked up the pace, careful not to fall, but enough to beat Barb there. That'll teach her to stop to pee.

I reached trauma three with time to spare and went about setting up the room just so. Then I gowned up, got on my gloves and ear loop mask, then put on a pair of glasses. Ten hours into my last twelve-hour shift for a week and this case was probably going to take me right to the end of shift.

The overhead speaker called out again, *"Leila Matthews please call three-four-seven-six."*

UGH. Who the hell wanted me right now?

I was on my way to the nurse's station to answer the page, when I heard the paramedics calling out vitals and running down the hall with the trauma. As I rounded the corner back into the trauma corridor, I saw way too many cops for a single GSW.

My heart started pounding as it always did when I saw that many cops in the ER clumped together; it meant the GSW was an officer.

Silently, I said a prayer for the fallen officer. As I approached the room and pushed my way through the army of men, I could hear Dr. Miller hollering out orders.

"Page the trauma surgeon on call STAT. And call the OR and get a room ready now!"

Chapter Two

Leila

I made my way into trauma three to see Mary and Derrick rushing around working on the patient. I ran straight to the phone on the wall and paged Dr. Drake Thomas to the ER. I called up to the OR and had them start prepping a room the way Drake required for GSWs. As I turned back around, my whole world stopped and the bottom dropped out.

No way. This couldn't be happening. I rushed to the side of the stretcher and gasped in horror. "Drew, oh my God, Drew. Talk to me Drew, can you hear me?"

Mary looked up at me. "Leila, what the hell? Do you know this officer?"

Tears were streaking down my face. "This is my brother. Drew." Turning my attention back to him, I grabbed his hand. "Drew, can you hear me? Please open your eyes."

Derrick came around the stretcher, grabbed me and tried to pull me back, but I fought out of his grasp.

"Leila, you can't stay in here, you know this. He's your brother. You've gotta step aside. Let us help him. We've got this. You know we'll do everything we can to save him, but you gotta go."

Turning around, Derrick got the attention of one of the SWAT officers that came in with Drew. "Hey man, can ya please get her out of here, she doesn't need to see this."

Jasper Smith, sergeant of the narcotics unit, stepped forward and scooped me up in a hug, and guided me to the glass front door that was swung wide-open. "Leila, I tried to reach you in route before we got here. I didn't want you finding out like this."

Jasper was a fifteen-year veteran of the North Charleston Police Department and had kept an eye out for Drew over the last ten years. Jasper had been Drew's sergeant when he started with NCPD, at the ripe old age of twenty-one. Drew eventually moved out of Narcotics to the K-9 unit and now onto the SWAT team, but they stayed close. Jasper and his wife, Donna, had Drew and I over for many Sunday dinners. They didn't have any children of their own. So after Mom died, they sort of became our surrogate parents.

I took a deep breath to try to regain my composure, but failed miserably and ended up rattling off questions like an interrogator. "Jasper, what the hell happened? How did this happen? I talked to Drew before my shift and he said it was gonna be a quiet night. Y'all only had one warrant to serve and it would be a piece of cake." Fisting Jasper's shirt, I cried, "How'd he get shot?"

Standing back, Jasper scrubbed his hand down his face. "We got shitty intel and…I don't know. It's like they knew we were comin' or somethin'. We always hit these houses at crazy hours, when most people are sleeping, so we've got the element of surprise. But these fuckers were waitin' in the house for us."

Shaking my head, I couldn't process what he was saying. "I have to find out what's going on with Drew." I turned and stalked back toward trauma three and was met just outside of the door by Barb.

"Oh no, don't tell me I missed all of the fun. The patient didn't come in DOA did he?" Barb joked, and then stopped. "Wait. Leila, what the hell is going on? Why are you out here?"

"Barb, you have to get in there. You have to help him," I demanded.

"Leila, you aren't makin' any sense. What're you talkin' about? Help who? Why aren't you in there?" Barb started to rush down the hall, getting closer to the room.

"It's Drew. Drew is the GSW. Oh God, Barb, it's bad. It's so bad. Please. You've gotta get in there," I pleaded with her.

Barb stopped short of the doors, turned back to me to say, "I promise, I'll do everything I can," then sprinted into the room.

"Barb, wait. I want an…update." But it was too late, the door was closed and the curtain drawn. Now I had to wait, something I didn't do well under ordinary circumstances. Being on this side of the door was a horror I had never contemplated.

Pacing the corridor, I thought of the times I came out here myself telling patients' families to have a seat and someone would be out shortly with an update. Heaven help the person that tried to say that to me right now. Chances were good I'd punch them in the throat if they did. I really didn't know the extent of Drew's injuries, but I knew enough to surmise they were bad. Really bad.

Standing across the hall from Drew's room, I shed my gear, then leaned back against the wall and slid down until I clutched my knees to my chest. Dear God. This was *not* happening.

Our father walked out on us when I was nine years old, then my mom was killed in a drunk driving accident two weeks before my eighteenth birthday. There was no way God would be cruel enough to take Drew from me too. Silently, I prayed to the heavens above not to take the only family I had left. Drew wasn't just my brother, he's my rock. He has always been there for me, even when I didn't want him to be.

Pulled from my thoughts as a strong, hand landed on my shoulder, I looked up from my not so comfy spot on the floor to see Bobby Gray, Drew's best friend and partner. He held out a calloused hand to help me up from the floor.

Wrapping his strong tatted arms around me, he pulled me into a tight hug and whispered, "I am so sorry Lei. What can I do?"

Tears threatened yet again, but I pushed them down. "There's nothin' we can do. They won't let me in there with him. They haven't even come out to tell me anythin'. I don't know what to do right now…damn it. Please tell me y'all got the asshole who did this."

"Yeah, we did babe. Drew actually got him. Clean shot right between the eyes. Dead before his sorry piece of shit body hit the floor." Whispering so quietly I could just barely hear him, Bobby added, "'Tween me and you, I put another one in 'em just for good measure. Seems like he deserved it."

Bobby released me just as the curtain and door to Drew's room flew open. Barb was perched on top of Drew, counting out chest compressions as they ran down the hall toward the elevators that went up to the OR. Dr. Miller nodded once, signaling me to walk with him.

"Leila, quickly. We're lookin' at a single GSW, left chest with hemothorax. We got a chest tube in and are movin' to the OR. I'm not gonna lie, it's bad, but we've seen worse cases come in and walk out. Drake's on and Barb said she is staying with him. I'm gonna go up and assist. And before you ask, he's not regained consciousness. I'll send you a text in a while to update you," he said hastily looking back toward me while still moving toward the elevator.

In the blink of an eye, he was gone and my heart sunk. Although I was surrounded by a truckload of officers I considered friends, I felt hopelessly alone.

I couldn't lose my brother.

Mustering courage I didn't feel, I gestured to the crowd. "Hey, y'all don't need to sit around here and wait. I'll tell Bobby as soon as I have an update. Ya know, it's probably gonna be hours before Drew comes out of surgery and the waiting room up there isn't very big. Go on home. Bobby'll send out a text as soon as we know more."

Heads nodded in agreement and after a few mumbles, the SWAT guys slowly filed out of the corridor. Everyone left, except for the two who I knew wouldn't budge. Bobby and Jasper. They were family.

Jasper walked over, draped his arm around my shoulders and pulled me toward the elevator. "He's gonna be okay sweet pea."

Bobby shook hands with the last few guys as they were leaving then turned to follow us up to the waiting room to wait for news about Drew.

Chapter Three

Leila

More than two and a half hours had passed, and several of the nurses and techs from the ER stopped by to ask about Drew. I must have heard a half dozen times that I needed to go downstairs and take a break or go get something to eat. Politely, I shook my head and told every one of them I would not leave until I knew Drew was okay.

After I had paced the same pattern around the chairs in the waiting room for what seemed like the hundredth time, I heard a smooth, deep voice ask about Drew. I turned toward the information desk, set just inside of the surgical waiting room, to see a man I'd never met. He was dressed in a sharp, custom-tailored suit. Cautiously, I moved toward the desk. When he turned to face me, I stopped dead in my tracks.

Holy. Shit. He was fucking hot with a capital H.

A face defined by a strong, chiseled jaw, he had sensual, full lips and dark unruly waves adorned his head. At least six-two, maybe even three, he was a hell of a lot taller than my five-foot-three-inch frame. He sported a subtle scruff that screamed sex god, and had piercing baby blues to complete the devastating package. Then, as if all that wasn't enough, he gave me a rock star smile when I started toward him.

That smile could melt the panties off a lesbian.

Shit. I could feel all of the blood rushing to my face. Oh great, now *would* be the time my body betrayed my completely inappropriate lustful and wicked thoughts. There were several very bad things I wanted to do to Mr. Blue Eyes and a few he could do to me.

Damn it Leila! Stop drooling over the man candy. Your brother is fighting for his life.

"I'm sorry, I couldn't help overhear you ask about Drew Matthews. Who are you?" I tilted my head.

Glancing down at my badge, Blue Eyes smiled softly and held out his hand. "Hi. I'm Brody. Brody Davis. You must be Drew's baby sister, Leila."

I hesitated before shaking his large, beautifully manicured hand. Squinting, thinking back to a few of Drew's comments over the years, I remembered hearing the name Brody on several occasions. "Yeah, I'm Drew's sister. How'd you know Drew was here?"

Brody stared down at me. "I happened to be watching the news while running at the gym. It said that Drew was shot while serving a narcotics warrant with SWAT this morning. I'm terribly sorry we're meeting under these circumstances."

Finally releasing my hand, he stepped back then undid the button holding his sleek, black, designer suit jacket closed. "How is he? I mean, do you have any idea how it's going in there? Have they said anything?" I could hear warmth and compassion in his questions.

Touched by his obvious concern, I answered honestly. "It's really bad. He has a hemothorax and they put in a chest tube. A friend of mine, Drake Thomas, the surgeon working on Drew, is the best. My BFF, Barb, is the RN who went up from the ER with him. Someone's supposed to text me, but I still haven't heard anything." I stopped abruptly and pinched my nose between my thumb and middle finger. "Oh God, listen to me ramblin' on. You must think I'm crazy."

Half smiling, Brody reached out and rubbed his hand down my right shoulder. "No, I don't think you're crazy. I do, however, think you're stressed and probably need to sit down and take a deep breath."

"Why does everyone keep saying that? I'm fine. I don't want to sit down. I don't want to take a deep breath. I don't want coffee or something to eat. I just want to know what's going on with my brother. Is that too much to ask?" I shouted, flailing my arms about like a damn lunatic.

As soon as the words left my mouth, I was so embarrassed I dropped down to one of the chairs and buried my face in my hands. "Oh shit. Brody, I'm so sorry. I didn't mean to totally flip out on you. It's just I am so…" Scared. But no way am I admitting that to anyone. "…worried. I didn't mean to take it out on you. Everyone keeps tellin' me to go eat, or go take a walk or a nap."

"I think you're entitled to have a small meltdown, all things considered. If you weren't a little frazzled I'd be worried." He took the seat next to mine. "Would you mind if I waited here with you for a while?"

"Of course not, please feel free. And don't take it personally if I get up and start pacin'. I just can't seem to make myself relax."

At that moment, as I took my phone out of the front pocket of my scrubs, the waiting room door opened and in walked Drake. The look on his face did not help the uneasy tension that had settled in my gut. Brody stood up beside me; without realizing it, I reached for Brody's hand. Jasper and Bobby crossed the waiting room in a flash to hear the news.

"Hey Lei." Drake approached and pulled me close, kissing the top of my head before releasing me. Looking down, silently he sought permission to speak freely.

"Hey Drake." Introducing the men, I indicated, "This is Brody, a friend of Drew's," tipping my head toward Bobby and Jasper, "and Bobby and Jasper work with Drew. It's okay, you can talk in front of them."

Drake nodded. "We were able to get the bleeding under control and he's stable, for now. But I wasn't able to get the bullet out. There was just too much blood in the field to visualize it when we first got in there. My main focus was to repair all the damage and stopping the bleed. I'm gonna send Drew down for a CT, to get a better idea of where the bullet is. We'll probably have to take him back in to remove it in a day or two." Drake paused and pulled me to the side. "After CT, he'll be moved up to ICU. You should probably go get something to eat and take a break for a while. I know you worked downstairs all last night. You have to be exhausted."

"I'll be okay. I just wanna see Drew," I pleaded. "Just for a minute."

"Leila, you know it's gonna be a few more hours before he's settled. He's gotta be moved from recovery to CT, then up to ICU. Let us take care of him. I know that's especially hard for you to do." He squeezed my hand. "Listen you can't help him if you're run down."

"I have to agree with him sweetheart." Jasper stepped forward. "You need to recharge your batteries. Go home, change, eat and then you can come back."

Bobby's phone started to ring. "Gray…. I'm still at the hospital with Drew's sister. Can't it wait? I understand that IAB wants their statement. You can't hold them off for an hour or two? No, Sergeant, I get it. I'll be there in ten." Ending the call, Bobby walked back over to us. "Lei, I'm sorry. I have to go to the station. You'll call me if anything changes?"

"Of course."

"Jasper, any chance you're goin' to the station? I rode in with Drew in the ambulance," Bobby asked after hugging me goodbye.

"Yeah, I have to drive past there, I can drop you off. Leila, do you want me to run you to your place after I drop Gray off?"

Brody was only three feet away and came over. "I can take Leila." he turned to me. "Why don't you let me take you to get a quick bite, then I'll bring you right back. Promise."

I started to disagree when Drake chimed in. "Good idea. Leila let Brody take you to get somethin' to eat. He can even stop by your house and you can take a quick shower, change clothes and deal with Ruger."

I sighed, signaling my annoyance, knowing I wasn't going to win this fight. Especially not with Drake, who was just about as stubborn as I was.

Drake waved me off. "I can tell you're gonna be a brat about this, but stop your poutin' and let Brody take you out of here for a little while. I'd do it myself, but I'm on call for another six hours." Drake looked down at his watch. "Okay, it's almost eight a.m. now and I am officially banning you from ICU until eleven a.m. And before you even think about callin' anyone who you might know up there, I will be callin' in favors of my own just to keep you out."

With a lazy smile Drake, pulled me into a hug. "Drew is gonna need for you to be at the top of your game and that means takin' care of yourself."

As a nurse, I knew what I needed to do, but as a little sister, I was terrified of losing my brother. Huffing once, I finally gave in.

"Okay, okay I'll leave…for a little while, but I'll be back at eleven and I *will* see my brother." Turning to Brody. "I have to run down to the ER locker room and grab my stuff. Can I meet ya down at the entrance to the ER?"

Brody grinned and nodded. "Of course, I'll pull my car around and meet you outside."

Brody turned on his heel, tucked his hands into his pockets and headed toward the elevators. I couldn't help but watch as he exited the room. Everything about him captured and piqued my interest. I was starting to understand why I had only heard stories about this handsome stranger and why Drew kept him away. Brody was the type of guy I didn't need in my life, if the stories Drew shared were true. I wasn't looking to get married any time soon, but I wasn't about a few random hook ups either. The vibe coming from Brody screamed player with no remorse.

Right then and there, I resolved to just enjoy the view.

Chapter Four

Leila

I entered the locker room, which, thankfully, was empty. I was not in the mood to answer any questions or have to put on a fake-ass smile. I changed out of my scrubs and threw on a pair of khaki shorts and plain white ribbed tank top. I shoved my Danskos in the locker, pulled out my favorite tan flip-flops and grabbed my striped handbag. Even at 8:00 in the morning, Charleston was hot. According to the weather app on my phone, it was already eighty-seven degrees, but with the humidity it felt more like Hell.

I left the locker room and made a beeline for the exit. As the doors slid open, I was hit with a blast of hot, muggy air and the sight of Brody on his phone. It had stopped raining, but the humidity was off the charts ridiculous. He was leaning against a palladium silver GL550 Mercedes SUV and hadn't noticed me yet, so I took the opportunity to gawk at this magnificent man. Damn, he really was gorgeous. The slight breeze caught his thick, chocolate brown locks, whipping them across his brow. Turning into the wind, he saw me as I stood near the ER doors. He ended the call as I approached and opened the passenger door with a devilish grin.

"So what would you like to do first? Breakfast or shower?" He paused and a flash of panic zinged through his sapphire eyes. "Sorry, that didn't come out right. I mean, do you want to get something to eat or go to your house so you can shower and change clothes."

"Shower. I live over on East Bay."

I felt the heat rise to my cheeks as I imagined Brody sneaking into my shower, pushing me up against the cold travertine and glass tiles, taking my mouth, and then moving slowing down my neck to my breasts. I was shaken from my little fantasy as we neared my condo. I pointed out a spot to park that was within walking distance.

*****

Brody

I was out of the SUV and opening her door before she could even pick up her handbag. I held out my hand to assist her from the car. The electricity that slid between us caught me completely off guard. I dropped her hand like it was on fire.

Thankfully, Leila didn't seem to notice. I wasn't sure why it freaked me out as much as it did, but I was trying to ignore the impulse to hop back in the car and haul ass out of there. I had to push my own self-preservation aside and remember Leila needed me. Drew needed me. Drew is one of my only true friends, I couldn't let him down. Drew always talked about how much he loved his little sister and how she depended on him.

Leila unlocked the front door to her condo and ushered me through into the living room. From another room I heard a deep, daunting barking. *Hmm, she must have a dog and from the sounds of it, a rather large one.*

As Leila put her purse down on the beige leather sectional, she turned to me. "Can I get you something to drink?"

"Coffee or a bottle of water would be great, if you have it," I replied, still feeling like I needed to get away from her.

"I've got bottled water in the fridge. Make yourself at home. I'll try to hurry, I just need to let Ruger into the back." She tossed the TV remote to me. "All the ESPNs start somewhere in the two hundreds." She turned to the wrought iron staircase and made it up three steps before my voice stopped her in her tracks.

"What makes you think I want to watch ESPN? What if I wanted to watch CNN or something a little more stimulating?"

*****

Leila
Oh, Mr. Davis. I know the game you're playing and I won't be falling prey.

"I'm sure you'll find somethin' to amuse yourself with. I'll be back in a few." I let Ruger, my 100-pound German shepherd, out of his crate in the downstairs guest room and opened the door to the small fenced area I called a backyard. It was the size of my bedroom, but it worked when I didn't have time to walk him. After allowing him to take care of business, I sat on the floor by his crate for a few minutes to give him some loving.

"I know buddy, I hate to put you right back in there but I don't know when I will be home and I don't need you cleaning out the fridge again. Your vet is already fussin' at me about your weight." I opened the crate door and he stalked in. "There's a good boy. I'll see you soon." I closed and locked crate, knowing we didn't have time to introduce Brody to Ruger. If I just let him roam the house like normal, chances are Brody would be pinned up against the front door by his throat or crotch. Ruger retired from the NCPD K-9 force and now was exceedingly protective of me.

I climbed the rest of the stairs to the master bedroom and shut the door. Quickly, I stripped my clothes off and started toward the bathroom, stopping to turn on the stereo. No matter how bad my day was, I always found music to help me weather the storm and today's storm was a hurricane.

Looking through the iPod playlist, I finally settled on a little Counting Crows "Raining in Baltimore." Fitting song, it matched my sorrowful mood. I reached in and turned the shower on until the water was steaming up the glass shower door. Tossing fresh towels over the towel bar, I stepped into the shower and let the hot water sluice over my face and down my body. A quick shampoo, then I scrubbed my body with the coconut lime bodywash. As I rinsed the conditioner from my hair, the weight of the day came crashing down on top of me. Falling to my knees, the storm clouds broke loose and, as I knelt on the shower floor, I sobbed uncontrollably, finally letting go of all of the grief and worry I worked so hard to hide from everyone.

Without warning, the door flew open and a frantic Brody searched the bathroom until his gaze found me. In a ball. On the shower floor. Naked.

Oh fuck me running. Could this day get any worse?

"Are you okay?" He turned his head slightly, but I noticed him peeking out the corner of his eye. "Sorry I just burst in, but I heard a loud thud and thought you were hurt."

Mortified at Brody seeing me naked and sobbing on the floor of my shower, I reached out and ripped a towel off the bar to cover myself.

"I'm fine." *Yeah, right.* "I'm gonna get dressed and I'll be down in a minute."

*****

Brody

I hesitated for a split second, before walking out the bathroom, descending the stairs back to the living room, then plopping down on the couch. The image of her naked in the bathroom was seared into my brain. Dear God, the things I want to do to her. I imagine wrapping my arms around her and pulling her to me; kissing her breathless and sucking on her perfect, pink nipples.

Jesus, my friend was fighting for his life and here I was lusting after the man's sister. I raked my hand through my hair, disgusted with myself. "Ugh, what is wrong with me?"

"Sorry, what was that?" Leila was standing at the top of the stairs. She had thrown on a pair of tight white capris, a tank top and her tan flip-flops. She left her hair wet, but pulled it back on top of her head. "I thought I heard you say something."

"Oh...no. I was just thinking out loud. You all set? Ready to go?" I was itching to get out of there. The longer we stayed, the harder it was going to be to stop myself from throwing her over my shoulder and carrying her back upstairs. I stood and nonchalantly adjusted the bulge in my suit pants, hoping Leila hadn't noticed how hard she made me by just walking into the room.

"Uh, yeah, give me just a minute. I want to grab a sweatshirt for tonight. The ICU tends to be a little chilly. I'm gonna let Ruger out one last time." She ran back upstairs.

I headed back to the kitchen to grab another bottle of water. By the time I returned to the living room, Leila was back. She was holding a grey sweatshirt with SWAT imprinted in yellow on the back. It must have been Drew's because it looked way too large to be hers.

She looked down at her watch and groaned. Shaking her head, she asked, "What the hell am I supposed to do for two hours?"

"Well, we could go get something to eat if you are hungry?"

"I am a little hungry, but I really don't feel like goin' out. I'll just throw something together here. Are you hungry?" She tossed the sweatshirt on the couch.

"Actually, I am. I didn't have a chance to eat before coming to check on Drew. How about I cook for you? You have to be exhausted. I could throw something together. You have the basics in the fridge, right? Eggs, butter, bacon? I saw some bread on the counter. I make a pretty mean bacon, egg and cheese sandwich," I said with utter confidence.

"Oh, you do, do you? Hmm, that does sound pretty good, but I can cook. You don't have to cook for me." She smiled sweetly.

"No, really, I insist. It's no trouble and like you said, you're tired. This way you can sit down and relax like that doctor what's his name said." I didn't wait for her to answer before opening the fridge, and taking the all of the ingredients. "Where are your frying pan and utensils?"

"Frying pans are in the island and the spatula is in the canister next to the stove. Anything I can do to help?" She pointed around the kitchen as she spoke.

I looked across the island as she sat down on one of the swivel barstools, staring briefly at her natural beauty. "Sure. You can just sit there and look gorgeous." Leila blushed three different shades of crimson, which made me even harder.

"Wow, that's gotta be one of the corniest lines ever." She shook her head.

"Okay in all seriousness, you could tell me what happened upstairs earlier. I'm sorry to have all but knocked down your door without permission, but I seriously freaked when I heard that noise. I just needed to make sure you weren't injured."

Drawing in a deep breath, she looked at her hand and starting picking her cuticle.

"Sorry, I had a slight meltdown. But don't worry, it won't happen again. It's just that I was finally alone and it all hit me so hard. I guess I wasn't ready for it. I'm sorry you had to see me like that."

"I am not sorry at all for seeing you like that. It's okay."

Leila hid her face in her hands at my comment.

"Leila, you don't have to be so strong all of the time. You're allowed to be scared and even freak out a little. Maybe next time you can lean on me. I've got some pretty wide shoulders." I grinned.

She turned on the stool, ignoring the comment. "Since we are gonna stay in, I'm gonna let Ruger out. Just don't run from him and you'll be fine."

Wait, what? Don't run? Why would I run? Fuck me, this can't be good.

Two minutes later, she came back with a large tan and black shepherd at her heel. He hesitated at the sight of me and growled.

"Pfui," she commanded in a deep, stern voice, and he quieted. "*Platz...bleib* Ruger. Brody walk over to me, he's not gonna hurt you. I just put him in a down stay, he won't move."

"He's not going to use me as a chew toy, right?"

She laughed as the dog cocked his head and whined a little, as if to say "Really?"

"No, just stand next to me. Ruger *fuss*." He trotted over to us. "Good boy."

She reached down and scratched the underside of his neck. I reached down and let him sniff me, then rubbed his head. He couldn't seem to care less. He walked back over and lay in his large, downy bed.

*****

Leila

If he flexed his muscles like that one more time I could not, and would not, be held liable for what I did. Doesn't he see me drooling over here? His witty comments were definitely helping to lighten my mood. Oh, and how could I forget the cheesy pickup lines?

"Thanks Brody, I appreciate the offer. I lean on Drew. He's been my rock. Oh God, I don't know what I will do if I lose him." Great and here were my tears again. "I can't lose him, he's all I have left."

Brody came around the island and enveloped me in a comforting hug. "It's gonna be okay. Drew is a fighter and he's one of the toughest guys I know. He's gonna make it through this, but he'll need you to help him."

Holding me for another second, Brody slowly pulled back, and then paused when he was a few inches away. I looked up at him as he gently wiped away my tears. Our gazes locked, and I thought he might kiss me when I smelled the eggs and looked toward the stove.

"Uhh, you might want to flip those eggs, 'cause I think they're burning." I tried to suppress a chuckle.

Brody pulled away and rushed back to the stove. "Shit, I think you're right...damn it. Maybe we should just run down to the deli, grab something and bring it back. That way you don't really have to face anyone and you'll get a sandwich that's not extra crispy. PS, I'm totally blaming that on you."

"Me? I didn't burn the eggs." I looked at him, feigning disbelief and shock, while holding a hand to my chest.

"Yes, you, it's your fault. You distracted me," he said with a flirtatious smile.

"Really? And just how did I distract you?" I asked, having a damn good idea where this was going, but kept playing the game.

"Oh, don't pretend like you don't know. Looking up at me with those gorgeous brown eyes and chewing on your bottom lip. It's enough to make even a monk want to tackle you." Brody watched my eyes widen in surprise. "What? Don't tell me you don't know how beautiful you are. You're easily the most gorgeous woman on the east coast."

This time I didn't have to feign shock, because I knew he was totally bullshitting me. Don't get me wrong, I knew if I took the time to do my hair and makeup, maybe I could pull off pretty. He was laying it on awfully thick. "Wow, I have to hand it to Drew, he was right."

Looking confused he asked, "Right about what exactly?"

"The fact that you think you can smooth talk your way out of or into anything you think you want. Applause, applause, that was smooth, but I'm most certainly not the most gorgeous woman on the east coast, let alone in Charleston. You, obviously, have not seen me in the dead of summer or just after it's rained. My hair looks like Simba when he jumps out of the water and shakes off."

"Wait, what? Who the hell's Simba?" he asked, totally befuddled by my reference. It didn't go unnoticed that he didn't deny or defend his Rico Suave nature. *Nice dodge.*

"Are you kiddin' me? Simba. From *The Lion King*." Brody stood there still looking at me like I had three heads. "It's a Disney movie and a Broadway play."

He squinted his eyes and then nodded. "Oh, right, that cartoon movie about the lions. Anyway, let's go get something to eat and we can talk on the way. It's already nine-thirty. Do you want to walk or would you prefer to ride?" Brody asked, opening the door for me while I grabbed my keys and purse.

"Let's walk. It's just a few blocks and we won't have to look for a parking spot," I answered, turning right out the front door toward East Bay Deli.

I left Ruger out of the crate since we would only be gone a few minutes. I didn't bother setting the alarm since the backup security was in place.

Chapter Five

Leila

Brody and I walked down East Bay Street, stepping over puddles from the recent storms, and returned to the condo. We brought home two bacon, egg and cheese sandwiches, a Mountain Dew and a large coffee.

"I don't know how you can drink coffee when it's so hot outside. Geez, it must be ten degrees hotter than when we left the hospital." I used my hand to fan myself.

Brody looked down at his half cup of coffee and shrugged. "I don't know, I just have always had a thing for coffee. What I don't understand is how you can drink that Mountain Dew shit. It's like straight sugar."

Grinning at him, I opened my soda and took a small sip. "Ahhh, so good. You should try it," I said, shoving the drink toward a leery Brody.

"Ugh, no thanks," Brody said, turning his nose up. "That shit probably has as much acid as a car battery."

Shoving the keys into the dead bolt on my front door, I rolled my eyes and smiled at his comment, then made my way over to the kitchen and took two plates out of the cabinets. I sat them down on the bar in front of Brody as he removed the sandwiches from the brown paper bag. He opened the aluminum foil wrapped sandwiches and sat one on each plate.

It'd been nearly half a day since I last ate and I was famished. Sitting on the barstool next to Brody, I took a bite into the bacon, egg and cheese. It only took a second before I realized I got Brody's sandwich.

"Eww, I think you have mine. I ordered turkey bacon, egg whites and cheese. This must be yours." I handed over the sandwich and snatched mine right out of his hand as he was about to take a bite. "If I ate that, I'd have to spend an extra thirty minutes running this afternoon," I said without thinking and quickly dropped my head, fighting back emotions I didn't have time for. I wouldn't have time for a run, because Drew was in the hospital, near death.

*****

Brody
I noticed the sudden and swift change in her demeanor and my immediate thought was I had to distract her. I finished my sandwich and took a gulp of coffee. I watched as she pushed away the last bit of her breakfast.

"Hey, why don't you sit down on the couch, put your feet up and relax, maybe even take a quick nap? We still have an hour before your doctor friend will let you in to see Drew."

"No, I don't want to sleep. I know if I fall asleep, I'm not going to get up." She gazed up at me. "Ya know, we could go head back and see if Drake'll lemme in a little early."

Why does she have to look at me like that? As if I have any control over her getting in to see Drew. I hate not being able to help her or Drew. Powerless is not something I'm accustomed to feeling. "Not gonna happen. I promised *Drake*," I emphasized Drake a little too much, because frankly the good doctor irritated me, "I'd keep you out of the hospital until at least eleven. What kind of a guy does it make me if I break my promise?"

*****

Leila
Knowing I wasn't going to win, I gave up and went to the couch, put my feet up on the matching ottoman and flicked on the TV. I turned on my go-to movie and tried to allow it to distract me.

Brody came around the island after placing the plates in the dishwasher and joined me on the couch. His sandalwood cologne surrounded me as I closed my eyes and inhaled him. I couldn't help it, I imagined smelling him on my sheets and on my skin. Before I could open my eyes, I felt him watching me. And damn if I wasn't right. I opened my eyes and found him staring directly into them.

Feeling uncomfortable, I decided to break the silence. "Uh, what kind of cologne are you wearing? I mean it's nice. It's clean and subtle. Not so heavy and pungent like some men wear. Ugh, some of the patients that come through the ER smell like they bathed in their cologne. Seriously, sometimes less is more." Great, I am rambling again. He had to see how nervous he made me.

"It's Burberry," he answered in a smooth, silky voice, still looking deep into my eyes.

As if caught in a trance I couldn't look away. His brilliant blue eyes were mesmerizing. I had never seen eyes that color before. At that very moment, my stupid cell phone blared out Kings of Leon "Sex on Fire".

Damn, if that wasn't what I was just thinking.

I pulled back with a groan and ran for my purse, pulling out my cell. "Hello? Yes, this is she." I paused, listening to the caller. "Okay, I will be there then, thank you for calling."

"What's up?" Brody asked.

"That was Brooke, the nurse in ICU. They called up from CT and it will be eleven thirty before they can get him in. Drake had her call me and push back visiting hours to twelve thirty. Although, I get the feelin' somethin' else was going on. You don't think Drew had a setback, do you? Drake'd tell me, right?" My mind was going to dark places. "If there was somethin' goin' on, it would make sense Drake wouldn't call me himself. He knows I'd be able to hear it in his voice." Panic was setting in as I rambled like a mad woman.

*****

Brody

I really didn't like these unfamiliar feelings bubbling up in my gut when she spoke of Drake. No way am I jealous. I don't get jealous. I have to figure out if she has a thing for this asshole doctor.

"No, I don't think there is anything else going on. They probably just got busy. I mean, you and Drake seem pretty close. Don't you think he'd call you if something happened?" There let's see how she responds to that.

"Drake and I aren't close in the way you are obviously thinking Brody. We've worked together for three years. Besides, he'd much more likely be into you than me," she quipped.

"Reason I thought maybe you two had a thing…ya know, the way he consoled you earlier, y'all seemed…familiar."

"Well, yeah, I mean he's been a friend for years. We met in the middle of a code. Some kid got himself shot while dealin' and Drake started baggin' the kid while I jumped on the stretcher to do compressions. We sorta hit it off. He and Barb are probably the only two friends I really have besides Drew." Her head drooped.

I took her petite, soft hand in mine. "No, you've got me too, if you want me. I'm here for anything you need Leila. All you have to do is ask." Leila turned back to look at the TV as I wondered what we were watching. "What is this anyway?"

She turned, jaw dropped, mouth open wide. "Are you freakin' kidding me? Please don't tell me you've never seen *The Notebook*!" I looked at her like she was speaking Swahili.

"Is it a chick flick? Because if it is, then rest assured, I've definitely not seen it," I replied dryly.

"Well, we don't have time to watch the whole thing, but you'll have to watch it with me sometime."

I leaned in and whispered in her ear, "If it means spending time with you in the dark, count me in." Ruger stood up, repositioned himself so his eyes were locked onto me.

Damn, this dog makes me nervous.

It took everything in my power to sit and watch that movie next to her. Every fiber of my being screamed at me to act, to launch myself across the couch at her. I was waging war inside my own head. This was Drew's little sister. He is one of my only true friends. I didn't want to break that trust and bond we had. But I could not deny the chemistry or the emotions she evoked in me. I've never wanted any woman like I want her. As the devil and the angel bickered back and forth on my shoulders, my head told me the phone call was a sign. Leila had so much going on right now. Maybe I should just back off. At least until we knew what's going on with Drew.

Yeah, I will wait and talk to Drew. I should get his consent and blessing. That way, if I royally fuck it up, he won't be too pissed. Who am I kidding? If I fuck up with his baby sister, he'd kill me and have his SWAT buddies help him bury my body.

I looked over to where Leila was snuggled down into a fuzzy crimson blanket and found her sleeping serenely. As much as I know she needed the sleep, I decided I'd wake her at noon, so we could head back over to check on Drew. This way she got a little rest and I got to stare at her stunning face without being too creepy. She really was quite exquisite. She had flawless, bronzed skin and perfect, pink, pouty lips that just begged to be sucked on. She was petite, but she had the most mind-blowing curves and in all the right places. I kept imagining her tight, little body under me, moaning as I slid into her; I'd bet she was as tight as a vise. The thought made me unbearably hard.

As if imagining her being naked and thoroughly fucked wasn't enough, she moaned.

"Mmm, Brody…hmmm," she squirmed, mumbling in her sleep.

Ruger's head shot up in warning, eyes glued to me. I put my hands up.

"Don't look at me dog, I didn't do it," I said, trying to reason with him. Christ, I'm explaining myself to a dog. Granted, the dog in question could probably rip off my arm and my leg.

Fuck. I was going to have to excuse myself to her bathroom if she kept this shit up. Maybe I should just wake her up.

No, I can deal for a while longer, she needed to sleep. I'll wake her up soon enough.

Sooner, if she kept making those sexy little noises.

*****

Leila

Brody reached out and pulled me to him. I could feel every rippled ab and hard plane of his chest. As his lips seized mine, my legs quivered and I almost combusted right there in his arms. The heat pooled between my legs and my clit throbbed its own craving. He pushed me up higher against the wall, allowing me to wrap my legs around his perfect waist. Grabbing my ass, he started grinding into me. Even through his clothes, I could feel his thick, hard length and I couldn't stifle the moaning any longer.

"Mmm, Brody." He pushed into me a little harder. "Ahhhhhh." I was so close to my first orgasm in almost a year I wanted to cry. He rolled his hips forward again; I threw my head back on a loud moan. "Harder, oh God. Brody don't stop."

But then he started shaking my shoulder and calling my name. When I opened my eyes to look at him, he wasn't holding me against the wall.

I was on my couch.

With a very real Brody.

Oh dear God in heaven, it was a dream.

That's when the dread set in and the humiliation plowed through me like a steamroller. It was like I had rocks sitting in my stomach. Please, please, please tell me I didn't talk in my sleep.

"Hey, you fell asleep and I didn't want you to sleep past noon. It's almost time to go see Drew." He looked flushed.

"I hope I wasn't talking in my sleep." Silently praying he said no, but by the smirk on his face I knew these prayers weren't going to be answered.

"Actually, you did say a few things. But for the most part, I couldn't understand what you were saying," he answered, grinning. I had a sneak suspicion there was more to it than he was letting on. But for now, I had to let it go and get to the hospital.

"What time is it?" I asked, looking around for my cell.

Brody handed my phone to me. "It's eleven fifty. If we leave in twenty minutes, we should have enough time to get you back over there and find a parking spot just in time for visiting hours. Do you mind if I use your bathroom?"

"Um, sure. There is one down the hall past the kitchen, first door on the left," I answered, still somewhat sleepy and disoriented by my dream.

After Brody left for the bathroom, I stood up and stretched my arms high above my head and yawned. I got up, took Ruger out, and then put him back in his crate. As I came back into the living room, Brody strolled back in. I was waiting with purse and phone in hand. "Hey, I know it's early, but I can't wait anymore."

Brody walked over to the door and grabbed his keys off the small, antique wooden table near the front door. "I completely understand, I feel the same way," he said. "Do you need to do anything with the dog?"

"No, I already took care of him. My poor guy, he's back in his crate."

Chapter Six

Leila

We arrived back at MUSC in less than ten minutes. Brody drove around the parking garage searching for a place to park, as he called it, his baby. After we drove around the first three levels I could see the frustration starting to creep across his face.

"What the hell? There are no damn parking spots in this whole garage. Where the hell do you park when you're working? How do you have this state of the art, technologically advanced hospital and have one small shitty-ass parking garage?"

I sat back, trying to remain straight-faced, but doing a horrific job. His eyes flicked to me. "This isn't funny Lei. This is the definition of insanity."

I bit the inside of my lip to strangle the giggle bubbling up inside. *He's really cute when he's angry.*

"I don't drive; I walk to work. For many reasons, one of which is the ridiculous parking problems. Employees aren't allowed to park here. We have to park a few streets over and either walk or catch the bus."

Well, that did it. Brody looked like a monkey was going to fly out of his ass at any second. *Heehee.* Again, I tried to rein it in, when I really wanted to burst out laughing. Thank God for a little self-control and a now numb bottom lip.

Brody slammed on his brakes and stared at me with utter seriousness. "The bus? They make you ride a fucking bus? Around here, a bus?" He started driving again in search of a spot. "Don't they understand it's not safe for a woman to wait around for a bus in the city? Especially at night? Wait, you walk home? What the hell Leila? That's worse." He was awfully adorable when he was sputtering and cussing upper level management decisions.

"Don't worry. Barb and I walk together. Oh, and Drake lives a couple of blocks down, so he occasionally walks with us too. But don't worry, I carry pepper spray with me at all times. See," I said, pulling my keys out. "It's right here on my key chain."

Now probably wasn't the time to tell him I have a CWP and a 9mm. Of course, I don't carry those at work. We have strict guidelines against that, otherwise I would.

Finally, we found a spot on the fifth level. Happily, it was near the elevator. Brody was around the car and opening the passenger door before I even heard his door shut. I stepped out into the parking garage, and even with the wind whipping, it was repressively hot. Heading over to the elevator, I started to get nervous.

As if sensing my anxiety, Brody stood behind me in the elevator and ran his knuckles up, then back down my spine. Even though his touch awakened some primal urge deep within me, it soothed my apprehensions. No words were needed. He said it all with the traces of comfort he left on my body.

We made our way up to the fourth floor ICU. I stopped at the nurse's station to check in with Brooke and found out what room Drew was in, then headed that way. Just as I was about to walk in, Drake came out of his room holding Drew's chart.

"Hey Lei, we just got him settled back in. He's stable and he regained consciousness about thirty minutes ago. He's extubated but I gave him four milligrams of IV Dilaudid about an hour ago, so he's pretty out of it right now. We'll set him up on a morphine pump to try to keep the pain at bay," he explained. "I am waiting on the CT results to decide what to do about the bullet."

Relief washed over me. "He's really stable? Oh, thank God!"

"Drake, my name is Drake not God. But if you ins—" He almost got the rest of his self-assured, cocky retort out before I punched him in the shoulder. "Ow. Damn it Lei, I was just playin'." He backed up with his palms up in surrender.

"You're not as funny as ya think, Dr. Thomas." I turned and headed into Drew's room with Brody in tow. I hesitated before going in and Brody walked right into the back of me.

"Sorry, I need just a sec before I go in." I took a deep breath and pushed the curtain aside. Amazingly enough, Drew was still awake when we walked in his room. He looked away from the television and smiled a lazy smile.

"Lei, you're here." He sounded groggy. "Drake said you'd be here soon."

"Shhh, don't try to talk too much, you need to save your energy." I rushed to his side, while Brody hung by the door. "Look who I found wandering around earlier." I nodded for him to come join us.

Drew started trying to lift his hand to greet Brody. "Bro, put your hand down and take it easy. You're going to have Leila in a tizzy if you don't chill. She's been freaking out all morning."

"I'm sorry Lei. I hate that I scared you, but I'm okay. It's gonna take a hell of a lot more than some punk banger to take me out." He looked up at me with glassy, Dilaudid eyes.

"Okay, if you're gonna insist on talking, then tell me what the hell happened." I wanted to know what had gone so horribly wrong.

Slowly and slurrily, Drew got out the story about the narcotics warrant that they rolled up on, only dozing in and out a few times. Once he got to the part about entering the house I stopped him.

"Jasper and Bobby already told me the rest. I don't wanna hear it again. You need to rest for a while. Brody, why don't we—" I was interrupted.

"Brody is gonna hang with me for a few minutes. Why dontcha run down and check your schedule or somethin'." Drew all but pushed me from the private room. Before I left, Brooke came in to check his vitals and make sure we weren't stressing him out too much.

She came and went pretty quickly, but I couldn't help but notice how she stared and all but drooled at Brody. What really confused me was the sudden pang of jealousy. I wanted to jump up and tell her to keep walking, but of course I didn't. Brody was not mine and I had no claim to him. Besides, I was sure he was used to women swooning at his feet. I mean he looked like a Greek God. He probably had a harem waiting to take care of all his needs. He certainly didn't seem like the type to be a one-woman man. There was no way on God's green earth that I would share a man. Especially this one.

"Okay, I will give y'all a few minutes, but I will be right back. Don't let him talk you into anything." I gave Brody a threatening look.

Why in the world would Drew need to talk to Brody without me? Knowing my big brother, he was trying to convince Brody to smuggle him in cheeseburgers or some other greasy takeout food. But something in Drew's voice had me second guessing myself.

Then again that could just be the drugs. I left the men to their own devices and made my way down to the ER locker room.

*****

Brody

I couldn't help but ogle Leila's ass as she left the room. I turned back to see Drew looking at me with uneasy concern. I knew why he wanted me to stay behind. He had to have seen the way I looked at his little sister. How was I going to explain to him that I wanted his blessing? That what I was feeling was truly different than the normal weekend pussy I went after. Well, here goes nothing. I prayed I didn't lose my friend, but I wasn't backing down where it concerned Leila.

"Listen Drew, I wanted to talk to you." I raked my hand across the back of my neck. "About Leila. Listen, I know she's your sister…"

"Whoa, whoa, whoa, stop right there. Yeah, she's my sister an' I love her immensely, but she's a big girl. I'm not gettin' involved in her relationships. She's more than capable of makin' her own decisions, whether I agree with 'em or not. And I'm not sayin' I agree with you pursuin' her. Jus' remember, she's not one o' your hookups. She doesn't date, an' I don't wanna see her get hurt. So, 'fore you go there, make certain this isn't 'nother conquest thing an' that you can give her wha' she wants an' needs," he said reaching for the button to the morphine pump.

Pausing to think for a split second, I answered, "This is different. I don't know what it is and I can't tell you in words, but I feel this unrelenting pull toward her. Shit man, when she walks into a room…it's crazy," I tried to explain, but I just couldn't.

"All I'm sayin' is treat her like a princess. She deserves the best and nothing less. If you don't, there will be someone else waiting to scoop her up. Don't hurt her man." Drew's words became slower and slurred more as the pain meds made their way through his veins. Then he blinked a few times and was out.

I stood and turned to leave the ICU room when Nurse Brooke returned. She leaned over Drew's bed, making sure he was hooked up properly to all of the machines.

"Since he's asleep, I think it's probably best to leave and let him rest. Maybe you can walk me to the Starbucks downstairs and we can get a drink." She batted her eyelashes and spoke in what must be her "fuck me now" voice.

"Please, don't mind me. I'll stay with Drew while you two…go get coffee and do whatever it is you were talkin' about doin'." I turned to see one very livid Leila standing in the doorway. She plowed past me, sat down over by the window and pulled out her phone.

"Uh, actually, I was just getting ready to say no thank you." I turned back to the nurse. "I'm not interested, I'm seeing someone." I tried to smooth over Leila's ruffled feathers and make it clear to Brooke I was not now, nor in the future, interested in coffee, dinner or a quick fuck. Well, at least not with her.

Leila's attitude seemed to thaw as Brooke exited the room. I walked over and stood behind her. I leaned down and quietly whispered in her ear. "You're the only person I want to go get a coffee with, or a Mountain Dew as you prefer."

Lightly, I kissed her temple and straightened. "Listen, why don't you let me take you back home? I know you're exhausted. You only slept forty-five minutes on the couch earlier." Going for extra leverage, I added, "Ruger will probably need to go back out. I'll stay there with you and if your phone rings or there's any change, I'll wake you up and bring you right back here, promise."

Hesitating, she looked at Drew, then back to me. She got up, looked at his morphine pump and his stats, then sat back down. "Okay, but here is the deal, I'll sleep after Drake calls with the CT results. And I am comin' back first thing tomorrow or if they call and say there's a problem. Visiting hours or not, I will be here at seven a.m. Even if that means I have to throw on my scrubs and sneak in." She paused and looked back to Drew's prone body. "But if you could give me a ride back home that would be great. I can walk back tomorrow morning, after I get some sleep and am not draggin' ass."

I looked on, confused. "I just said I'll drive you back whenever you want. So if that is tomorrow morning or tonight at three a.m., it won't make a bit of difference to me. If you don't want me to stay with you tonight that's fine too. I just thought it would make it easier whenever you decided you wanted to get back over here. You wouldn't have to wait for me to get here from Johns Island." I prayed she would reconsider and let me watch over her tonight. I didn't know where this protective instinct was coming from but I couldn't shake it.

Chapter Seven

Leila

Brody brought me back to my place and insisted on going to pick up something for dinner, even though I assured him I could cook. He dismissed my offer, saying I had enough going on, that I didn't need to worry about feeding him too. I smiled, slightly relieved I could just curl up on the couch and not worry about food. Brody suggested Chinese for dinner, which I had to admit, sounded simply delicious. I sat down on the couch and started to doze off when I heard my phone start singing.

It was Drake calling with the CT results and the plan to go ahead with surgery on Sunday. He wanted to give Drew enough time to regain a little strength before opening him up again. The bullet fragment was lodged near his scapula, thankfully. This would be a much easier surgery since it was away from his lung that was previously damaged by the bullet. Drake was confident he'd be in and out, which was a huge relief.

I was lost in thought, when I heard a knock at the door. I looked down at my watch and realized it was already 7:00 p.m. Hopping up from my spot on the couch, I made my way over, then answered the door. I was greeted with an elegant bouquet of white calla lilies, green zinnias and light pink hydrangeas. "Oh wow, they are beautiful!"

They were lowered and there stood Brody, who had gone home and changed. He wore a snug fitting gray cotton V-neck that accentuated his tan, sculpted arms, and a pair of low hung vintage Polo jeans that were slightly frayed at the cuffs. He had food and flowers in hand and all I could think about was dragging him in and mauling him like a lioness who hadn't hunted in eons. Internally, I was salivating like a caged, hungry predator that had just locked eyes with her next meal.

He grinned back and walked in. "I didn't want to just walk right in. I thought a little surprise might cheer you up a little. Ready for some sesame chicken and lo mein?"

"I am," I answered as I ushered him into the house. Feeling grateful, I quietly turned to Brody. "Thank you…for everything."

Trying not to get caught up in my own emotions, I took the food and whisked it to the kitchen. I had already set the table and even put out candles. I took the cartons of Chinese food from the bag and brought them to the dining room table.

We started opening the cartons and piling food on our plates. "So, what do you do for a living?"

Of course he had a mouthful of food when I asked. He finished chewing and wiped his mouth with a napkin before answering. "I'm in real estate. My parents were in real estate and when they died the business was handed over to me. More than anything, I buy land and build on it. I own a few businesses, a couple of restaurants, a small boutique that my mother acquired and a hotel."

He was so casual about the whole thing, slipping the hotel in at the last minute under his breath. Like owning a hotel wasn't a huge deal or anything. I almost choked on my lo mein.

"Oh, well, I guess that keeps you pretty busy, huh?" I tried to recover without making a fool of myself.

"You could say that. I've got people who run the businesses. I'm there for the big decisions, but that's about it. I prefer to concentrate on building. I like the gratification I get from making something out of nothing." He returned to eating, consuming his first bite of sesame chicken.

"How old were you when your parents passed away? I mean, if you don't mind me asking," I quickly added.

"No, I don't mind. I was twenty-two when they died in a plane crash. They were on their way to the house in Parrot Cay on North Caicos." Anguish washed over his face and I immediately regretted asking.

"I'm sorry Brody. I didn't mean to upset you. I know how hard it is to lose a parent." I look down at my plate. "I still think about my mom every day and I miss her like crazy." I lifted my gaze across the candlelit table to Brody's pained stare. "My dad, on the other hand, I don't miss. He's still out there somewhere and I don't care if I ever see him again. He waltzed out of our life more than twenty years ago and never looked back. After our mom died, I thought he might reach out, but he didn't. Part of me wanted him too, but I knew better than to hope." Tears collected in my eyes. "After that, he was basically dead to me. He can't hurt me if I don't think about him, hope for him or expect him to come to his senses, right?"

After a few long beats of silence, he asked, "What do you like to do for fun?" quickly changing subjects. He must have thought I was such a big baby.

"Fun, hmmm... I don't know, normal stuff I guess. Ya know, like going to the beach, reading, yoga, oh and I love riding horses. Since I moved downtown, I enjoy walking around the Open Market. I never buy anything though. I just love to see all of the neat things. And I love going to the gun range. What about you? What do you do for *fun*?" I raised my eyebrow.

"When I am not giving rides to nurses?" he teased. "Just kidding. I guess the same as you." He shrugged. "I like surfin' at the beach, walkin' around downtown, golfing, hunting and fishing. Basically anything outdoors. And I have to say, I love how you slipped the gun range in there at the end. Can't say I know many women who like guns. Let alone going to a gun range."

We continued with the small talk, finished eating, and then I cleared the table, taking the dishes to the sink. He followed me into the kitchen and put our glasses on the island. "Would you like a glass of wine or a beer?" I offered.

"A beer would be good, thanks."

He grabbed the beer I took from the refrigerator. I poured a glass of Riesling and followed him to the couch. He sat on the end directly in front of the TV and patted the spot beside him. I sat my glass of wine down and dropped onto the couch next to him. He grabbed the remote from the coffee table and handed it to me.

*****

Brody

"What would you like to watch? We didn't get to finish that movie from this morning, want to watch that?" I looked over at her hoping she wouldn't tell me to pick. I don't have time for TV or movies, so I don't really know what's on these days.

"Yeah, let's finish that movie." She bit down slightly on her bottom lip and just like that I was rock hard. "Lemme turn off the lights in the kitchen and we can start it over. You have to see if from the beginning."

She jumped up and went to the kitchen. I took that time to adjust myself, trying to be as discreet as I could. She turned off all of the lights in the house and blew out the candles on the dining room table.

"I'll be right back, I'm gonna change really fast." Ruger followed her up the stairs.

"All right, take your time, I'm not going anywhere," I pronounced as I watched her dash up the stairs. Damn. That ass.

I used her absence to try to relax. I thought maybe without her so close, my raging hard-on would subside. Boy was I wrong. The only thing I could think about was what she was changing into. I imagined she would come down the staircase in a sexy bra, panties and thigh-high stockings. Oh and red fuck-me heels. Clearly, that didn't help my physical predicament. I was pulled from my fantasy by the sound of her padding down the stairs and turned my head to see she was in a pair of green plaid men's boxers and a pink tank top. Fucking hell, I was going to come right there in my pants. She didn't have a bra on. I could totally see how hard her pert nipples were through the sheer cotton.

Thank you air-conditioning.

She had a soft, fuzzy blanket folded in her delicate arms as she came around the sectional and sat back down next to me. She pulled her knees up and spread the blanket over her lap.

"You know what, I have a pair of Drew's pajama pants upstairs if you want to get comfy too," she offered innocently, tilting her head.

"Yeah, if you don't mind that would be awesome."

"I sat them out on my bed. Feel free to change up there." She grabbed the remote and started scrolling through the DVR list. "Oh, and Ruger is in his bed up there, just so you know."

"Cool, I'll be right back," I said, taking the stairs two at a time. I reached her bedroom and saw the black flannel pajama pants sitting atop her large king-size bed. I stripped my jeans off and pulled on the pants, immediately noticing the tent I was sporting. I looked over at the dog.

"Great, what the hell am I gonna do about this?" He cocked his head in response.

Quietly, I made my way to the bathroom and threw some cold water on my face. Looking in the silver gilded mirror, I thought of Drew. My friend was just shot in the chest and here I am taking advantage of his sister. No, I wasn't taking advantage of her, nothing had happened.

Yet.

I took a quick piss and headed back down to Leila. She was yawning as I came down the stairs. "If you want to call it a night and go to sleep, I will completely understand."

"No, I'm fine, let's watch the movie. Although, I'm not gonna promise I'll make it to the end." She smiled.

"Well, if you fall asleep, I'll make sure you get to your bed."

About thirty minutes into the movie, she looped her arm through mine and snuggled against my shoulder. We sat like this for a few scenes, until I decided it wasn't enough. I lifted my arm and pulled her into my side. Sneaking a peek from the corner of my eye, I caught her with a huge grin spreading slowly across her little face. I placed a soft kiss on the top of her head as she settled in and resumed watching the movie.

*****

Brody

Sometime in the middle of the night I picked my head up off the back of the plush sofa and looked around. The movie had ceased playing and it was now on infomercials about some hair crap. Clearly, I had been exhausted too.

I felt the heat from her tiny body before I realized she was still curled up next to me. For the first time ever, it didn't completely freak me out to be cuddling with a woman. Surprisingly, I was pleased to be there with her just like we were. There was no urge to run out; in fact, I had the exact opposite idea.

I looked down at her angelic face resting on my chest and her thin arm draped across my stomach, reached over and gently rubbed her arm up and down. "Leila, Lei...Wake up sweetheart." She blinked a few times before she opened her big brown eyes and yawned, making the most adorable little noise at the end.

"What time is it?" she asked, rubbing her eyes while looking around the room. Finally seeing a clock, she mumbled, "Oh geez, it's three a.m. I can't believe you let me sleep on you this long, you had to be so uncomfortable."

"Actually, I must've fallen asleep at some point too. I just woke up and realized how late it is. Why don't you let me carry you up to your bed? If it's cool, I'll just crash on the couch."

"It's okay, I can walk." She rubbed her neck. "But you are welcome to sleep upstairs. I have a huge bed and we're both adults. Beside, Ruger will wake you up if you stay down here, and this couch is great for sitting on but it really sucks for sleeping."

My mind did somersaults. Sleeping in the same bed and sleeping? Next to her? Sounded great in theory. In practice? "Yeah, okay. I didn't realize how tired I was and, honestly, I'm relieved I'm not driving back to Johns Island at this time of night." I tucked the blanket we had snuggled under during the movie beneath my arm then took her hand in mine. We made our way upstairs to the master bedroom and climbed into her bed.

Certain I'd spend the night worried how I'd keep, my hands off her, my body clued me in to the stress of the day; by the time my head hit the pillow, I was back to sleep.

Chapter Eight

Leila

I woke to the smell of sandalwood permeating my senses and immediately beamed from ear to ear. Brody was in my bed and cuddled right up behind me. I glanced at the clock on the bedside table, 7:09. Damn, it was early. I lay there for a minute, trying to figure out if he was awake yet. Based on the steady, slow rhythm of his chest against my back, I guessed he was still asleep.

Well, most of him.

He was as large as I had fantasized, and it was nudging me to prove it. His heavy arm was draped over my waist, holding me in place like I was going to escape. I haven't slept with anyone in months, like eighteen. Normally, this would be the point in time where I slid quietly from the bed and snuck out. There was nothing worse than a clingy man.

Don't get me wrong, I wasn't into one-night stands, but I definitely didn't need someone following me around like a lost puppy. I was not ready for that. Hell, I don't think I would ever be ready for anyone needy. But, here and now, wrapped in Brody's arms and tangled in his legs, I felt safe.

For the first time in a long time, I felt at ease with a man. I pushed back against him, trying to snuggle down and go back to sleep, even for just a little while. Before I could enjoy that possibility, a warm, wet nose nudged my hand. Ruger. We went downstairs to potty, then came back up and I crawled back into bed, wanting to soak up as much Brody as I could. Surely as soon as he woke he'd want to take us over to the hospital; then he'd be on his way.

I must have drifted back to sleep because I woke to soft, delicate kisses on my shoulder. Smiling, I turned my head to see Brody propped up on his elbow.

"You are so beautiful," he said with a sleepy grin.

Quickly, realizing it was down and the curls were probably 'fro-ing, I grabbed a hair tie from the bedside table and pulled my hair back in a sloppy bun.

"I must look a hot mess."

"Not a chance, you look gorgeous," he said in a suggestive deep voice.

With that, he rolled me under him and caught my face with his hands. He looked into my eyes like he was seeking permission, then, finally, he pressed his lips to mine, ran his tongue along the seam seeking his way into me.

He nibbled on my bottom lip, sucking it into his mouth, while his tongue traced a pattern along it. He turned his head slightly, allowing his tongue to delve further into me. I welcomed the invasion with a soft moan. Our tongues intertwined, dancing and caressing one another. The heat flooded my body and in a matter of seconds I needed new panties. Brody grabbed my leg behind my knee and pulled it up to his hip. Moving between my legs, he rolled his hips, grinding into me. I wrapped both legs around his waist and kissed him like it was my last day on earth and he was my salvation.

He was moving himself against me in just the right spot. My clit was throbbing, pleading for more attention. I could feel every single, thick inch of his cock as it massaged my folds and clit. I knew this was too much, too fast for me, but I couldn't stop myself. God help me, I wanted him. So bad, I was considering having sex with a man I had met only yesterday.

This was not me. I didn't want to just be a quick fuck, so I pulled back.

Brody looked at me knowingly. "We don't have to do anything you're not ready for. I got carried away. Leila, you've got no idea what you do to me. I've wanted to do that since I saw you walking toward me from across the waiting room, but I get this is fast. Maybe we should get ready and go check on Drew."

Relief flooded me, thank God he understood. I hoped he wouldn't be upset and think I was a bitch. I pulled his face to me and kissed him slowly and deeply, trying to express my gratitude for his understanding and patience.

"You're a good man Brody Davis, even if my brother thinks you're a man whore," I teased him. "You can shower downstairs in the guest bathroom or you can wait until I'm done and shower up here." I untangled my legs from his and headed for the shower.

"So there is no third option of joining you in the shower?" He looked at me with a quirked brow as if I was Thanksgiving Day dinner. "You look like you could use a good, soapy massage," he said with a wink.

"Wow, does that work for you often? Because that's gotta be one of the worst lines ever." I burst out laughing.

He pretended to look devastated and wounded, clutching his hand to his heart. "So mean. I was just trying to be a nice guy and rub your back."

Still giggling I said, "Right, rub my back. You mean cop a feel. Well, Mr. Davis, it's gonna take more than Chinese food and *The Notebook* to get you in these panties." I smiled, and then sauntered teasingly to my bathroom, shaking my ass the entire way.

*****

Brody

She was going to be the death of me. I have never wanted anything the way I wanted her. I had to have her, and not just for a night, one night would never be enough. I loved the way she didn't back down, the way she teased me and the simple fact that she thought more of herself than to just let me fuck her in the first twenty-four hours after I had met her. Leila surprised me at every turn. She actually had morals, a quality most of the women I slept with didn't have. No, they only cared about being seen with me and my money. Well, my family's money.

Funny; my dad always told me I would find my greatest fortune when I wasn't looking for it and I didn't expect it. All of these years I thought he was referring to a business deal, in that moment I realized he wasn't. His and my mother's love was his most priceless possession.

I lay back down and waited. Thinking back to the way she felt underneath me, so small and delicate but so vivacious. Jesus, I could've exploded just kissing her. She was breathtaking, funny, smart, kind and sexy. Damn was she sexy. The best part, she had no idea just how amazing she was. I was going to get the privilege of making sure she knew just how incredible she really was.

I wanted to plan something for her, maybe a nice dinner at my place, overlooking the water and then a ride on the boat. Yeah, she said she likes being outdoors. That way I can prove to her that I am not just looking for someone to warm my bed.

Remembering what Drew said, *"Treat her like a princess or someone else will,"* I knew I had to take my time and get to know her. I wanted to know what her deepest, darkest fears were. I wanted her to share her dreams and aspirations. I was so lost in my thoughts I didn't even hear the shower turn off or her come out of the bathroom.

"Hey, I'm done, feel free to hop in." She paused in the doorway to her closet, wearing nothing but a towel.

A cold shower, yep, I definitely needed to take a really long, really cold shower.

I climbed down off the bed and made my way over to the bathroom. I reached in and turned the shower to lukewarm, I didn't want to literally freeze but I needed to get rid of this raging monster in my pants. I stepped out of the pajama pants, opened the heavy glass door and entered the large two-person shower.

Shit, I shouldn't have thought about it being for two people, because now I was picturing myself pinning her up against the glass wall and taking her from behind. Her breasts pressed again the glass, her hands grasping for anything to hold onto as I slam into her tight, hot pussy. No cold shower was going to alleviate the fully grown beast now.

I grabbed the bar of soap and began to scrub my body. Trailing my hand down, I stroked my hard cock, thinking about how sweet her pussy must taste and how warm it would feel. I could see her moaning and screaming in ecstasy when she came, while I am driving deep into her, paying extra attention to her clit so her orgasm didn't stop. The last thought pushed me over the edge, and I jerked faster and faster until a thick, hot stream shot all over the shower wall. While I was still rubbing myself, I realized that relief was temporary; this was going to be a really long day.

After I dried off, I wrapped the towel around my hips and went in search of my clothes. The bedroom was empty and I found my clothes on the upholstered bench at the foot of her bed. Dropping the towel, I grabbed my boxer briefs. Just as I was pulling them up, I heard her suppressed gasp. "Oh crap. I'm sorry. Uhh, guess I should have knocked first."

When I turned around, I found her cheeks flushed with embarrassment as she twirled away to face the door. "Don't worry,

I'm not shy. It's only fair, I saw you naked first. Besides, it's your room."

I sat down and pulled on my jeans as she crossed the room and stood in front of her dresser. She was dressed in a pale yellow sundress that buttoned up the front and her flip-flops.

"I just needed to grab my watch and earrings. I'll be outta here in just a sec." She was so embarrassed, she couldn't even look up to speak to me. I walked over and stood behind her; wrapping my arms around her tiny waist, I kissed her soft neck.

"You're more than welcome to stay, I just need to throw on a shirt. And for the record, I plan on you seeing much more of me naked, so get used to it, babe." With that, I smacked her on the ass, pulled my grey V-neck over my head and strutted to the kitchen.

Chapter Nine

Leila

We arrived at MUSC; this time Brody decided to forego the parking garage of ridiculousness. We pulled through to the valet in the front of Ashley River Tower where Brody handed over the keys to his car. We rode the elevator up to the fourth floor and made our way down the corridor toward the ICU. Just as we rounded the corner, he reached over and took my hand. As we walked past the nurse's station hand in hand, I couldn't help but smile as we passed Brooke. Brody, being the polite, well-mannered gentlemen, bid everyone a good morning.

"Good morning Mr. Davis," Brooke said, and then snidely acknowledged me with a subtle eye roll. "Nurse Matthews. Drew had a quiet night, but an eventful mornin'. He apparently does not care for our, and I quote *'tasteless slop'* so he's refusing to eat. He said he'd talk to you when you came in this mornin'."

"All righty then. Let's go see our cranky patient, shall we?" Turning, I smiled sweetly at Brody.

"Of course, maybe you can cheer him up."

The minute we walked in, Drew started up. "I see you don't waste any time, huh Davis?"

"Drew, that's rude. Just because you're in pain and don't want to eat what they're serving you, doesn't mean you need take it out on Brody," I said irately.

Brody chimed in. "Leila, it's okay. I think Drew and I need to talk. Why don't you run to the cafeteria and get him something you know he'll eat."

"No," I said indignantly. "Why don't y'all talk in front of me? It's fuckin' obvious you'll be talkin' about me when I leave the room, so man up and say it to my face."

"All right sis, I'm sorry. Of course you can stay, but after we finish discussing whatever it is that's going on here"—pointing to me, then Brody—"will you please get me some decent damn food?"

"Yes, you know I will, just as soon as I see your chart and see what diet they have you on," I answered.

"The tasteless, shitty food diet apparently," he mumbled under his breath.

"Okay Brody, what did you need to say to Drew that I couldn't stay for?" I looked at him curiously.

"It wasn't anything bad or nefarious. I just want to explain to Drew that nothing happened between us. We're just getting to know each other and I plan on taking things slow, but that I do have feelings for you and I will not ignore them. I made my intentions clear to him yesterday." Brody turned to Drew. "Drew, I promised you I'd be a gentleman and I have been. I want this and I don't plan on fucking it up."

Well, that was *not* what I had expected him to say. I was so shocked I got up and just walked out of the room without saying a word to either of them.

Holy shit, Brody seemed dead serious as he declared his feelings and his intentions. My inner lioness was purring in satisfaction as I walked past Brooke. I caught the elevator and went to the cafeteria to find something for Drew to eat. Shit, in my haste I forgot to look at his chart, I pulled out my cell and phoned Drake.

"Hey baby girl, what's up? How's Drew this mornin'?" he answered, sounding like he was in a great mood.

"Hey honey. Drew's in a shitty mood this morning because he's eating hospital food. Actually, that's why I called. What diet did you put him on? I'm in the cafeteria now and was gonna get him something but thought I should double check." I wandered through the cafeteria looking at the options.

"Uh, get him whatever, as long as you think he will be okay eating it. I trust your judgment. I haven't been up to do rounds yet, so I haven't seen him. But I imagine if he's giving the nurses shit, then he's okay to eat solid food."

"All right, thanks, honey. I'll see ya later." I hung up and decided on scrambled eggs and grits. I mean I came so close to losing him yesterday, a little eggs and grits won't hurt. I ordered, paid with my badge and made my way to the Starbuck's and ordered Brody a coffee.

I rounded the corner to see Brody standing in the hallway outside of Drew's room. "What's goin' on? Why are you out here? What happened?"

"Whoa, whoa, slow down Lei. Everything's fine. The doctors came in and wanted to look at his incision and I didn't want to see that shit, so I came out here. Luckily, Nurse Brooke was needed in the room to assist or I imagine she'd be propositioning me again. I don't think she hears no very often," he laughed, trying to calm me down, but the mention of her name grated on my nerves.

"Sorry, I just got worried, I didn't mean to freak out," I apologized. "Here, I got you a coffee, since I didn't have any at my place. I'm gonna go in. Are you sure you don't wanna go with me?"

"Actually, since you're back, I will." He slid his hand into mine, leaned in and gave me a quick kiss. "Thanks for the coffee that was very sweet of you."

We returned to Drew's room as they finished. Drake came in behind us. "What's up Drew? I hear you're keepin' the nurses on their toes up here."

Drew shook his head. "I don't know what you've heard, but I'm the perfect patient."

Drake shook with laughter. "Yeah, sure I believe that, like I believe I've got a chance with Channing Tatum."

Unable to stop himself, Drew burst out laughing, and then clutched his chest. "Oh God, dude stop, I can't laugh, it hurts," he said, trying to stop laughing.

"Okay, you two, this *is* ICU not Jake's," I said, referring to the bar down the street. "So is the plan still to go back in tomorrow to get the bullet out?" I asked Drake.

"Yup, that's the plan. Drew, you seem more than strong enough, so I'll give you the day to eat and drink. Then NPO after midnight, I wanna set up to start by seven a.m., I have a nine thirty tee time I can't miss," he teased. Drake's idea of golfing was getting a bucket of beers, a bucket of balls and hitting the driving range. Turning back to Drew, Drake said, "I'll see you tomorrow in the OR and Lei, I'll call you after I'm out with an update, but I don't foresee any complications." With that, Drake left the room.

I turned my attention to Drew and placed the brown paper bag, holding his breakfast, in front of him. "Grits and eggs, it's the best I could do. Don't worry, I put salt on them. And yes, I tasted them first," I answered him before he had a chance to ask.

"I'll take it." His eyes popped open wide with enthusiasm. Drew snatched the bag, causing him to wince. Taking out the small

Styrofoam container, grabbing the spork from the tray, he started inhaling the food.

"Jesus, Drew, slow down, you're gonna choke," I admonished him. I started to take the container away, and he stabbed me with the white plastic spork. "Ow. What the hell? You just stabbed me." I started laughing while I jerked my hand back and rubbed it.

Brody snickered and rolled his eyes. "Can't tell you two are siblings or anything."

The door opened and Brooke came waltzing in. "Visiting hours are over for the morning. Y'all will need to leave. You can come back this evening from six to eight p.m."

Ugh. What a bitch. She made me want to stab her with a spork, even if it was plastic.

"Drew, try to get some sleep and don't give them any more trouble," I warned. I looked over at Brody. "You ready to go *honey*?"

Without skipping a beat, Brody sweetly put his arm around my waist. "Whenever you are, babe."

We made our exit from Drew's room with Brooke watching. I so badly wanted to shove my tongue down his throat right in front of her. The lioness had her claws out and ready, daring her to touch my man.

Whoa! Where did this shit come from? I'd never felt possessive about a guy before. Especially one that wasn't even mine. Yet.

As we hopped back into Brody's car, he asked, "Hey, why don't you come to my house? We can take a ride on the river and get some fresh air. That is, unless you have to go to work."

"Nope, next shift is in two days. And, yeah, that sounds like fun, but we need to be back at six to see Drew. Would you mind stopping by my place so I can take Ruger out and hang with him for a little while? Plus I need to grab a few things and change."

There was no way I was going to wear a dress on a boat. I could see it flying up and revealing my lacy white tangas. Nope, I needed shorts and a tank. I might as well throw on my bikini too.

He glanced over to me, and then turned his attention back to the road. "Sure, we can do that."

As we drove, I found myself trying to figure out what his game was. He was a handsome, wealthy man who could certainly have anyone he wanted. Why me? I was just a nurse with frizzy hair and I certainly wasn't rolling in it or part of high society.

Chapter Ten

Leila

Brody pulled into a spot right in front of the door, then came around the hood to open my car door for me.

"Hey, I hope you don't mind, I need to make a couple of business calls. I'll be waiting in the car whenever you are ready." He closed the passenger door. He watched me until I was safely inside my condo.

First, I let out Ruger, then played an energetic game of tennis ball with him, making sure he'd run up and down the stairs enough times to tucker him out. I gave him a treat, let him slurp up some water and then watched as he threw his body against the wall, turned upside down and went to sleep.

Quickly, I washed up while Ruger was snoring and changed my clothes. I threw on a pair of cutoff jean shorts and white cotton T-shirt over my peach colored string bikini, grabbed a towel, a light pink jersey sundress and some toiletries. With my crazy ass curls, the wind would whip my hair into a Medusa-like mess. I needed product if I had any hope of not sending Brody screaming into the hills.

I sent a text to Barb to check in since I haven't talked to her today.

Hey hooker going out w/ Brody for a ride on his boat, Drew's doing ok, sx again 2moro to rmv bullet. So much 2 tell ya, call ya later. SMOOCHES

I knew she was probably sleeping since she worked last night, so I didn't wait to see if she'd text back. I chucked my phone in the bottom of my handbag, then roused an exhausted Ruger, put him in his crate and left his little night light on. I turned out the rest of the lights and locked the door on my way out to Brody's car. He was out of the car and holding my door for me as I approached.

"Overnight bag?" He looked at my small duffle with a hopeful expression.

I decided to flirt with the devil. "Might be."

Nodding with a huge smile Brody pulled out onto East Bay and started heading to his house. "You're more than welcome to stay the night any time you want."

I cocked my head to the side and looked at him out of the corner of my eye. "Who said the sleepover was with you?" I couldn't wipe the sinful grin from my face.

"Damn, it's like that huh?" he teased right back.

I burst out laughing. "Okay, you got me. It's not an overnight bag," I explained. "I grabbed a change of clothes and some hair stuff for after the boat ride. I didn't want you to have to be seen with me in public looking like I stuck my hand in an electrical outlet."

"You could cover yourself in mud and I'd still be the envy of every man in the room," he said.

Smooth, and he seemed sincere. After his pronouncement to Drew this morning, I decided to give Brody the benefit of the doubt. Nonetheless, I deflected the comment.

"Ha. We'll see what you think after the wind has its way with me." I turned my attention out the window to take in the gorgeous day. The sun was finally out after a few muggy days of showers.

We pulled onto Route 17 south and drove for about twenty minutes before we turned off the main road to pull up to a large gated property. Brody put down his window and pressed a code into the keypad. The gates slowly swung open and we continued down the paved driveway through the meticulously landscaped grounds on a winding road. Along the way, we passed a small stable with three horses grazing in the paddock.

Oh, how I would love to go riding. I haven't been riding since my mom died.

We came through a small grove of trees into a large open area. A massive gray stone and stucco home sat off to the right. The multilevel home was wrapped with a warm, inviting porch adorned with potted plants, a large hanging porch bench and white wicker furniture, all decorated with large yellow and gray throw pillows.

We drove over to the matching four-car garage adjacent to the house and parked. As we walked up the front steps, it felt like I had just stepped into a picture from *Better Homes and Gardens*.

We entered through ten-foot mahogany and wrought iron double doors that opened to a two-story foyer. A modern chandelier with about twenty pendant lights, of varying lengths and crystals, hung above a black marble table. In the middle of the table sat an arrangement of fresh wild flowers. The floors were a rich acacia blonde hardwood that made the home feel welcoming, despite its size. Large homes always felt so intimidating, like they had personalities of their own and were looking down their noses at you. Brody's home had a cozy, lived in feel. You could feel the love and warmth that cloaked this home. The walls were painted a neutral, but rich taupe color and decorated with tasteful artwork. I couldn't tell you a thing about the artwork or the artists, other than they fit the home's personality.

Brody placed his hand on the small of my back and ushered me through the foyer, down the wide hallway toward an extravagant kitchen. Chefs from around the world would give their right kidneys to cook in this kitchen. Stainless steel appliances set throughout toffee colored quartz countertops and custom cabinets. It was a dream kitchen.

We traveled past the kitchen to a set of French doors that opened out to the veranda overlooking a large in-ground pool and spa. Off in the distance I could see a lengthy dock leading out to the Stono River.

He steered us to a large circular teak table that had been set for lunch. "I hope you're hungry. I called ahead to my assistant and had her prepare lunch."

"I am a little hungry. This was really sweet of you Brody. What are we havin'?" My stomach started to grumble in anticipation.

Brody pulled out my chair. "Grilled chicken Caesar salads. Drew told me it's one of your favorites."

With a smile I nodded and took my seat.

"You have a gorgeous home Brody." I lifted my napkin from the table and placed it across my lap.

"Thank you, but I can't take credit. This was my parents' home. My mother decorated the whole thing herself, down to the knobs and hinges on the cabinets. She loved this place. When they died, I couldn't bring myself to sell it and it was too large to keep as a memento when I had a place of my own. So, I ended up selling my place and moving out here. It's definitely further from work, but it has its advantages. It's peaceful out here. I'm close to the water and can jump on the boat and be in the ocean in minutes. But it gets lonely. Jane, my assistant, lives here too, but she usually keeps to herself. She'll have dinner with me occasionally and then we'll talk for a while. She's kind of filled the motherly role the last few years," he explained.

"Do you have any other family around the area?" I was trying to change the subject because I didn't want to Brody to dwell on losing his parents.

"Not here in South Carolina, but I have an uncle in Philadelphia. How about you? Have any family around other than Drew?" he asked.

Well, there's a loaded question. "Honestly, I'm not sure. I have a dad out there somewhere, but I don't consider him family anymore. Not after he abandoned us almost twenty years ago. What kinda man just up and leaves his family?" Oh crap, I went there. Taking another bite of my salad, I decided I didn't want to talk about him anymore. "I'm sorry Brody. I didn't mean to sound so bitchy. Guess it's a sensitive subject for me. How 'bout we not talk about family?"

"Sounds good to me. How's your salad?" He continued eating, watching me intently.

"It's really good, what do you think? You don't look like you enjoy salads much." I watched as he pushed the lettuce around the plate.

Brody chuckled. "What gave me away?"

"Gee, I don't know, maybe the fact that you have only taken one bite and I'm almost done. You should've picked something you liked. You didn't have to eat this on my account." Though, the sentiment was sweet; I was flattered.

"I asked Drew what your favorite meal was and he said this. So that's what I wanted you to have, your favorite." He reached out and took my hand in his. "I want to give you whatever your heart desires, because you deserve it, so I planned an afternoon I thought you'd enjoy. After we finish here, we'll take a walk down the dock to the boat that is ready and waiting for us. From there, we can go anywhere you want."

God, this man was too good to be true and certainly too good for me. There has to be a catch or something. I already knew he wasn't overcompensating for a small dick. Please don't let him be bisexual or into really weird shit. Don't get me wrong, I was down for some kinky stuff, but I wasn't into someone whipping me or bringing someone else into sex. It wasn't like I've had a whole lot of practice with the whole three men I have been with and it's been *long* months since the last time I had sex. Four years since I had good sex, not mind-blowing, earth-moving sex, but at least I had an orgasm that I didn't have to fake. If sex with Brody is anything like I imagined, we will need to board up the windows and batten down the hatches.

"Well, if I'm being honest, I'd much rather stay here. Maybe we could swim or take a walk around the property…or go see the horses. I just worry with the summer weather we might get out there and get caught in a thunderstorm. I'm sorry. I know you had this whole thing planned and now I'm ruining it." Before he had time to answer, I said, "Never mind, let's take the boat out. Besides, it's not like we are gonna go miles offshore, right?" I shook the doubts from my mind. *Chill out Lei*, I scolded myself.

"No, we can stay here. We'll just go out another time, when we have plenty of time and nowhere to be." He walked over to the veranda kitchen and picked up a small tablet, walked back over to the table and handed it to me. "Here, why don't you find some music to put on? It's connected to the wireless speaker system outside. I'm going to go inside and change." He leaned down and gave me a quick, sweet kiss, sucking my bottom lip between his lips and nibbling slightly. By the time I opened my eyes, he was walking through the French doors into the breakfast nook.

I grabbed my phone and synced my playlist to the tablet. Soon Luke Bryan's "Play it Again" was resonating through the veranda. Shucking my top and shorts, I threw them on one of the cushioned wicker lounge chairs. I was standing next to the side of the pool singing along when a strong pair of arms scooped me up and jumped in with me. I came up laughing and choking on water.

Brody popped up next to me for a split second and then disappeared again. I took that as my queue to give chase. I swam after him, but yet again he surprised me by turning and swimming right toward me. Quickly, I scrambled to turn around, knowing I was no longer the hunter but the hunted. Damn, that man was fast. He was on me before I could even reach the side of the pool to escape. He circled his arms around my waist and pulled me back into him. I spun around coming face to face with this gorgeous man—who wanted me.

Sweet baby Jesus, he took my breath away. I wrapped my freshly shaven legs around his sculpted V muscles at his lickable hips and my arms around his neck. He slid his hands down my thighs, then around to my ass. Just as he started to kiss me, Jason Aldean came over the speakers singing "Burnin' It Down." My God, if that wasn't a sign I don't know what was.

Brody kissed me deep and slowly, then quietly sang, "I wanna rock it all night, baby girl will you rock it out with me?"

Holy sheep shit Batman, the man is singing…to me. Of course he chose the sexiest, most provocative lines of the whole song. Damn you Lei for having morals, because so help me God, I would take this man right here, right now. The lioness was purring and ready to hunt. Brody was still kissing me, but I had to get away or I was going to falter.

I pulled back slightly, breaking the kiss and let the biggest grin ever spread across my face. He tilted his head to the side as if confused, that was my opening. I released my legs and shoved his head under water and swam away, giggling, as fast as I could. I heard him splashing behind me in pursuit, but this time I made it to the steps and flew out of the pool like it was filled with piranhas. I ran around the large rectangular pool on the concrete decking toward the diving board. Once I reached the diving board, I leapt off in a perfect swan dive into the ten-foot cool blue waters. As I hit the water I heard him laugh, a few seconds later I felt him jump in behind me.

I broke the surface and threw my hands up in retreat. "Okay, I give up, I give up." We were both cackling as he caught me.

"No, stop I can't breathe." I was laughing so hard I was crying.

He paused, slid his hand into my hair and hauled my lips to his. He kissed me like it was the end of time and we'd never have another one again. He stirred up so much passion within me I never knew existed. When he kissed me, it left me feeling things that scared the shit out of me. I didn't know him well enough to have these kinds of sensations. My stomach was filled with butterflies trying to escape and my whole body just wanted to scream in exhilaration.

We floated around the pool, talking and kissing for almost an hour, then the skies opened up and starting pouring on us. The heavy downpour felt like an ice bath in contrast to the tepid pool and sticky air. We scrambled out of the pool, grabbed our towels, my clothes and ran for the covered veranda.

"See, it's a good thing we stayed here. It would suck to be stuck on a boat right now." A huge bolt of lightning ripped across the sky making me take notice. As I was about to suggest we dry off inside, a loud clap of thunder startled me, causing me to jump.

"Let's get you inside, I'll show you to a bathroom. You're welcome to take a shower if you'd like to get warmed up," he offered as we entered the breakfast area off of the expansive kitchen.

"Oh, a shower would be great. It was like ninety-five degrees out there twenty minutes ago, but that rain was freezing," I said, shivering.

Jesus, Mary and Joseph. What did he set the air conditioner to in here, North Pole? My poor nipples were hard enough to cut glass.

Brody walked back to the foyer and climbed the lavish, wrought iron and hardwood staircase as I followed. He passed several doors to the left and right until we came to the last door on the left. He opened the door to, what I quickly figured out was, the master bedroom. It was seriously the size of my entire condo. There had to be nine hundred square feet in here. It was elegantly decorated with a massive black king-size bed with tall balusters, a suede upholstered headboard and a thick panel footboard on the right side of the room. There was an oversized wood-burning fireplace and a sitting area with a couch and coffee table to the left. Walking past the bed, straight ahead was a wall of large glass accordion doors that lead to a balcony overlooking the backyard and river. Turning around the room, I noticed a wet bar and small stainless refrigerator near the door where we came in.

"The bathroom is right through those doors. There should be towels already set out on the vanity. I'll wait for you to finish, then I'll get cleaned up." He turned toward another set of doors.

I looked back over my shoulder as I entered the bathroom, and saw him open a set of French doors. My mouth gaped open as my eyes were met with a walk-in closet that could have had its own zip code. No joke, in the quick glimpse I saw a large island, sitting area, two large floor to ceiling mirrors and walls of clothes, shoes, hats and ties hanging in perfect order. This was my Disney World. Brody's closet should have a turnstile and admission booth. Women would line up and camp out to walk through a closet like this.

He looked back at me. "Everything okay?"

"Huh, oh yeah, everything is fine. I'm gonna take a quick shower, but I'll be sure to leave some hot water for you." I winked and then sauntered into the bathroom, shutting the doors behind me.

WTF, I was so busy drooling over the closet, I hadn't noticed the swanky ultramodern bathroom done in all white. White limestone tile floor with walk-up sunken tub large enough to fit three or four people. Two of the shower walls were white glass and gray limestone mosaic tiles while the others were pure glass. It had a rainfall showerhead in the middle of at least a seven square foot area and body jets mounted throughout the walls. This was like a shower on steroids.

Oh, I can't wait to get in there.

Carefully, I opened the large glass door and turned on the water. I stepped out of my bathing suit bottoms and threw them in the sink, then untied my top and tossed in on top of my bottoms. I took my hair down and put the hair tie around my wrist, opened the door and tested the water. It was just right, as Goldilocks would say. Stepping in, I let the water cascade down my body, then shampooed and conditioned my hair before soaping up. I rinsed off and grabbed a gray, fluffy towel to wrap my hair in and then another to dry myself with. I looked around the posh bathroom and realized I left my duffle downstairs. Shit. I guess I was going to have to sneak down there and grab it.

Slowly, I opened the door and poked my head out. Looking around the room I didn't see Brody, so I walked out and started toward the door leading back to the hallway. I only made it halfway before the door was opened and in walked Brody, carrying my clothes and duffle.

"Here," he said, handing it to me. "Thought you might like to have your clothes. Although, I must say, I definitely prefer the fuzzy towel look." He smirked.

"Thanks, but I think I should put some clothes on. I'm all done in the bathroom. Thank you for letting me go first." I walked over to the bed. Knowing he was watching, I took my black lace VS panties out and slid them on under the towel. Keeping my back to his gaze, I dropped the towel and picked up the matching 34D bra from the bed. I took my time putting my bra on, just to tease him that much more. I heard him groan loudly and stalk off toward the bathroom. I knew I would pay for it later, but I couldn't help myself. I just didn't care anymore.

Dear God I wanted him. To hell with my morals, I was letting the lioness out of her cage.

Chapter Eleven

Brody

Fuck, she was going to give me an aneurism. My blood was boiling I was so turned on. No chance in hell a cold shower or my hand would relieve the pent up testosterone and sexual frustration. Nope, the only way that was going away was with my dick buried balls deep in her pussy. I had to find a way to calm myself. She wanted to take this slow and I didn't want to fuck it up. She was more than worth waiting for. Hell, I would wait as long as she made me, but not too long, *please*. This raging hard-on was going to be difficult to hide, I wasn't small. Turning on the shower, I stepped in, not even waiting for it to warm up. I looked up into the showerhead and tried to let the tension leave my body.

Deep in thought, I was trying to put my libido back in the bottle when I felt the tiniest hands on my lower back.

"You look like you could use a good, soapy massage," she whispered, kneading my skin.

"That might be the best pickup line I've ever heard," I teased.

"Would you like some company?" she asked quietly, still massaging. How did she not know the answer to that question?

I turned around and, without saying a word, I captured her in my arms and pushed her small, hot body up against the wall. As her warm skin met the cold glass and limestone tiles, she let out a small shriek. She reached up and wrapped her arms around my neck.

I crouched down, so we were nose to nose, eye to eye. "You sure you want this? Me? I'll wait if you aren't ready. I do *not* want to rush you or for you to have regrets later." I paused, searching her face. I could see the conflict in her eyes as she chewed on her bottom lip. I leaned forward, and seized her plump, pink lips between my teeth as I pulled her hands above her head and pinned them to the shower wall. She never closed her eyes; they never left mine. I sucked her bottom lip in and traced it with my tongue, then released it. My tongue pushed past her parted lips, swirling around her tongue and gently flicking back and forth. Finally, I pulled away, breathless and afraid to ask again, but I had to be sure.

"Are you absolutely sure you're okay with this? You can say no, I won't be upset. We can get dressed and take a walk around the yard."

She answered without hesitation. "The only walk I want to take is to your bed. With you. I'm sure this is what I want. *You* are what I want. I've never been more sure of anything before."

With that, I turned off the water, opened the shower door and grabbed our towels. I wrapped one of the gray cotton towels around my waist and started toweling Leila off. I wanted to take care of her, not rush it. I took her hair in the towel and gently squeezed the water from her heavy ringlets. I wrapped her in a dry towel, bent over, scooped her up in my arms and whisked her out of the bathroom.

I crossed the room to my large bed in four quick strides and placed her into the middle. She lay back on her elbow, reached up and pulled her towel open. For the first time, I was able to stand back and take her all in. She was truly magnificent. She had a petite frame with large, full breasts and hips that don't lie. I love that she wasn't rail thin or bony. She had a real body, something I could hold onto and not worry about snapping in half. I reached down and pulled the towel the rest of the way off of her and threw it on the floor. Immediately, she placed her hands over her pelvis. I lay down next to her and pulled them away.

"Don't hide from me. You're way too beautiful to cover up."

She blushed. "Sorry, it's been a while since…I've been with anyone. I guess I'm a little self-conscious."

"Oh baby, you don't have anything to worry about. Your body is perfect. Perfect neck." I place a chaste kiss on her neck. "Perfect breasts." Kissed her left breast just above her nipple. "Perfect nipples." I kissed and gently swirled my tongue around her right nipple. "Perfect stomach." Kissed from her sternum down to her navel. "Mmm, and I can't wait to kiss you here on your pretty little pussy. I bet you are wet. Hmm, I think I should be sure." She threw her head back and moaned as I slid my middle finger over her damp clit, between her folds and softly eased into her hot, wet pussy. My dick was harder than it had ever been and bounced in delight.

"Fuck, Leila, you're so wet. Goddamn, I can't wait to have you wrapped around my cock."

Her arms gave out as she fell back onto the bed, her legs parted just enough I was able to see her completely. She was completely bare, with the exception of a tiny patch of hair adorned just above her clit. She had miniscule pink lips surrounding her delectable pussy. I rolled over on my stomach and caught her left leg and threw it over my shoulder. I scooted all the way up until my face was just inches away from her. I lightly pushed her other leg up to grant me full access to her trembling body. She was looking down at me, biting her lip in approval. I used my fingers to pull her folds apart so I could see her clit. Using my thumb, I grazed it ever so gently, sending a jolt through her body and earning myself a deep throaty whine. I rubbed back and forth a few more times, before thrusting two fingers into her soaking wet cunt. I curled my fingers around and stroked her G-spot as I continued to rub her clit with my thumb. Her greedy little cunt clamped down on my fingers as I pulled out and pushed back into her. Her body was buzzing with pleasure as her hips thrust to meet my fingers.

"I can't wait to taste you any longer." I extended my tongue and lapped straight up from her quivering entrance to her hooded clit. Honey. She tasted like the purest honey, fresh from the hive. Circling the nub as I pumped my fingers, I felt her beginning to tense. Needing her to succumb quickly, I add just a tad more pressure as I licked back and forth. I could feel it coming and swirled around one last time.

She moaned and her body shook. "Oh God Brody, mmmm yeah, ohhhhh don't stop. I'm coming, don't stop, oh God, ahhhhhh."

She screamed out my name as she finally came, all over my fingers. She picked her head up, looked at me and breathlessly said, "Wow…that was…wow."

"Oh, sweetheart, that was just the beginning. I'm going to watch you come apart several more times before I'm done with you." I stood and dropped my towel exposing my eager cock. Dropping back down to the bed, I took my place again. "Starting right now."

I slipped my hand underneath her ass, pulled her to me and buried my face between her legs. Licking her sweet pussy, flicking my tongue back and forth over her swollen clit, I listened to her moaning and screaming in ecstasy. She started to convulse under my carefully guided attention and pressure to her nub.

Secretly, I prayed she'll find her release quickly. I was two minutes away from coming all over myself. She had me so fucking hard I could pound nails through a wall. Shit, I couldn't wait to feel her grip me as I thrust into her and milk my dick as I came. I pushed two fingers into her and sent her over the edge.

*****

Leila

"BRODYYYYYYY!" I wailed his name louder than I'd intended. "Oh God, Brody, holy shit." I tried to pull away from him to give my poor overly stimulated clit a break, but he snaked his arms up over my legs and held on tight.

"Wait," I begged, gasping for breath. "I need a minute, there is no way I can come again right this minute. My God, I've never come twice in that short of time before."

He grinned and slowly released me. "What can I say, I do what I can. We have all afternoon, I'm in no rush." He stood up and walked to the head of the bed and pulled the garnet comforter back, sat down and reached into the bedside table, moving things about. He was obviously looking for something.

"Oh, no, please tell me you have a condom?" I prayed he had one. I was not prepared or planning on this, but now that we were here I couldn't wait any longer. I needed to have him inside me, filling and stretching me. As much as I wanted this, there was no way we weren't using a condom, not after the man-whore stories I'd heard about him.

"Yeah, I was just getting one out and wanted to make sure I had a few more." He tossed one on the pillow and then set his sights on me. A few more? Geez, he was energetic.

"Time's up." He grabbed my left leg and swung me around to the edge of the bed. He took both of my hands in his and pulled me up so I was standing in front of him. He circled his arms around my back and lifted me up so we were eye to eye. I ran my fingers through his dark hair, tilted my head and captured his mouth.

Gently, he laid me on the pillows without breaking the kiss. I kept my eyes open, focused on the passion and lust growing in his cool blue eyes. He slowed his kiss to gentle pecks, trailing down my neck and across my collarbone. He reached over, took the condom from the pillow and then looked back into my eyes. "You're sure?"

I nodded lightly and whispered without breaking his gaze. "Yeah."

I heard the crinkle and rip of the wrapper and started having a wave of self-doubt. What if I'm not good? He'd been with way more partners than I had. What if he can't climax with me? Oh God, why did I say yes?

He positioned himself between my legs and propped up on his elbows; looking down at me, he smiled. It was a sweet, tender smile that instantly calmed my fears. It made me feel like I was the only woman in the world and that he wanted only me. He rubbed the thick head of his cock over my clit and stopped just before he entered me.

"Tell me if I hurt you," he said softly.

"I will." The anticipation had built so much I didn't think I could wait any longer. I opened my hips and pulled my calves up to flank his. Slowly, he pushed into me, stretching me so much it burned. Immediately, my whole body went rigid and he knew it. He stopped moving, allowing me to adjust to his girth. As I relaxed, he pushed the rest of the way in.

Sweet Jesus, he was huge. It's one thing to see it and think, *fuck there is no way that's gonna fit*, and it's another to have it impale you and prove it can.

He pulled out slightly and then drove back in. "Damn babe, you're so tight."

I grinned and then clenched my pelvic muscles around his hard cock buried in my pussy. "Holy fuck, Leila, you're gonna make me come right now and I'm not nearly done with you yet."

He quickened his pace, driving into me as I moaned. Sex had never been so amazing. Even if he only lasted five minutes, it would still be the best sex of my life. He slowed, angled his hips and hit my ever elusive G-spot. Well, at least I think that's what it was since no one had ever found it before. He grabbed my ass, lifted it, giving himself deeper access, and starting fucking me harder and faster than I had ever been fucked. My hands released their grip on his taut biceps and found themselves a new home digging into his lats. Trying to hold myself in place, as I got closer and closer to my climax, I locked my legs around his waist.

"Oh fuck, Brody, oh God don't stoooooop, yeaaaaah, ooooooooooh GOD BRODYYYY!" My orgasm hit me like a ton of bricks. Brody slowed, extending the climax.

"I don't think I have ever wanted to come so bad in all my life. You're so tight and God, feeling you come all over my dick was fuckin' amazin'." He tried to pace himself but I could tell he was ready to shatter into a million little pieces.

"I want you to fuck me hard and fast Brody," I said between gasping for air. I couldn't believe the words that were actually coming out of my mouth. I've never done the dirty talk thing before, but with Brody it felt natural, like I could say anything and he wouldn't think I was a slut or a nympho.

I placed my hands on the sides of his face and pull him to me, kissing him deep and fast. Our tongues tangle in the exploration of one another's mouths. Brody thrust once, harder than before, causing me to cry out from the sting. He stilled, pulled his hips back, looked down at me, then slammed into me hard again. Throwing my head back and closing my eyes, I prayed he wouldn't stop, even though it felt like he might tear me in half. With the pain and sting came pleasure and excitement.

Again, he stilled and looked at me. Something in his eyes had shifted. The look of hedonism and pleasure replaced with worry and concern.

"Oh fuck. Leila, are you okay? I was too rough wasn't I?"

I felt a lone tear escape my eye. "I'm okay, really, I'm fine, don't stop."

"Jesus, you're crying. I hurt you, didn't I? How can you say you're okay if you're in pain?" He looked like he was going to pull out of me, so I locked my hand behind his neck.

"I'm not crying in pain because you hurt me. You just feel so damn good. Okay, it did hurt a little, but it was good pain. I never knew that you could get so turned on from a little bit of pain, so don't you dare stop. Please," I explained. No way in hell was he going to stop; it felt way too incredible.

"Oh baby, you have no idea the kind of pleasure that pain can bring when applied the right way."

His comment gave me pause, but then he slammed deep into my body again making me forget everything, included my own name. Pushing himself up, he sat back on his heels, grabbed my right ankle and, in between thrusts, threw it up on his shoulder. He pushed my left leg out to the side, spreading me sideways across the bed. He increased his pace and lessened the intensity of his drive. He wrapped his arms around my right leg and held on to me as he continued to fuck me into oblivion. I could feel his cock growing and hardening the longer he drove into my wet pussy. He reached down with his thumb and found my swollen clit. He rubbed lightly as he plunged into me over and over again. Within a minute, I found myself teetering over the cliff and I was just about to fall.

"Wait Lei, wait, not yet. Come with me. I'm close. I want you to come with me," he pleaded. I squeezed his dick as hard as I could, knowing that would send him over the edge. He reached down and squeezed my clit between his thumb and middle finger, causing my whole body to convulse. No way could I hold off any more.

"Oh God, Brody, I need to come, I can't hold it anymore," I begged for my release.

"Not yet, wait for me." He fucked me hard and fast, rubbing my clit with his thumb. Then he screamed out my name. "Now Leila, now. Come for me."

That is all I needed. My hands sought out my breasts and squeezed my nipples as he impaled me roughly. My sex clenched as I felt his cock harden and twitch. He grunted, slowing his unrelenting assault on my throbbing, sore pussy, as he came. Brody massaged my clit through my orgasm until I was spent. We stilled for a few moments before he pulled out of me and went to the bathroom. I drew the comforter up to cover myself; his absence left a chill on my skin.

"Jesus Christ Brody," I huffed. "I never knew sex could be so...intense."

I could barely breathe, let alone absorb my astonishment over the best sex ever. Seriously, before Brody I was lucky to have one orgasm during sex. And that was usually if I did it myself. Shit, this...this could be addictive. Sex like this surely can't last with one person for very long. Maybe this is why he bounced from bed to bed.

Damn it, why did I have to go there now? Why couldn't I just enjoy this moment?

"Lei, believe it or not, it can be better that. It'll definitely get more intense. If you want it to, that is," he said in a challenging tone as he sauntered back over to the bed.

I rolled to my side as he climbed back into the bed. He lay down and pulled me to him, nestling me against his chest. "I seriously don't think it can get more intense Brody. That was...transcendent."

"Let's just say if we were to add some toys, the pleasure could be...heightened. Remember what you said about feeling good. The pain you experienced is mild and brought mild pleasure." He lay there looking up at the ceiling. I suddenly felt a little uneasy.

I shot up in the bed.

"Toys, like as in paddles or whips and shit?" My voice was at least three octaves higher in response and I'm sure my eyebrows had never reached that height before.

He burst out laughing. "No, I'm not talking about beating you. Relax babe. Take a breath. You look like you're gonna pass out."

"Okay, then what are you suggesting?" I settled back into his side and he pulled my arm across his masculine chest, entwining our fingers together.

"Let's start out light and then, seeing how you like it, we can go from there. Maybe a blindfold and some well-placed ice cubes." His playful, yet devious smile returned, and in kicked my curiosity.

"Ice cubes huh? I think I can handle that. Just don't plan on pulling a Christian Grey and go paddlin' my ass, 'cause I can guar-damn-tee you, that shit won't fly," I told him, shaking my head.

"I promise you, I won't do anything that you won't enjoy. By the time we are done, you'll love it and be begging for more." He sounded so cocky.

"Oh really, you think so, do you?" I said just as smugly. "And if I don't? Does that mean this," I motioned back and forth between us, "won't work out?"

He flipped me onto my back and was on top of me so fast it took my breath away. "Not a chance in hell. If we had sex like today, every day until the end of time, it would be more than enough for me. But I'm not going to lie, I like to push boundaries and try new shit. That doesn't mean you'll like it. I only want to give you pleasure, babe. It's a huge turn on to watch you moan and come at my hand. If you don't enjoy it, then neither do I."

I studied his face, while my thoughts prattled away. Could I like this? I mean, I did. A little. But, can I trust him not to make me do something I don't want to do or didn't like? Maybe just a little experimenting would be okay.

"Okay."

"Okay, as in…you want to try?" His eyes beamed with desire.

"Yeah, just don't go all S and M on me," I quipped.

"How about we go shopping? That way we can pick out things together and there are no misunderstandings and I don't take it too far." He leaned down and kissed my nipple, swirling his tongue in circles until it pebbled.

"Mmmm." I was trying to focus on the stimulating sensation he was giving me and not on his "take it too far" comment. Brody switched breasts and started to nibble gently on my nipple, while he was tweaking the other between his fingers.

"Ahhhh," I moaned, conceding to the pleasure.

I started to notice the increased pressure as he sucked, tongued and nipped at my breast. He started to lightly grind his teeth over my nipple. Not so much it really hurt, but enough it provoked just the right amount of pain to be pleasurable.

Holy shit, that's what he meant.

Oww. Okay, that hurt a little bit more. I got this; it wasn't too bad. The pain caused heat to flood my sore, swollen sex. Now it throbbed in both desire and from the pounding it took earlier. Damn, this man was relentless. As I started to eagerly imagine the afternoon's events, his phone started ringing.

He groaned, releasing my nipple from his mouth with a pop, snatched the phone from the bedside table and answered it. "Hey Sara, what's up?"

Sara, my lioness popped her head up. Who is Sara?

Whoa, wait, I have no right to be jealous. Besides, I didn't know who this Sara chick was; she could be nobody. I hoped like hell he wasn't taking a call from some random chick he used to fuck, while I was still, literally, lying in his bed.

"No, Sara, I told you if he can't make the meeting we already have in place, then that's tough. No, I don't give a shit about any sob story. If he wants me to invest in his restaurant, then he'll get his ass in my office at eleven a.m. Monday morning." He leaned over and started trailing delicate, quiet kisses from my ear down my neck, back to my breasts.

Still on the phone, he said, "Okay, Sara, I'll push it back one hour, that's it." Kiss. "Listen, I have to run...something just came up." His eyebrows jumped. Kiss. "I'm unreachable for the rest of the day. If anything else comes up, handle it or it'll wait until tomorrow. Thanks Sara." He hit end on the cell phone while she was still talking. He stood up and took the phone over to the coffee table, then came back over and jumped on top of me.

"Where was I? Oh, right, I was right here." He palmed my breasts and squeezed my nipples, giving each one a quick lick. He hopped up and strutted to the bathroom. I heard a flush and then water start running. I thought he must be washing his hands, so I took the moment of peace to shove my face into one of the down pillows, squealed and kicked the bed.

"Ahem."

Oh dear God in heaven, shoot me now.

Embarrassment washed over me, I left my face buried in the pillow. "Please tell me you did not just see that."

"Sorry babe, I can wait in the tub, if you're not done." He chuckled.

"No, smart-ass, I'm done." I sat up and threw the pillow at him and dragged myself out of the massive bed.

"Smart-ass, huh?" He bent over and threw me over his shoulder and smacked my ass.

I let out a little yip. "Put me down Brody. Come on, put me down." I was trying to be serious, but I couldn't help but laugh and roll my eyes. I mean, come on, who could be serious while being toted upside down with this man's backside as their view.

Damn, there is not an angle in which he didn't look hot.

He carried me through the bedroom, to the bathroom and over to the small, indoor swimming pool he called his bathtub. He walked up the wide limestone steps to the tub and stepped down into the inviting warm water.

"I thought you might like to soak for a little. Since I mauled that tight little pussy of yours," he gloated.

I hid my eyes and pushed my fingers up my brow. "Was it that apparent?" I asked, embarrassed at my inexperience.

"Hey, don't do that. I was just playing." He pulled my hand away. "I just wanted to help you relax a little. I know, despite everything we've done today, that you're still tense and worried about Drew."

"Sorry, I guess I'm a little self-conscious. It's been a while since I've been with anyone." I sat there in the tub with my back to him not sure what to say.

"Leila, I'm going to be completely honest with you. I was not expecting this. I don't really do relationships. I'm sure Drew has said as much. I work a lot and I have to travel often, but we can try if you want to." He laid it all out there.

"Listen Brody, I didn't sleep with you today thinkin' this was gonna be some whirlwind romance." I started to feel pretty damn indignant. "I'm sure you have plenty of women waiting and I don't want to get in your way." I jumped out of the tub, grabbed a towel and stalked out of the bathroom, leaving Brody stunned. I grabbed my clothes and ran for the door. I got as far as the stairs before I heard him behind me.

"Leila, what the fuck?"

Remembering the hall bathroom was the first at the top of the stairs, I ducked in and locked the door. I threw my clothes down, frustrated with myself. Damn it, Lei you had to know better. Did you think Drew was making all that shit up?

A gentle knock on the solid wood door pulled me from my thoughts.

"Leila, please open up. Talk to me, what did I say?" He sounded sincere.

I dried off and put on my bikini, shorts and tank. "Brody, please just leave me alone. I obviously made a mistake. I thought I could do casual sex with you, but hearing you say you would *try* if I wanted to, just sort of solidified the fact that casual sex is all you do."

"Come on Lei, opened the door so we can talk. That's not what I meant. I was just trying to be honest. I *do* want to try…with you. This is honestly the first time I have ever said that to anyone. I've never been in any sort of monogamous relationship and," he huffed, "I guess I am fucking this up already, but please understand, nothing about this is casual."

I sat down on the toilet as he spoke, trying to figure out what I should do. He probably thinks I'm a fucking nutjob, running out soaking wet. But you can't get hurt if you walk away first. Well, at least that has always been my reasoning. I walked over and unlocked the door and sat back down.

Chapter Twelve

Brody

I stood in the hallway, looking at the door trying to figure out how to make this right. When I heard the click of the door being unlocked, I waited a second and when it didn't open, I turned the knob. I pushed the door open and she was sitting there on the toilet, eyes filled with tears and cheeks pink.

"Hey, let's go back to the bedroom and talk." I held my hand out to her and nodded toward my room.

She stood, taking my hand, not saying a word and let me lead her back down the hallway she had just ran through trying to escape me. I walked her past the couch over to the bed. I wanted to hold her and set her mind at ease. I wasn't trying to be a dick. I just wanted her to understand I wasn't going to always be around, but that I still wanted to be with her. I lay down on my side in the middle of the bed and pulled her down in front of me so we were facing each other. I propped myself up on my elbow and looked into her beautiful brown eyes.

"So, when I said I don't do relationships, I should've said I've never done a relationship before now. I really like you, Leila. You make me feel something I haven't felt in a really long time. I feel alive with you." I pulled her closer and kissed the tip of her nose. "I'm probably going to fuck up a million times along the way and say things I don't mean or just say the wrong thing. You'll have to be patient with me. I do want to try, not just because you want to but because I really want to. There's no one waiting in the shadows to jump into bed with me."

"I'm sorry I freaked out and ran from you. If we're both being honest, my whole adult life I've avoided serious relationships. I have a really hard time trusting. I can't get hurt if I am the one who walks away first," she clarified her statement.

"I have to say that's the first time a woman has literally run away from me." I grinned. "Although, there have been a few that I wish would have," I added, teasing.

She rolled her eyes, trying not to let me see her smile.

"Ahhh, there it is, your stunning smile." Proud of myself, I beamed back at her. "I want you to know that I'll never cheat, that's not me. If I don't want to be with you, then I'll respect you enough to tell you. I expect the same from you. If you are with me, then you're mine and I don't want to see some other man's hands all over you. Just promise you'll talk to me before you haul ass again."

She was quiet for a minute; I could see her processing all that I had just said.

"I don't cheat either, so that won't be an issue. I can't promise I won't run, but I'll promise to try to talk to ya before I do."

"Deal. Now come here." I wrapped my arms around her, rolled and pulled her tiny body on top of mine. I held her face in my hands and looked at her. She was so gorgeous. I leaned up and kissed her, tracing her lips with my tongue.

Chapter Thirteen

Leila

We lay in bed talking for the next couple of hours. We talked about traveling the world, books and sports. Brody seemed to be shocked that I liked football. He couldn't seem to wrap his head around the fact that from September through January I did not work on Sundays simply because of football. He nearly fell off the bed when I told him I played fantasy football. His words, "I found the perfect woman." I laughed and told him I was far from perfect.

We laughed and shared silly stories about our childhoods. I brushed over most of mine since I didn't have as many funny stories to share. Brody must have sensed my anxiety and quickly started talking about cooking and food. I could understand why he invested in restaurants. His voice came alive when he talked about food.

"Let's get dressed and get something to eat on the way to see Drew. That salad didn't do shit for me. Plus, I worked up an appetite," he teased, waggling his eyebrows.

"Sounds good to me, where do you want to eat?" I asked.

"Doesn't matter, what are you in the mood for? California Dreamin' is on the way and pretty close to MUSC, or there is—" I stopped him.

"California Dreamin' is perfect, I love that place." I jumped up and gathered my small duffle and handbag. "They have the best salad on the planet."

"What is with you and salads?" he asked.

"What? I like them. It's not like all salads are healthy, like the California Dreamin' salad with its hot bacon dressing," I educated him. "Go get dressed before I smother you in my boobs," I ordered.

"No way, I'd rather smush my face in your tits. Come here." He chased me around the bed.

"Go! Stop. And go get dressed." I jumped on top of the bed. "We'll never leave if you don't go," I admonished him.

"Party-pooper." He retreated with a pout all the way to his closet the size of Rhode Island.

He returned wearing dark jeans, a snug, white cotton tee and brown oiled-leather Sperry's. Holy shit, I should have waited downstairs. He looked so fucking hot. I'm so glad I took the opportunity to change into my dress. At least, I was dressed like I deserved him, even though I probably didn't.

Holding his hand out to me he asked, "Ready to go babe?"

I smiled. "Yes, sir, I am." Sweet baby Jesus, get me out of this room before I rip his clothes off and tie him to the bed.

We left the house around 4:30 p.m. and started back toward downtown. As we exited the property, the horses were galloping through the field. The sight made me want to go for a ride. The power and grace they exhibited as they ran was spectacular. Maybe if things go well Brody would invite me back out here and we would saddle up. I bet Drew would love to come out with us. Well, once he was feeling better. I hoped he hadn't given the nurses too much trouble.

Ugh, macho men make the worst patients. Just like the BBB (big biker baby) from the other night. Either they go all alpha male on you, insisting they can just walk off the 9mm GSW to the quad or they damn near faint at the sight of a little 22 gauge needle.

I had this sexy-as-fuck guy come in about two weeks ago, who had an "accident" with a knife. He had a laceration from his wrist to the middle of this forearm, clearly a defensive wound, and he wanted me to just put some glue on it and wrap him up. When I laughed at him and told him he needed sutures he refused. Told me he didn't have time for all that bullshit, just to wrap it up. He, of course, was a biker. But he, unlike BBB, was the epitome of the word biker. He was strong, rugged, drop dead gorgeous with messy golden blond hair and a scruffy beard. He wore a ripped up pair of jeans, white tee, leather vest with patches on it and had massive arms covered in full sleeves of tattoos. If he hadn't been a biker, I probably would have taken him up on his offer for a drink.

"You're awfully quiet over there, what's going on inside that head of yours?" he inquired.

"Huh, oh, I was just thinking about work"—busted—"and Drew. And your horses. Watching them run reminded me of when I was a kid. Drew and I used to go riding when my mom was alive. She had a friend who had horses out near Walterboro. We would go ride her horses on the weekends that my mom actually had off." I stared out the window thinking about my mom.

"Why don't we plan on all going riding when Drew has recovered?" He glanced over at me, then back to the road.

"I would really like that Brody."

I was so in trouble. I swear this guy can read my mind. He was either really smooth or really sweet. I hadn't settled on a verdict, but I was leaning toward sweet. I wasn't ready to let my guard down just yet though.

We drove past the marina and pulled up to the restaurant a few minutes later. We walked up to the hostess stand and were immediately taken to a table. They sat us near the bar with a picturesque view of the water. We ordered two glasses of sweet tea while perusing the menu. I don't know why I even bothered. I only ever ordered the California Dreamin' salad with the hot bacon dressing. The waiter brought back our drinks and a basket of honey drenched croissants. *Damn him.* They were mouthwateringly delicious, but as much as I loved them, they loved my ass even more. I didn't have time to run them off, so I had to pass.

"You know what you're gonna get?" I asked, placing my menu on the table next to me.

"I think I'm going to get a steak. Probably the rib eye with a baked potato," he said, making my mouth water.

"Oh, that sounds yummy. I wish I could eat a loaded baked potato, mmmm. Carbs are my favorite enemy." I giggled at my own comment.

He let his menu fall away from his face. "You do realize you're thin, right? You can eat whatever you want."

I burst out laughing. "I'm 'thin' because I don't eat whatever I want. That, and because I run like I'm being chased by a clown with a bloody knife. Thank God I have Ruger, he loves to run." I smiled at the thought of my slobbery best friend.

The waiter returned and Brody ordered for both of us. Returning to our conversation, Brody asked how I came to own a drug-sniffing retired police dog.

"He couldn't work anymore. He's seven years old, which is young for a K-9 to be retired, but his hip dysplasia made it difficult for him to run down a suspect," I explained. "I have to keep the remote close when I watch TV because if he hears sirens, he runs to the door and freaks out. And God forbid if Drew shows up in uniform or in a marked car. Ruger still has the drive, but his hips are too arthritic."

"Poor guy, that sucks," Brody sympathized. "I hope I never have to be put on the sidelines and watch people do my job." His cell phone started buzzing on the table.

"Damn, sorry I thought I put it on silent, not vibrate," he apologized, picking up the phone. "Shit, Leila, I'm sorry I have to take this. I'll be right back." He answered the phone and walked back toward the front of the restaurant.

As busy as it was, I knew our food wouldn't be out anytime soon so it wasn't a big deal. He'd be gone only a minute or two. I turned, looking out the window and watched the boats on the choppy water, when all of the sudden I heard a deep, sultry, yet gravelly voice.

"Excuse me, don't I know you?" Turning around I was staring at the sexy-as-fuck badass biker from two weeks ago. Damn, is it possible he's even hotter than before? Shit, what was his name?

"Yeah, you're that nurse from the ER, aren't ya? The one who patched me up and then refused to let me buy ya a drink."

"Uh, yeah." Shit, shit, shit. Horrible fucking timing, dude. I tried to look around him to see if Brody was on his way back.

"Why don't you let me buy you a drink?" he offered.

"Actually, I am here with someone. He just stepped out front to take a phone call; he should be back any minute." Silently I begged for tall, dark and slightly dangerous to leave before Brody got back.

"Leila, right?" he asked.

"Right, but how do you know my name? I certainly don't remember yours."

"It's not every day that a woman turns me down. I tend to remember her name, and since there's only ever been you, it's a short list." He stopped a waiter, took his pen and check pad, scribbled something down and placed a page in my hand.

Geez. Conceited much?

"Call me when you're ready for that drink. Only live a few miles from here so if your *friend* doesn't come back, call me." He nodded and walked away. I looked down at the crumpled paper. Jaxon. I stared at the name and number and shoved it in my purse.

Thank God, that was close. I didn't see Brody taking too kindly to Jaxon's offer to take me out. Speaking of Brody, where the hell was he? Just as I started to look around, our food arrived. Okay, what the fuck? It had been more than five minutes. I looked at my watch. Crap, it was almost 5:30, visiting hours started in thirty minutes.

Do I get up and look for him? I didn't have his cell phone number to even call him. I'd wait another minute or so and then if he wasn't back, I'd walk out front and find him.

Tick...

Tock...

Tick...

Tock...

I took my napkin out of my lap and stood up to walk out when I saw Jaxon standing at the bar. He was wearing jeans and a maroon button down, rolled up to his elbows showing off his tats.

Okay, I had to get past him without him seeing me. I waited until he was talking to the tall, beefy, bald man next to him and made my way to the front door. I could see Brody on the phone outside on the sidewalk. He was pacing and swinging his hands. He looked pissed, almost as much as I was. I walked out the front doors, down the stairs and right up to him and just looked at him.

"Hang on," he barked into the phone. "I'm sorry Leila, I'll be inside in a minute." Then he continued to yell into his phone about having this discussion too many times.

"Just thought I'd let you know your dinner is getting cold. You finish your call. I'll see you later." I spun around and walked back inside. I reached the table, grabbed my purse and took out my phone. I decided to call Barb and see if she could come pick me up. I'll be damned if I was going to miss visiting hours.

I flagged the waiter down, got the check and paid for dinner. Barb answered and said she'd be here in five minutes. Rolling my eyes, I had a feeling she'd be here before Brody came back. I got my salad to go and left Brody's food on the table. I took out a pen and an old receipt and wrote:

Don't worry I paid for dinner before I left.
Thanks, Leila

Of course, as my luck was running, I literally walked right into Jaxon coming out of the bar. *Shit Lei, you have to stop texting and walking.*

"Sorry, I wasn't paying attention," I excused myself.

82

"No worries, where's your friend?" Jaxon asked and I was almost too embarrassed to answer.

"He got pulled away on business. I'm actually on my way out. My friend is waiting out front for me. See ya." I smiled quickly and then rushed out the door. I skipped down the steps, passing Brody, walked over to Barb's topless black Jeep Wrangler and hopped in. Brody came running down the stairs.

"Leila, I was just coming back in. Where are you going?" He seemed stunned I wasn't waiting like a good little girl.

"Well, Brody, considering it's almost six o'clock, I'm going to the hospital to see my brother. Since you were too busy on the phone, I called Barb," I responded.

"Wait, it's almost six? Shit! Leila, I am sorry. The call just got away from me. I was trying to…uh." He stopped, stumbling over his words.

"Look, you obviously have things you need to handle and I need to spend some time with Drew. I'll talk to you later Brody."

"Wait, let me take you," he pleaded.

"No. Why don't you just call me later?"

"Okay, you're pissed. I get that, but I told you I suck at this." He pulled out his business card. "My cell is on there, text me your number, I don't have it."

I looked at the card and back into his baby blue eyes, took a deep breath remembering the last forty-eight hours. "Fine, I'll text you. Bye Brody."

He leaned in and kissed my cheek and whispered, "I'm really sorry Lei. Please, don't run far."

Just as I looked back up at him, I saw Jaxon coming down the stairs. I turned to Barb. "Let's go, I need to get outta here."

She put the Jeep in gear and drove away. I couldn't help but look back at Brody. He was walking to the front door of the restaurant with his head down, but I could see Jaxon walking over toward him. Dear God, please let his car be near Brody's and that be the reason he was walking in that direction.

"What the hell is goin' on, Lei?" Barb shouted over the wind howling around us as we drove back to the hospital.

"Long story, girl." I rolled my eyes and starting giving her the short version of the events over the last forty-eight hours.

Chapter Fourteen

Leila

Barb dropped me off at Ashley River Tower and went back home since she had been in to check on Drew after her shift ended this morning. I made my way up to Drew's room, stopping at the nurse's station to see if he had been behaving himself. His new nurse, Melissa, assured me he was having a better afternoon. She also informed me Drew was back to his old self, flirting shamelessly. I laughed, not surprised, and took it as a positive sign.

I walked in the room to find Drew sitting up watching ESPN *SportsCenter*. "Anything good on?"

"Hey sis. Nah, I'm just watching the same recap for the third time. Where's Brody? Parking the car?" He looked around me to the door.

"Uh, no Brody is…"

"Right behind her. Sorry, had to use the restroom." Brody appeared in the hospital room out of thin air. I hadn't noticed him when I was in the hallway. He walked over and sat down in one of the chairs next to Drew that was facing the television. "What's on? *SportsCenter*. Hmm, no baseball games?"

"Nah, they don't have a whole lot of channels to choose from here. But at eight the Saturday night game comes on, so I have that to look forward to. My luck, it will be the Yankees or Mets." Drew hated New York sports teams; he was a Braves fan. Brody chuckled quietly.

"Hey Drew, has Drake been back up to see you since this morning?" I wondered if he had a chance to talk to Drew yet.

"Yeah, he was here about an hour or two ago. It's hard to keep straight with the pain meds." Drew shook his head. "But he said surgery is a go for tomorrow and that you should call him later because he knows you're a, and I quote, FA-REAK," he said, making his voice jump an octave.

"Shut it Drew, you're lucky you're in pain or else I'd beat your ass," I threatened. Brody was trying not to laugh at us bickering back and forth like children.

Drew started to laugh and clutched his abdomen. "Stop Lei, I'm gonna pop something."

"I hope you do, serves you right for makin' fun of me." I sat on the foot of his bed and grabbed my bag. I reached in and whipped out his phone. "Here, Bobby gave it to me when you were brought in. I charged it for you."

He took the phone from me. "Sweet. Thanks for bringing it. Any chance you brought a charger with you?" he asked.

"Yeah, of course, I did. I also downloaded and logged you on as me on the DIRECTV app. You can watch On Demand from your phone if there is nothing on." I glanced at Brody who hadn't taken his eyes off me.

"Thanks kiddo, I appreciate it." He patted my knee. "Ay sis, can you see if you can get me a coke? I'm dyin' of thirst."

"Of course, do you have a cup with ice already?" I looked around the room.

"No, the tech took it with my lunch tray earlier," he explained.

"Okay, I'll be right back, you two behave."

*****

Brody

Shit, I knew why Drew got rid of Leila, he was going to browbeat answers out of me. I looked at Drew, who was smiling watching his baby sister leave the room. Once she shut the door, his cut his eyes to me.

"What the hell is up with Leila? Did somethin' happen? She looks like somebody kicked her puppy," Drew grilled.

"We were at dinner and I got a call I had to take. I lost track of time and she called Barb to pick her up. She left me in the parking lot of California Dreamin'. Man, she was so pissed, I don't know how I am going to make this up to her, but I will. She's agreed to talking a little later. After we leave here I'll take her home and then we can talk," I tried to explain.

"Who called Brody?" Drew's voice was stern.

"Don't Drew, it wasn't like that. I swear. It was a business call." I stood and ran my hands through my hair. "I've been working on a deal to buy a bunch of land near Summerville. It was all set to settle next week and now everything is falling apart and…. You don't care about that. Point is, it's not what you think at all. It was really business. It's not like I was blowing her off. I just got so consumed by the details, I lost track of the time. I am going to make it up to her."

"I hope so," her tiny voice filled the room. She carried a Styrofoam cup with a straw floating around in it over to Drew's tray table.

"Here, I got you water too." She sat it down in front of him without so much as a glance in my direction. "Is there anything else I can do?"

"No, just sit and relax. Tell me what ya did today?" he asked innocently.

I could see her panic starting to set in, so I chimed in. "I took her out to my house, we had some lunch and went swimming. Just hung out, talked and got to know each other."

Drew looked at Leila, who was smiling at me with a sweet but scary smile. "Yeah, then we tried to go to dinner, but it seems you've already heard about that. Now, we're all here."

"Any plans for tonight?" Drew asked her.

"Actually, n—" Leila began to speak, but I cut her off.

"I'm going to take her home, possibly stop for a drink or two. Then maybe take Ruger for a walk along the Battery." I prayed she didn't shut me down cold, though she had every right to. I had told her I worked a lot and that I would fuck up along the way.

Who the hell was I kidding? It was a bullshit excuse.

Damn, I didn't even make it twenty-four hours. *I could do better, I know I can. I will do better.* She deserves it. I never wanted to be the one to put that look on her face again. She was pissed, but she also looked devastated. I felt horrible.

Drew chimed in. "That sounds like a good idea. No offense sis, but you look like you need a stiff drink."

"Wow, thanks Drew. Do I really look that bad?" Her face fell.

I walked over to where she was and pulled her in for a hug. In that very moment, I decided to hell with what anyone else thought and kissed her. Not anything crazy or X-rated, just a quick innocent kiss to remind her how good I thought she looked.

"For the record, I think you look hot." Then I leaned in and whispered, "And I can help with the *stiff* drink." Pressing a light kiss to her temple I let her go. She was blushing and couldn't make eye contact with Drew anymore.

Drew groaned and adjusted himself in the bed. "Hey Lei, can you get the nurse? I think it's time for my pain meds. My chest is killin' me."

"Where's the pump?" she asked.

"The morphine was makin' my chest hurt more. I don't know, it kept makin' me feel like an elephant was sittin' on my chest, so they took it out," he grimaced as he explained.

I don't know if he was in much physical pain or if he wanted the drugs to knock him out, so he didn't have to witness any further interactions between his best friend and little sister.

She started toward the door. "Ya know you're not supposed to wait for the pain to get out of control, right? It takes more meds and longer to get it back in check than if you'd just let them give it to you when you are scheduled."

Drew rolled his eyes. "Yeah, yeah, yeah. Go get my nurse."

"I see the eye rolling is a family trait?" I joked with Drew and in response he tried to keep a straight face and not laugh.

"Bro, you know I love ya like a brother, but if you hurt her I'll shoot you and dump you in a ravine," he retorted with a half smile. I didn't think he was joking.

Melissa and Leila came in the room a few minutes later and Drew's eyes lit up at the sight of the needles. "There's my favorite person in the whole world."

Melissa grinned back. "Right, I'm sure if she," nodding toward Leila, "walked in with your pain meds, she'd be your new bestie and I'd be a fleeting memory."

"Not gonna lie…that's probably true," Drew replied with a smile.

Melissa administered his IV meds and then slipped out of the room. Drew's eyes glazed over and his face relaxed. We sat around watching TV until Drew's head started to bob.

"I think we should head out and let him sleep. He's trying to stay awake when he should probably just knock out," I suggested.

"Yeah, you're right." She turned to her brother. "Drew, we're gonna leave. I'll see you in the morning after you get out of surgery, okay? I love you."

Drew mumbled something incoherent and then passed out. I nodded toward the door and Leila followed me out of the room, down the hall and into the elevator.

"Can you just take me home? I'm not in the mood to go out." Her mood had shifted, again. She seemed hurt and disappointed.

Fuck, for just a moment I had forgotten. It had slipped my mind what a total jackass I had been at the restaurant, which reminded me of the guy who approached me after she pulled away with Barb.

"So after you left this guy came up to me and asked what I had done to make you run off. At first, I thought he must have overheard our conversation, but then he told me that *'Leila deserved better'* than me. And it dawned on me, he knew you and you knew him. Care to share why he was so concerned over our relationship?" I tried not to sound piss off, but I was. Some guy telling me how I should treat anyone pissed me off.

She sighed loudly. "Can we not do this here? I'll explain on the way to my place."

"Fine," I said abruptly, staring at the elevator door and didn't say another word.

Chapter Fifteen

Leila

We didn't say another word to each other until we got into Brody's Mercedes, then he finally spoke. "Look, I know we haven't known each other long and I don't know all your friends, but he's not someone I imagine as your friend. I was completely honest with you about my situation. If there's anything you want to add about yours, now would be a good time. Are you seeing this guy?"

Oh geez, where do I start? I turned to look at him.

"You're right, he's not one of my friends. He was a patient a few weeks ago. I can't go into details, but he asked me out. I politely declined. End of story. Uh, well, I thought it was. When you were outside on the phone earlier, I was staring out the window, watching the boats and he approached me at the table. It was very innocent, I swear. He came over because he recognized me and asked if he could buy me a drink." I looked back out the windshield. "I told him no, because I was there with someone. He said he understood and then he went back to the bar. Oh, and then when I was leaving, I ran into him. Like, literally, walked right into him as he walked out of the bar area."

"So that's it? He was just a patient that asked you out?" Relief flooded his voice. He let out a deep breath. "Thank God. You have no idea the thoughts that were running through my head."

I looked back over at him and decided to make him sweat a little. "Really? And just what were these thoughts?"

"Huh, oh, uhh, well, the first thought was that he was an ex. Then I started wondering if you were seeing him too." He looked so damn hot when he got jealous.

"So what, you think I'm some sorta slut?" I pretended to be outraged.

"What! No! I didn't say that. That's not what I meant at all," he backpedaled.

"Oh, it's not what you meant, hmm." I looked out the window, trying to hide the smile that was spreading over my face and regroup. "So, if I was seeing him and you, what would that make me Brody?"

He let out a huff. "That would make you someone I couldn't trust, and I can't be with someone I can't trust. In business, I have to watch my back everywhere I turn and I will not do it in my personal life. I'm sorry if that sounds selfish or arrogant, but it is what it is."

Okay, now I felt like a total bitch. No more games.

"Well then, I guess it's a really good thing that he's just a patient and I'm not seeing both of you, huh?" I turned back to him, grinning from ear to ear.

He looked back and forth between the road and me and then realization set in. "You were totally fucking with me, weren't you?"

I grinned and looked back out the windshield. "Maybe. I am glad you were honest with me about trustin' people. It's important to earn and deserve trust. The fact is that we don't know each other that well—"

He cut in, "Yet…We don't know each other that well, yet. But we will," he declared.

"I was gettin' there." I shook my head at him. "I'd like nothin' more than to get to know you and see where this is going."

He reached over, took my hand in his, brought it to his lips and kissed my knuckles, then the back of my hand. "Good, I'd like that too, babe."

He took me to a little bar down the street called Jake's for a few drinks. We sat at the bar near the back, him sipping his scotch, yuck, and me with my Captain 'n ginger. We talked about his crazy work schedule and upcoming opportunities. We tried to make a plan to be able to spend time together. With my shifts always being overnight, it conflicted with his schedule. He suggested that I spend the night with him tonight. I protested, citing my dog as the biggest obstacle in his well thought out plan.

But Brody Davis is a relentless man when he wants something. He's a shark that can find a few drops of blood or, in this case, doubt in an ocean of excuses.

He finally convinced me to go home, pick up Ruger and then go back out to his house. I was hesitant, but he got me when he told me Ruger would be able to run around the yard. Oh, and the promise of a long hot bath together may have helped sway my mind…a little.

What? Come on, that bathtub was astounding. What girl could resist? *Don't judge me.*

We stopped at my place so I could pack another bag and pick up Ruger. We drove out to Johns Island and back down the long, winding driveway to Brody's beautiful estate. He called it a house I called him delusional. We fell into a good rhythm, teasing each other back and forth, and flirting shamelessly.

Once we parked the car, he opened the back door and let Ruger off his leash. He hopped down from the backseat and proceeded to sniff his way over to the first large tree. I guess something caught his eye because he took off running toward the backyard. He didn't run off too long before he was back next to me as I made my way up the front porch steps.

We went inside and decided to watch some TV in Brody's bedroom. He got a blanket out of his closet and put it on the floor by the side of the bed for Ruger to lie on while I flipped through the channels. Finally settling on *Identify Thief* with Jason Bateman and Melissa McCarthy. Brody had seen it, but I hadn't. He assured me it was worth watching, and it turns out he was right. I laughed 'til I cried and couldn't see. After the movie we were both exhausted, but I reminded him of his promise.

"Come on, you promised. It's time to pay up mister." I grabbed him by his arm and attempted to drag him off the bed to the bathroom.

"Okay, come on." He let me lead him to the bathroom. "You get undressed and I'll fill the tub."

I don't know if he even reached the tub, because as soon as I took my dress off, he was kissing my neck. "Oh no you don't, we are taking a bath. That can wait until after, or maybe during, if you're good." I waggled my eyebrows at him.

"Party pooper," he teased, but ran the water and drew the bath. He disappeared out into the bedroom and returned naked, hard and carrying an antique-looking blue glass bottle. He poured a little into the tub, replaced the cap and set it on the white granite vanity with a clink. Noticing me watching, he lifted the bottle.

"Bath oil, I had Jane pick it up earlier. Thought it might help you relax; its lavender and vanilla."

"Aww, that was so sweet of you." I stepped down into the warm water. I sunk to the bottom, the water came all the way up to my chin and it wasn't even full. He threw two large bath sheets on the steps leading up to the tub, stepped in and then turned the water off. I sat up and he slipped in behind me. I leaned back and put my head on his shoulder. There is something quite intimate about taking a bath with someone. A vulnerability. He wrapped me in his arms and pulled me closer, so his already hard cock was grinding against my butt.

"I'm really sorry about earlier." Brody said. I tried to interrupt him but he kept talking. "I know I apologized for the call and for acting like an ass about that guy, but I need you to know that I'm truly sorry. I warned you I'd mess up and I did, it didn't even take me twenty-four hours."

"Okay, first of all, stop apologizing. I accepted your apology earlier." I turned my head so I could see him. "We're both new at this whole relationship thing. We're bound to screw up from time to time, but like you said, don't run too far. We need to learn to trust each other and talk to each other. That's the only way this will work. Deal?"

"Deal." He kissed me then sat me forward. For a split second I wondered why, and then he started to rub my shoulders.

"Mmm, that feels so good. You're really good at this." I hung my head and relaxed. "I may have to come take a bath with you every day if you're gonna do this."

Slowly he started kneading lower and lower, until he was massaging my sacral spine. I felt his lips ever so lightly start kissing down my spine, to the middle of my back and then back up. On the way back up he continued kissing, but added a tiny swirl of his tongue. It sent electrical jolts through my entire body. It was so sensual and erotic. All he had to do was graze my clit and I would shatter into a thousand tiny pieces. Like he was reading my mind, he let one hand come around and dip between my legs. Not messing around, he went straight to my clit and massaged small circles around the nub. I moaned and groaned, begging for him to make me come.

He stood behind me, in an attempt to leave the tub. I took the opportunity and grabbed his hard cock that was only inches from my face. The oil in the water allowed me to glide my hand up and down his thick, long shaft. He stopped, eased his head back and whimpered.

"Fuck babe, that feels so fucking good."

Before he could say another word, I turned and kneeled in front of him. I licked from the base of his cock all the way to the tip of his head. I sucked just the head into my mouth and swirled my tongue around, tracing the ridge around the thick tip. Without warning, I took him all the way in my mouth, trying not to gag when he hit the back of my throat and then sucked as hard as I could as I pulled back painfully slow.

"Holy motherfuckin' shit Leila, if you keep that up I'm gonna come into that sweet little mouth of yours." He slid his hands into my curls to hold on to me. He started to slowly thrust in rhythm as I slid him in and out of my mouth. I reached up with my hand and started to rub his heavy sac. He cursed and thrust hard and deep, gagging me slightly. He picked up his pace, so I ceased my movement and let him take control.

"Oh damn baby, I'm so close. We have to stop, let's…ahhhhhh, go to the bed." He started to try to pull away, but I wrapped my arms around the back of his legs and grabbed his ass, holding him in place. I looked up at him from my knees.

"It's okay, baby, let go. I want you to come in my mouth." I resumed sucking his cock.

It only took a second for him to return to controlling the situation. He started sliding himself in and out of my lips. As I rubbed his sac, I felt it tighten and his cock get stiffer than ever. "Oh fuck baby, I'm gonna come, shit."

I felt the hot, salty fluid explode from his dick and slide down my throat. When he was finally finished, I reached down into the tub and splashed some water on my face. He came so much I couldn't swallow it all and it dripped down my chin.

"Damn baby, that was fuckin' amazing." He pulled me up and we stepped out of the tub, wrapped up and dried off.

I just smirked and winked at him. "What can I say? I do what I can."

He burst out laughing. "You sure love throwing my own words back at me don't you?"

"I do love givin' you a hard time," I flirted.

"Oh, I'm going to give you a hard time all right." He dragged me to the bed, ripped my towel off me and pushed me down, climbing on top of me after dropping his own towel. He used his lips and tongue to explore my body. It felt like heaven, until he got to my ribs. I tried so hard not to squirm or giggle, because if he knew how ticklish I was he'd never leave it alone.

He must have sensed the tension in my body and mistook it for reluctance. He stopped kissing me and lay beside me. "I understand if you're still pissed and aren't in the mood. I guess I misread you in the bathroom."

Well fuck me running, now I had to tell him, damn it. "Brody you didn't misread anything, I absolutely want you."

"You might say that, but your whole body tensing up tells me you're not into this." He seemed so bummed out as he stared at the ceiling.

I had to tell him. "Okay, I wasn't gonna say anything—" I tried to explain but he cut me off.

"See, I knew it." He blew out an exasperated breath.

"What I was trying to say was that when you were kissing my ribs I tightened my muscles to stop from laughing. I'm ticklish as hell."

"You're not pissed?" He sat there stunned. "You're ticklish and you didn't want me to know?"

"Yep, that's it. Nothing bad, I promise," I assured him, then rolled over and straddled him. I hadn't noticed before, because I was worried about him tickling me, but his dick was fully erect again. I rolled my hips, gliding my damp pussy up and down his stiff dick.

"Oh God babe, you're so wet. I would love to feel you just like this." He was implying sex without a condom. *Not a chance buddy.* "I've never *not* used a condom. I'm certainly not ready for kids. But, God, I wanna feel you bare, with nothing between us."

I was confused, was he seeking permission or was he just wondering what it would feel like. "I've always used condoms and I take the pill too. I am definitely not ready for kids either, I want to travel and spend a few more years in Shock Trauma." All of this talk about birth control reminded me that I needed to be careful for the next week or so. I just recently finished a Z-Pak for a sinus infection and my birth control pills wouldn't be as effective.

"Speaking of which, we definitely need to be cautious for a little while, I just finished an antibiotic. As long as we use condoms it should be fine, since the pill's really just backup," I explained.

"Good to know," he said as he flipped me onto my back and kissed me senseless. He rolled back over to his bedside table, dug out a condom and rolled it down his length. He pulled me to the side of the bed by my ankle, grabbed my hips and flipped me onto my stomach.

"I want you on your knees baby," he ordered. He kneeled behind me, spread my legs and began to lick and suck on my engorged nub. I was just about to come when he stopped and stood up.

"Ugh," I moaned in protest. "Don't stop, I'm so close."

I felt him rub the head of his cock at my entrance briefly before slamming it into me in one deep push. He buried himself deep inside of me and stilled with a low rumble.

I threw my head back and pushed my ass back into him, allowing him to delve deeper, and dear God did he. He started pumping into me as I grasped at the comforter, trying desperately to hold myself in place. I had to keep pulling my knees back underneath of me, as he slipped an arm around my waist, fixing me in place.

"Harder Brody, fuck me, oh God, yeah," I whimpered as he slammed into me repeatedly without hesitation. Without warning his hand met by ass with a sting. There was no way I could keep up with him. "Brody don't stop, I'm gonna come, oh Jesus, right there."

Brody reached up and grabbed for my hand. "Lean on your forearm and give me your hand."

I obeyed, resting my forearm on the bed and hanging my head to watch his every move. "Brody, mmmm please don't stop."

He took my hand in his, reached between my legs and slipped my own fingers over my clit. He released my hand after we made a few small circles.

"That's right, baby, rub that tight little pussy of yours. I want to watch you make yourself come all over my dick." He smacked my backside again, just enough to sting but not hurt. "Fuck, babe, if you get any tighter I'm not going to be able to move in you."

I wasn't sure if it was the dirty talk or the spanking that threw me over the edge, but I fell headlong into an abyss of pleasure.

"AHHHH," I screamed as he fucked me ruthlessly and I massaged my own clit. It was easily the most intense orgasm I had ever had. I stilled my motion, but kept two fingers firmly over the sensitive button; it felt like it would never end. As it finally did, I slumped over onto the bed and Brody pulled out of me. I hissed at the emptiness he left in his wake.

"Roll over and get up on the pillows," he commanded. I complied, too spent to argue about his alpha tendencies. He grabbed a pillow and shoved it under my hips, lined himself up again and slowly pushed into my tight opening.

"God, Leila, you are amazing. I can't get enough of you," he exclaimed as he slowly and deliciously slid in and out of my overworked sex. He leaned forward and took my nipple in his mouth, licking and sucking on it as he drove into me over and over, each time bottoming out into my G-spot.

"Mmmmm, Brody, you're gonna make me come again." I pulled his face to mine and kissed him. Then whispered, "I love the way you feel inside of me." I wrapped my legs around his waist and dug my nails into his back ready for the next flood of intensity to rack my body.

"Come with me, baby. Now." He plunged into me wildly as he climaxed. He leaned back, and his fingers found my clit and set off my explosion. He rode out the rest of his orgasm and then collapsed on top of me.

"Uh, Brody, can you pull the pillow out? This is not very comfy."

"Yeah, sorry I didn't mean to crush you." He started to roll off of me. I locked my legs around his body, preventing him from moving.

"I didn't want you to move, just the pillow." I shrugged my shoulders. "This just feels right."

He pulled the pillow out.

"I need to take care of this." He went to the bathroom then returned with his black Calvin Klein boxer briefs on. He crawled back into bed and covered us up with the fluffy down comforter. I snuggled into him and quickly fell asleep.

Chapter Sixteen

Leila

At some point in the middle of the night, I woke to a cell phone ringing. Brody sat up in the bed, looked at the caller ID displayed and hit ignore. It didn't go unnoticed that his jaw tensed and eyes narrowed. Whoever was on the other end of that call had Brody annoyed. He rolled back over to face me, pulled me back to his chest and kissed my forehead. I started to ask who was calling in the middle of the night, but I decided I didn't want to know. Well, I didn't want to know at too-fuckin-early o'clock.

While I was drifting back to sleep some not so pretty thoughts ran through my head. It wasn't like we had been together for more than a minute. I'm sure his past is unaware of our current situation, so why wouldn't women be calling him in the middle of the night? I tried to quiet the nervous chatter bouncing around my brain as I fell back to sleep swathed in Brody's heat.

✱✱✱✱✱

Leila

Brody and I pulled up in front of 82 Queen. As we waited for the hostess to ready our table Brody leaned in and whispered in my ear, "I can't wait to for you to see what I have planned for you tonight."

The short blonde hostess reappeared and asked us to follow her. As we wove our way amongst the tables and patrons, Brody let go of my hand and moved faster away from me. I tried to keep up, but I felt like I was frozen in place. I called out to him, he spun and looked back. He was almost to me when some leggy blonde walked up to him, cutting off his path to me. She grabbed the lapels of his suit and pulled him into a sensual embrace, shoving her tongue down his throat. He kissed her back, wrapping his arms around her thin waist and acted like I wasn't even standing there. I tried to pull him away from her, but he shrugged me off, telling me they were not ready to order yet. I looked down and I was dressed in a black shirt, black pants and long white apron, not in the black cocktail dress I arrived in. I looked around the room and no one looked up at the train wreck playing out before my eyes. Had nobody even noticed that this bitch just walked up and took my man? WTF?

I started to try to run from the restaurant, but the hostess grabbed my arm and stopped me, spinning me around to face her. She started shaking me, but when she shouted my name it came out garbled. She opened her mouth to yell again, but this time it sounded different. It wasn't her mousy little voice but Brody's strong voice. "Lei."

"Lei." My whole body shook. "Leila wake up, you're having a bad dream baby. It's me, Brody, wake up honey."

I shot straight up in the bed, gasping and out of breath.

"Holy shit. Brody, you…oh God, it was just a dream." I blew out a slow deep breath as he rubbed his hand up and down my back. Even though I knew it wasn't real, I shirked away from him. I tried to rationalize to myself that it wasn't really him in the dream. He didn't kiss anyone else.

"Hey, you're okay. It was just a bad dream. Just breathe baby, I got you," he coddled me and this time I let him. "Do you want to talk about it?"

"No," I practically yelled, pulling away from him. "Sorry. No, I'll be fine. It was just a bad dream like you said."

There was no way in hell I was telling him. *Oh no, I'm just a neurotic mess and am already imagining you cheating on me.* He'd run screaming for the hills before the sun rose. No, I needed to relax and trust him. If this is going to work, I need to learn how to trust him with my heart. Which will be no easy task.

I settled back into the bed, pulling the comforter up to my chin and faced away from him. He tucked himself in behind me, wrapping an arm around my middle and then quietly drifted off to sleep. I was determined to do the same thing; I need to get some sleep. I was exhausted and Drew's surgery had been circling my brain all day. I fought with my mind, but was finally able to turn it off long enough to fall back to sleep.

Later in the morning, I woke up to a cold wet nose pressed to mine. Ruger

"Okay, baby boy, give me a minute. Lemme get dressed," I whispered to him not wanting to wake Brody. I turned my head and realized the bed was empty. "Hmm, I wonder where he went. Ruger, where's Brody?"

He tipped his head to the side and perked his big pointy ears up. He looked at the door and then back to me. I looked at the clock. Ugh, 6:45 am. Why couldn't this dog sleep in?

I hopped out of bed, pulling the sheet with me and went in search of my clothes. Along the way, I was drawn toward his closet. Just a peek, I promised myself. I don't want him to catch me in here.

I opened the tall, white French doors. There were two tiers of hanging clothes on both sides of the closet in four-foot sections. Each area was backlit in soft white lighting. Separating each section was either a thin mirror or tall cabinet. As I walked further in there was a large island with drawers on both sides, the top absent of clutter. Just beyond the island the room split into a T. To the left I could see shelves of shoes, boots, flip-flops and slides lining the walls with a velvet bench in the middle. Off to the right was another room with ties, hats, vests, scarves and belts lining the walls and shelves. The far wall was a massive floor to ceiling framed mirror.

I turned and started to head back out when I noticed my duffle sitting on the most amazing antique Victorian rose carved armchair in the main room of the closet. My attention was diverted when I saw my clothes were hung neatly in one of the hanging sections.

Weird; there was nothing else hanging in that section but the couple of outfits I brought with me.

"I hope you don't mind," Brody's voice startled me from my exploration of his closet.

"Jesus." I jumped. "You scared the shit outta me. Don't you make any noise when you walk?"

"I cleared out a small area for you to hang clothes when you stay over. I hope you don't think it's presumptuous of me. I just wanted to be sure you understood how much I want you here. With me."

I stood in front of my new little section of the closet, wrapped in the sheet I pulled off the bed. I tugged it a little tighter to my body, feeling self-conscious under his scrutiny.

"I think it's sweet, and incredibly thoughtful of you to bring my stuff in here." I paused, sweeping my eyes around the room. "Just one question, where are my bras and panties?" I smiled sweetly at him. Grinning, he walked around to the near side of the island and pulled open the first two drawers.

"Here, I cleared out a few drawers for you too. Go get ready and I'll meet ya downstairs. Oh, and your toiletries are in the bathroom, second vanity." He gave me a quick kiss and exited the closet, leaving the doors wide-open.

Throwing on my sundress, I hightailed it downstairs to let Ruger out. After he sniffed every other tree in the yard, I scurried off to the bathroom to take a shower, taking the opportunity to truly appreciate the magnificence of this bathroom. I mean, mine was nice, but his was…freaking awesome. I angled the body jets to massage my well used muscles while I cleaned myself. I managed to figure out how to turn on the steam. Grabbing my razor, I sat down on the floating teak shower bench to shave my legs. I took my time and leisurely showered.

I didn't feel like dealing with my hair, so I wrung out as much water as I could with the fluffy towel and pulled it up. It was way too humid to wear it down. *If you're a girl and have curly hair, you know what I mean.* I had a hair tie in my hand at the mention of humidity or wind. Just a little bit of either while my hair was down and POOF! It was instantly rendered a giant rat's nest.

Heading back to the closet, I slipped on my black lace bra and matching thong. Threw on a pair of frayed cutoff jean shorts and a pink Salt Life T-shirt. I found my tan Sanuks near the upholstered armchair my duffle was sitting on and slid them on. Looking down at my toes, I made a mental note to make an appointment for a pedicure. The silvery purple polish was dull, but thankfully not chipped. I went back out to the couch in the bedroom, grabbed my cell and then made my way down to the kitchen. It wasn't difficult to find Brody; I simply followed the smell of strong Colombian coffee. He was sitting at the bar in the kitchen, coffee in one hand and newspaper in the other. There were several different newspapers stacked in front of him.

"Ya know, you could read the newspaper on a tablet and you wouldn't have to flip through all of those," I suggested sitting down next to him.

"I like the feel of a newspaper in my hands. It reminds me of my dad," he said grimly. Okay, I obviously hit a nerve, new topic…. Ruger.

"Hey, did you happen to see Ruger?" I looked around the room and out on the deck. "He came and woke me up earlier, we went out, but since I got out of the shower, I haven't seen him."

"Yeah, I let him out a few minutes ago. I should warn you, he's probably going to gain about ten pounds today the way Jane is giving him treats. She just loves dogs." He relaxed again. "She's agreed to keep Ruger here while we go to the hospital to check on Drew, if that's okay with you?"

"That would be wonderful. That way we can take our time and not have to rush back. Plus, I have a little stop I'd like to make while we're out today."

"And just where would you like to stop?" He raised his eyebrows.

"That, sir, is for me to know and you to find out." Changing subjects I asked, "What time do you want to head to the hospital? Drake said he was takin' Drew in about seven, so he should be done by eight or so."

I looked down at my watch and realized it was already 7:30.

"We can leave whenever you want. Let me just tell Jane we're leaving and then I'll meet you back here. There are homemade cinnamon pecan muffins over by the oven. Jane baked them fresh this morning for us." He nodded in the direction of the counter where the muffins were sitting before slipping out to the deck.

I grabbed a muffin and a couple of napkins, planning to take it with me. I was way too on edge to eat anything. I would definitely puke if I put anything in my nervous stomach. That is the last thing I want Brody to see me do. Okay, well, maybe not the last, but it was way down the list. Him attempting to run his hands through my hair. That was the bottom of the list. One does not run his hands through curly hair.

I was pulled from my imaginary list when I heard Ruger barking and carrying on just before I heard the door to the deck open.

"Okay, boy, relax. Hold your horses, I'm getting it," Brody said, looking down at Ruger.

"And just what, pray tell, are you gettin' him?" I sass as Brody walked toward the abundant butler's pantry.

"Oh, his treat. I had Jane pick him up some Greenies. I figured that would distract him long enough for me to sneak you away." He smiled deviously and winked.

"Ah. Okay."

Brody took the treat and walked back outside with Ruger hot on his trail. A few seconds later, he returned alone. He came over, gave me a sensual but quick kiss, nibbling gently on my top lip. "Ready to get on the road?"

"Mmm, yes. Even though I'd really like to take off all of your clothes and have my way with you right here on the floor." I wrapped my arms around his trim waist and raised up on my toes to kiss him again. Getting lost momentarily, we were brought back by a man's voice.

"Damn bro, where'd you find her?" a tall, lean guy asked Brody.

"Shit, Damon, I completely forgot we made plans." Brody rubbed his hand across the back of his neck. "Damon, this is Leila, Lei this is my buddy Damon."

"Leila." He nodded once and then turned his attention to Brody. "So, what's up, fucker? You bailin' on me or what? Cami said she'd meet me there and she's bringin' a friend."

Oh really? Interesting. I turned and started toward the front door when a strong pair of arms snaked around my waist, stopping me dead in my tracks. "And just where do you think you're going?"

"I was gonna step out front and call Barb to see if she would come get me. You obviously have plans and I don't wanna get in y'all's way," I said with all of the attitude I could muster.

"Don't do that. Don't run before I even have a chance to explain things to you, or for you to hear me tell Damon about you and apologize for bailing on him," he whispered in my ear still holding me tightly against his chest. "Give me a chance babe."

Hmph, I did it again. I tried to bail before I even knew the situation. I sighed. "I'm sorry, you're right."

Brody released his hold and interlaced his fingers into mine and pulled me back to the kitchen.

"Hey D, sorry I forgot about the races, but I'm not going. Lei and I have to get back to MUSC; her brother is having surgery again today. He was shot on Friday. Oh shit. I didn't tell you. You know Drew."

"Drew? As in Drew Matthews?" he asked.

"Yeah, how do you know my brother?"

"Holy shit, you're that Leila?" He looked back to Brody with a chuckle. "Damn bro, Drew is gonna fuckin' wreck you when he finds out you're bangin' his little sister."

I cleared my throat. "Shit, sorry girl. Drew, Brody and I are all members of the huntin' club. We've been friends for years."

"Really, years? I've been to the hunting club before and I've never seen y'all before." I stared doubtfully at Damon.

"Ha," he stifled laughter. "That's 'cause you're off limits, babe. Well, at least you were. So wait, Drew got shot? What the fuck bro? Can't call and give me a heads up?" Damon berated Brody.

"Sorry, I was more concerned about Drew and trying to make sure Lei was okay," he apologized

"Okay, now that everyone knows what's going on, can we go?" I was starting to get antsy. By the time we got back to MUSC he should be out of surgery and I wanted to be there.

"Yeah, babe, let's go. D, I'll call you later, but it's safe to say I won't be hanging out with Cami's friend…or anyone else's friend for that matter." He tugged my hand to follow him toward the garage door.

"Hey, y'all mind if I follow you to the hospital? I'd like to stop in an' see Drew. If that's okay with you Leila?" he asked politely.

"Of course, I'm sure Drew would love to see ya. Plus, he's pretty funny all doped up."

We exited to the garage and I stopped dead in my tracks. In the four-car garage were some of the hottest cars on the planet. In the first bay was the Mercedes SUV, next to it was a silver Bentley Continental, then a dark gray Hennessey Venom GT and at the end was my favorite by far. A 1966 Shelby Cobra 427 Competition in guardsman blue with white stripes. I stopped walking and dropped my jaw. Brody looked back and laughed.

"What're you gawking' at?" He followed my eyes to the cars. "Oh, my baby, the Venom right?" he said arrogantly. "She's—"

"Not a chance, don't get me wrong, it's a sexy car, but the sixty-six Shelby blows that thing out of the water. I didn't know you collected cars." I turned and looked at him briefly before walking over to the Cobra, circling it, taking in every line and each curve.

"I don't." He nodded at the Cobra. "My dad bought her, it was his prized possession. He used to take it out every Sunday and ride around in her. My mom used to tease him that he loved it more than he loved her. I sold most of his collection, but I couldn't part with this one. It will stay with my family and get passed down to my son and then his son. It's what my dad would've wanted."

"You ever drive it?" I asked.

"Twice a year, his birthday and the day they died." He cleared his throat and then walked back over toward the other cars. "Why don't we take the Bentley? That way you can drive from the hospital to wherever it is you're planning to take me."

Oh wow, he was serious. He's gonna let me drive his Bentley, which I am sure must cost close to a quarter of a million dollars. "Okay, but I can just tell you when and where to turn, I don't have to drive. That thing costs as much as a house."

"Leila." He cocked his head and gave me this look, like it was a Honda we were getting into.

"Don't *Leila* me. If I wrecked this thing it'd take me five years to pay for the repair bill alone. I am not driving it." I shook my head.

Brody just laughed. He started the car, opened the garage and backed out carefully. He took care in driving it slowly down the driveway out to the main road. He sped up a little, but he didn't drive like a maniac.

No, he saved those shenanigans for the highway.

"How about we see what she's got?" All of the sudden I was slammed back into my seat from the sheer force of acceleration. I looked in the side mirror and couldn't see Damon in his Aston Martin anymore. Glancing at the speedometer, I saw we were well above the speed limit, pushing 100 miles per hour. Brody was weaving in and out of cars like a dog on an agility course.

Jesus, he's gonna kill us.

"Hey, uh, Brody? Maybe you wanna slow down a little." It came out as more of a suggestion than a statement. But he backed off the acceleration a little and took us to 80 mph. Soon, I could see Damon again.

With a chuckle he glanced over at me. "I have a thing for speed."

"You don't say?"

We made it to the hospital in no time at all. We pulled up to the valet and Brody pulled the guy aside. I'm sure he was going on and on about taking care of his car, probably some shit about it being his baby and not joy riding in it. He slipped the guy some cash and then met me at the revolving doors.

"What? I just asked him to leave it parked in the front. I don't want it in that crazy, fucked-up garage. God only knows what would happen in there."

I laughed and made my way over to the bank of elevators. We waited for Damon and then went up to see Drew.

Chapter Seventeen

Leila

Drew's surgery was successful and there were no complications. Drake said it was textbook. *Thank you, sweet baby Jesus.*

I walked into Drew's room with Brody and Damon bringing up the rear and low and behold who did I find, Nurse Brooke. Great, my day just keeps getting better and better. Deciding against letting the green monster rear its ugly head, I settled on killing her with kindness.

"Good morning Brooke." I smiled so sweetly I felt my blood sugar spike off the charts.

"Good morning. Drew's doin' pretty good. He's still out of it, but his vitals are stable. We should be able to move him to a step down bed later today or tomorrow, barring any unforeseen issues."

"That *is* great news. Thank you so much for your help." I continued to lay it on thick. Brooke looked at me like I had ten heads. Just about that time Drew opened his eyes and scanned the room.

"Hey sis, where's my breakfast?" he mumbled.

Leave it to him to ask for food only minutes after getting out of recovery.

"It's downstairs in the cafeteria. You'll have to settle for Jell-o, crackers and ginger ale there pal."

"Hey Damon, what're ya doin' here?"

"Seriously, where else would I be dude? You got shot and I just heard about it this morning when I went to Brody's." Damon sat in the chair next to the bed.

"My bad man, not exactly like I've been able to call anyone," Drew countered.

"True, good point. I'll let it slide this time." Damon chuckled, nodding his head.

Then slutty Nurse Brooke chimed in with her singsong tone, "Hate to be a party pooper, but we have to limit this little reunion to two visitors at a time. I need one of you to wait in the hallway or waiting room around the corner."

Oh hell to the no. I knew what she was up to. She was trying to get Brody alone in the hallway to make her *I'm-an-easy-whore* eyes at him again and beg him to screw her in the supply closet.

Brody started to offer when I said, "You guys stay, I'm gonna run down to see if Drake is still here so I can thank him for taking such good care of my big brother."

That wench had the nerve to just stand there and watch me with daggers shooting out her eyes. I started to leave when Brody stopped me, pulled me into a tight hug and kissed me like I was going on an African safari for a year.

Holy crap. I needed a new pair of panties.

Drew and Damon all but cleared their throats as a way of saying *hey we're still here*. Brody released me and I stumbled backward and left the room. Brooke came out the room a minute later looking rather disappointed, and went back to the nurse's station.

I took my cell out of my bag and called Drake. Unfortunately, he had already left the hospital, so I had to settle for talking to him on the phone. I filled him in on the Brody situation and told him that he, Barb and I needed a night out soon. He suggested a day at the beach, which I agreed sounded spectacular. He said he would call Barb and let me know, which meant I would need to call Barb and figure something out because he wouldn't remember. He may be a brilliant surgeon, but he sucked at being on time and remembering things. After I finished my call I went back to Drew's room where the guys were talking.

"I'm gonna get out of here and let your sister chill with y'all for a while." Damon went to shake Drew's hand and then realized he couldn't, so he gave him some sort of awkward kind of wave/knee pat. Brody laughed at him and then gave him a quick man hug. Ya know, bumped shoulders with a quick one-pat-on-the-back man hug. Damon made his exit, but not before tipping his head at me. "See ya later sweetheart."

I wasn't sure Brody liked that because I heard a slight grumble come from his chest. Damn, was he was super sexy when he got all jealous, or what?

"Yeah, yeah, yeah, Damon. I'll call you later. Oh, and her name is Leila or Lei. Not sweetheart," he said with a glare.

Damon just sort of laughed it off as he walked out. "Right. Talk to ya later bro."

We sat around talking to Drew for a little while longer. I told him how much Ruger loved Brody's place and that Jane was spoiling him rotten. At 9:30, Brooke returned and brought his IV meds with her. We told Drew goodbye before she finished pushing the drugs since he'd be in la-la land in a matter of minutes. I kissed his forehead then walked out of the room.

Brody and I strolled down the hall hand in hand and got on the first elevator. As I pressed the button I could sense him moving closer; he wrapped his arms around my waist and pulled me back into him. His mouth nipped along my neck to my ear, teeth gently pulling on my earlobe.

"You're lucky we only have a few floors to go. Otherwise…" he trailed off, allowing my imagination take hold as his lips continued their exploration of my neck.

DING!

The elevator bell alerted us of our arrival on the lobby floor. Saved by the bell!

Brody held the door for me as we exited from the lobby. We waited to retrieve the keys from the valet attendant for the Bentley, which was still parked right where we left it. He handed them to Brody, who tossed them at me. Luckily, I was paying attention. I actually caught them instead of them smacking me in the forehead.

"Brody, I said I'll tell you how to get there. I don't need to drive." I tried to give him the keys back but he stuck his hands in his pockets.

"Babe, you're driving. It's only a car. You do know how to drive a car, right?"

Oh, this was how he was gonna play it, the smart-ass. "Yes, of course I know how to drive a car. And before you ask, I do know how to drive a manual."

"Good to know. Now let's go. People are staring at us." He looked around the driveway.

"Damn you Brody Davis, I can't believe you are making me do this." I slid into the driver's black leather seat. The quilted leather was soft, supple and screamed luxury. "You are so gonna pay for this…What if someone hits me while I'm driving?"

"I promise everything will be fine. Do you want to tell me where we are going?" He was trying to distract me.

"You really don't like surprises?" I asked, looking from the steering wheel over to him.

"No, not really. Well, sometimes. If it was you dressed in nothing, waiting for me at home in my bed, then yeah, I'd like that kind of surprise," he hinted.

"Well, that's not it. We're going to Badd Kitty to do some shopping. You owe me some toys mister," I teased.

"Oh hell yeah. I am down for that." He reached over and turned up the stereo as Metallica's Fuel came on.

As I took the on ramp to I-26, I decided to see just how fast she could get up and go. I pushed down on the pedal and the Bentley roared to life; before I knew it I was going 85 mph. I was shocked at how smooth the ride was; it certainly didn't feel like I was speeding. Looking back down, I was pushing ninety. I decided to let off and enjoy driving this fine piece of mechanical engineering.

We exited the highway and headed toward West Ashley to Badd Kitty. Of course, I had been to an adult toy store before now, but never with a man. I didn't know why I was so nervous. I mean, everyone has sex, right? My lioness purred in agreement. We pulled up out front and suddenly Brody looked uncomfortable.

"Hey, you okay?" I touched his forearm.

"Huh, uh oh, I just realized I might know someone here." His face was full of worry. "It was a long time ago, I met her at a bar and she happened to work here. We only hung out a few times."

"It's okay, I'm sure we are bound to run into exes from time to time. No biggie," I played it cool, while my lioness was growling and pacing in her cage. "Let's just go in and deal with whatever happens."

We entered the store and headed over to the 50 Shades area. I picked up a whip looking thing made up of several strands of quarter inch suede leather and soft fuzzy stuff. It didn't look like it would hurt much. I whipped it against the bare skin of my thigh.

Hmm, that was interesting, it didn't hurt really. The leather had a little sting but the soft fuzz soothed it at the same time. Maybe I could try something like this for Brody. If it was anything like his spanking earlier then I could definitely enjoy that.

He approached taking notice of the toy in my hand. "Ahhh, I see you've found the floggers."

I blushed as he caught me in mid-fantasy.

He raised his eyebrows in surprise. "Thought you said no whips?"

"This isn't really a whip. I mean, sure, it has little bits of suede but the fuzzy stuff is soft and can't hurt that much. So, if you promise to play nice, then I'll try it." I prayed I didn't regret that decision later.

"I promise to play nice. How do you feel about being restrained?"

"Restrained how? Like as in handcuffs?" I wasn't sure if I liked where this was going.

"We could start with some of my ties and if you like it, then maybe we can come back and get handcuffs," he said.

"And just how do you plan on restraining me?" I asked.

"I'd start by tying your wrists together and then maybe tying your wrists to the bed frame. But we can use a slipknot, that way if at any time you are uncomfortable you can free yourself. I think if you trust me and let me guide you, it will be extremely gratifying," he said leaning forward and giving me a quick peck.

"Now, what other sort of toys were you talking about the other night?"

"I think we should start with the silk ties, flogger and maybe a blindfold," he replied.

I walked around to the display of vibrators and started to check them out. Brody came up right behind me, put his arms around my waist pulling me back into him and whispered in my ear, "No vibrators or dildos. My cock or my fingers are the only things inside of your sweet pussy."

Oh sweet Jesus, I almost came right there. "Get a blindfold and meet me at the register, it's time to go."

He chuckled and went in search of a blindfold. I made my way through the store and back to the front to check out, stopping along the way to look at some lingerie and a few other things. Brody met me at the register with a lot more than a blindfold. While I set the flogger down on the counter Brody started to unload his arms. He set down a bottle of lubricant, condoms, a lipstick-size bullet, nipple clamps and of course the blindfold.

"You get to wear the clamps first there buddy." I never agreed to that shit. Those things look like they could do some damage. The girl behind the counter stifled a giggle, Brody just shook his head.

She finished ringing everything up as I dug into my purse for my debit card.

"Your total today will be one hundred fifty seven dollars and ninety eight cents." She said it like it she just finished ringing up groceries at Bi-Lo. I was a little shocked at the cost, but I presented my card to her anyway. Brody snatched it from her hand.

"I've got this." He handed my debit card back to me.

I put my hand up signaling the cashier to stop. "It was my idea to come, I'll pay."

"Please, just run the card." He ignored me and spoke to the poor cashier witnessing our struggle over who was paying. "Lei, I am paying, end of discussion."

Discussion? What discussion? More like end of your decree. I rolled my eyes, then took the bags off the counter and stalked out the front door.

Once outside, I got into the car, on the passenger side, and sat there fuming. I didn't like being dismissed like that, especially in front of someone. Hmph, it was one thing to be dominant in the bedroom, but it was a totally different thing to do it in public.

He got in the driver's side and I held out the keys to him, even though he didn't need them to start the car.

"Why are you so pissed off that I paid?" he asked, like he didn't get it.

"Brody, it's not just about you paying. It's more the fact that you dismissed me and were totally domineering," I explained.

"I'm sorry if you saw it that way, it wasn't my intention to dismiss you. I just wanted to be the one to buy these for you. I have more money than I'll probably ever be able to spend. You are the only person in my life that doesn't expect me to pay for everything. You challenge me at every turn and I love it. You don't expect or ask for anything and it makes me want to give you everything that much more," he explained. "I won't apologize for being assertive, that's who I am. I will try to rein it in a little while we are out in public though."

"If this is gonna work, you have to compromise some and let me pay for my own things." I tried to stand my ground.

"I'll let you pay for your own things. You pay your mortgage, electric bill, cable, sewer, water, phone and groceries. And while you're with me, I'll pay for our meals, toys, entertainment and other travel expenses."

"Why can't we split dinners?" I harped.

"We'll see," he seemed to relent. However, I didn't buy that shit for a second.

The Bentley roared to life as we pulled back out on Savannah Highway and headed back to Brody's house. Before we paid, I was excited to get back and try out some of our new toys. Now, I just wanted to take Ruger and go for a run. Running always cleared my head and gave me perspective on a situation.

Chapter Eighteen

Leila

Once we returned to Brody's I had calmed down some. The twenty
or so minute drive through the scenic Lowcountry had helped. We
rode home in complete silence. That kind of silence is deafening,
where every little noise sounded so much louder than it was. Yep,
that kind of quiet, with the exception of Brody asking if I was going
to speak to him. I didn't answer him.

Yes, I realize I am acting like a child.

"Are you hungry? I can have Jane make us some lunch, maybe a
salad?" His voice was quiet as we walked through the front door.

"Lunch would be good, but just have her make whatever you
want. I'm not in the mood for a salad right now." I tried not to sound
too bitchy. I looked around the house and wondered where Ruger
was. "Do you know where Jane and Ruger might be?"

"Either in the pool or down at the carriage house where Jane
lives. I'll text her and have her come up to the kitchen," he said as he
took out his phone. "There. She'll probably be here in a few minutes.
Why don't I take our stuff up to my bedroom?"

"I can do it. I need to use the bathroom anyway," I said, walking
over and taking the bags from him. As I started to turn and leave, he
tugged them back, pulling me to him. He gave me a quick kiss and
then smiled.

"I don't want to fight with you Leila. I will work on
compromising."

I kissed him back, energy rushed through my body. "That's all I
want, is for you to try. I'll be right back."

*****

Brody

Damn, she was killing me. Any other person on the planet and I
could give two shits whether or not they were seething mad at me.
Anyone, except her. The look on her face nearly broke me. I wasn't
trying to be an asshole by paying for the toys and shit, I just want to
take care of her. I know she can take care of herself and she has

enough money, but I have more money than I could probably ever spend and amassed more every day.

"Brody." Jane came in the back door with Ruger following her. "I got your text about lunch. What would you like to eat dear?"

"How about some sandwiches and fruit? Something simple. I'm going to call and try to get a reservation for dinner tonight. I need to smooth things over with Leila. She's upset with me." I scrolled through the contacts in my phone.

Jane looked at me with knowing eyes. "What did you do?"

"Nothing really, I just paid for some things while we were out shopping." Jane gave me the look that says *what else*. "Well, I may have taken her card from the clerk, gave it back to her and then paid myself. She wouldn't speak to me the whole way home," I explained.

"Oh." Jane's eyes widened.

"See, I don't see the big deal, I only paid for some stuff." I was totally at a loss.

"Oh my boy." She patted my shoulder. "It's not the money she's taken issue with. It's the way you commandeered the situation without her input or consent. Make sure you take her to a nice dinner and apologize properly."

"I will, thanks Jane."

"Now about lunch, I have fresh chicken salad I made earlier. I could toast some bread and make y'all sandwiches with that." She started pulling condiments and bread out.

"That would be great. I'll be right back, I'm gonna make a call. If she comes down distract her, would ya?" I asked as I walked out to the veranda, not waiting for the response.

I scrolled through the contacts until I found the listing for Halls, making arrangements for us to have dinner in one of their private rooms tonight at 7:00 p.m. Halls was the best steakhouse in South Carolina and I wanted Leila to enjoy a steak. I know she would say she'd need to run it off, but I had a better alternative planned for her tonight. She would need to eat plenty of steak and potato in order to keep up.

I returned to the kitchen to see Jane and Leila conversing over chicken salad sandwiches. What they were speaking about I couldn't say, but the second they realized I was back, they stopped talking, looked at each other and giggled. Oh hell, that can't be good. I started to worry what they had their heads together about.

"You two don't have to stop on my account, please finish your conversation. I'll just be at the bar eating my lunch." I picked up one of the sandwiches and sat down at the granite breakfast bar.

"Oh, don't worry, we were done. Weren't we Leila?" Jane started putting away lunch.

"We certainly are." Leila turned to me. "Brody I was hoping you might be able to take me home after we eat."

Shit, she's really angry. She's not even going to stay with me tonight. I hung my head over my plate and replied, "Yes, if that's what you want, then I'll take you home."

"I'd like to grab some more clean clothes and a pair of running shoes. I don't have to be back to work until Tuesday night, so I thought Ruger and I'd stay here tonight. If that's okay, of course." She batted her long dark eyelashes at me.

I stood up and walked over to her. "I'd love nothing more than for you to stay tonight."

I pulled her into a long, slow kiss forgetting Jane was in the kitchen with us. Ruger's barking pulled us apart. He was standing in the foyer barking at the front door, a few seconds later the doorbell rang.

Jane wiped her hands on a white dish towel. "I'll get that."

I walked over to the bar, pulled out Leila's barstool and sat her sandwich in front of her.

As we started to eat, I heard Jane telling the visitor that I had company and that they should call before coming over next time. That couldn't be good. I heard a female voice giggle, then high heels clicking annoyingly across the hardwood floors.

"Dude, where were you today? You told me that you and Damon were going to meet us out at the races." Sean walked in flanked by some blonde bimbo whose boobs might as well have been water balloons as fake as they looked.

"Hi Sean, how are you? Who's your friend?" I said condescendingly as I stood.

"Huh, oh this is Rachel. Rachel this is my boy Brody and…" Sean looked at Leila waiting for me to introduce them.

"Sean, Rachel, this is my girlfriend Leila." I smiled, standing behind her as I draped an arm over her shoulder.

Sean burst out laughing. "Girlfriend? You, Brody Davis, have a girlfriend?"

He must have seen the look on my face because he quickly changed his attitude. "Wow, I never thought I'd see the day you called anyone your girlfriend. Nice to meet ya, Leila."

"Likewise, we were just having lunch." I knew where she was going with this and it wasn't happening.

"So, why don't I call you and make plans for all of us to get together next weekend?" I interrupted her because I had things planned for us today. Sean and his piece of ass were not on that list. I walked over and shook Sean's hand.

"Cool, I just wanted to make sure things were all good man. I tried your cell, but it went straight to voicemail. That's mostly why I drove out; your cell's never off. Hit me up later." Sean strolled out with his POA following right behind.

"You didn't have to do that, they could have stayed and eaten with us," Leila said.

"Huh, nah, I don't want to share you with anyone just yet. I want to keep you all to myself." I sat back down and started eating my lunch.

"You do, do you?" she asked in a sweet tone.

I finished chewing then answered her. "I have plans for us for the rest of the day and they don't involve Sean or Big Boobs McGee."

She damn near choked on her food she was laughing so hard. "Oh. My. God. I can't believe you just said that. I seriously wanted to scream out *'Hooters, Hooters, Hooters,'* but I controlled myself."

We both laughed at our movie references to *Big Daddy*. Man, her laugh was awesome. It was real and wholesome, she laughed with her whole body. Not like most of the girls I "date." They would've laughed pretentiously and sounded as phony as their hair and boobs.

We finished our lunch and Leila insisted on cleaning up after us. She told me that just because Jane could do it didn't mean that she should have to. I tried to explain that's what I pay her for but Lei refused to listen.

I looked at the watch my father gave me and realized it was almost 1:00 p.m. I needed to take her to her house for clothes, but I had a few business calls I needed to make before I could relax and enjoy my evening. On our way up to the bedroom I figured out how to kill two birds with one stone, well with one Bentley.

"Hey babe, I need to make some calls and look over a few contracts that are supposed to settle this week. I know I said that I'd take you to your place, but I was thinking, maybe you could just take the Bentley and run out while I get some work done." I prayed she wouldn't freak out again about driving one of my cars.

She sighed. "Yeah, I can do that, but why the Bentley? That thing costs like two hundred and fifty thousand dollars. I know ya say it's just a car, but that's a lot of money."

"If it will make you feel better, then take the Mercedes." I pulled her into me and kissed her forehead. "See, I can compromise."

"Oh gee, thanks, only a Mercedes that costs a hundred grand," she said sarcastically before kissing me and walking into the bedroom. She picked up her purse from the couch, pulled out her phone and smiled. "Drew must be feeling better, he sent me a text asking where I was bringing him lunch from."

"That sounds like a great idea; why don't you have Jane pack him up a sandwich and some fruit," I suggested.

"Ooooh, that would be nice and healthy. He'll be so happy it's not hospital food, he won't even notice it's actually good for him." She laughed in a scary, up-to-no-good kind of laugh. It made me grin from ear to ear.

I walked her out to the garage, gave her the keys to the Mercedes and showed her which buttons opened the garage and the main gate. I also had her Bluetooth her phone so she would be hands free.

"It's really fine, I don't need to use my phone," she protested.

"If it's in your purse and you have an accident, it could go flying. This way it's synced with the car and you can call with a press of a button. It's safer," I explained.

"Yes Dad," she deadpanned.

"All right, go. Be careful." I dipped my head in and stole a quick kiss before she closed the door.

She shut the door to the SUV, adjusted the seat and mirrors, then backed out. Damn, she looked as nervous as a teenager driving alone for the first time.

She rolled her window down and waved. "Bye."

Oh hell, I was in trouble. And that trouble started with a capital L. She wasn't even out of sight yet and I found myself longing to see her again. I needed to get my shit together and quick. I didn't know what she was doing to me, but, God help me, I didn't want it to stop. She made me want things that, if I stopped too long to think about, would totally freak me out. In the short time I'd known this woman I have let her in my home, had her sleep in my bed and, hell, I've even *enjoyed* cuddling.

And, shit, don't even get me started on her beast of a dog. I woke up this morning and that fucker had made himself comfortable on my bed. *My* bed. He was curled up at her feet. He was her protector and for that reason alone, I didn't say shit. Didn't even freak out and make him move. Okay, I may have freaked a little on the inside, but I let him stay. Why? Because he made her feel safe and happy. It was obvious she loved that dog like he was her child. But, damn, that dog shed like a motherfucker. The Hair Club for Men needed to look into the hair loss–hair growth in German shepherds. In the twenty-four hours that dog had been at my place, he'd shed enough hair to make another dog.

Chapter Nineteen

Leila

I was thankful for the time I had alone to clear my head and reflect on the last few days of chaos. I always tried to find the positive in every situation, good, bad or indifferent. While I was devastated that Drew was shot, it brought me Brody. I choose to be positive. I really wasn't looking for any kind of relationship and I still wasn't sure how serious we would be, but I felt at home with him. He seemed easy and familiar and fun. And he made me feel safe. Safer than I have felt in a long time; I wanted to hold onto that feeling. We just had to work on his domineering tendencies.

I turned the radio on to my favorite country station and started singing along with Miranda and Carrie. Before I knew it, I was pulling into the Ashley River Tower driveway to valet, shaking my head. That crazy man and his hatred of MUSC parking garages. I couldn't help but let out a little giggle. I promised to valet park and not dare enter any of the evil parking structures. I didn't plan on staying too long, especially since it really wasn't visiting hours.

I made my way to Drew's room, but when I opened the door it was empty. Hmm, they must have moved him to a step down bed, I thought, but as I looked around the room, I started to think otherwise. His stuff was still up here. What the hell was going on? I left in search of a nurse or someone who could tell me where Drew was.

I reached the nurses station and started to ask about my brother. Brooke immediately hung up the phone and walked out to talk to me. The look on her face really freaked me out.

"I've been trying to reach you, Leila. Why don't we walk in here to talk?" She motioned to Drew's room.

"No, let's talk right here. Why were you trying to reach me? Where is Drew?" I started to feel frantic.

"Drew started having more chest pain about thirty minutes ago. He pressed his call bell and when I got there he was coughing up blood. We called Drake, who was just finishing up a surgery and he met us in the OR."

Oh God this isn't happening. "How much blood?"

"Enough that we needed to take him back into the OR to find the cause and stop it. Listen, Drake wanted me to call you and I did try a few times, but it just went to voicemail so I left a couple of messages. I was just calling Sergeant Smith when you arrived, since he's next on the emergency contact list," she explained. "Is there anything I can do for you? Anyone I can call?"

"No, thank you." Right, you think I'm gonna give you Brody's number to call? Like I don't know you would save it for later. I needed to call Brody and let him know what's going on. I stepped into Drew's room and took out my phone. Sure enough, three voicemails. I didn't listen to them, just deleted them and then called Brody.

He answered on the first ring. "Hey babe, miss me already?"

"Brody, Drew's in surgery," I blurted out. "He started having chest pain then started coughing up blood. They took him to the OR, and Drake is with him. Brooke said it was a significant amount. Oh God, Brody, I'm sorry I'm ramblin' again."

"Take a deep breath baby. Tell me when this happened," he said, trying to calm me.

"About forty minutes ago now." I slowed my breathing.

"Okay, what do they think happened?" he asked calmly.

"Most likely a vessel or artery they cauterized earlier didn't hold." The nurse in me took over.

"I'm in the garage now, I will be there in twenty minutes," he assured me.

Part of me wanted to tell him to just stay at home and not rush over here, that I would be fine, but the other part of me knew I would feel better with him here beside me. I worried about him driving. I knew he'd drive like a maniac to get here quickly.

"Hey Brody, please be careful. I couldn't deal with it if something happened to you because you were rushing to be here with me."

"Baby, I promise I'll get to you in one piece." With that he hung up.

I sat on the bed and was immediately reminded of my mother's death. The chaplain took Drew and me into a room and told us to sit down. I sat on the foot of the stretcher that was in the room, and then he broke the news to us. Drew held me while I sobbed hysterically. I shook my head. That was *not* going to happen with Drew. It couldn't. I loved him. I needed him.

"Brooke." I walked back out to the nurse's station. "I'm heading up to the OR waiting room. I have my cell, which is turned on. Will you please call me if you hear anything?"

She smiled weakly. "Of course I will Leila. Please call if you need anything."

I thanked her and then sent a quick text to Brody.

Will be in OR waiting room, same as the other day.

I dialed Bobby and filled him in on Drew and asked him to call Jasper and let him know what was going on. While I was on the phone a text message from Brody came through.

Ok I'll meet you there.

I got to the waiting room and found it empty. I guessed, since it was Sunday, there weren't too many surgeries happening. I flipped on the TV. Not that I was going to watch it, but I needed the background noise. I started pacing and then thought I would do some yoga. I mean there was no one here, so why not? It helped me relax and I desperately needed that. I bent over into a forward fold to stretch my back and legs. I slowed my breathing and focused on feeling the stretch throughout my body. I walked my hands out into a downward dog, holding my core tight and concentrated on my breathing. I held the pose for sixty seconds and then went into a plank position for another sixty seconds. I had walked myself back up to a forward fold when I felt a set of strong, masculine hands on my hips. I attempted to jump forward and away, but they held me in place. Then I heard his voice.

"Baby, I don't think it's a good idea for you to be bent over like this in a hospital. You'll start giving all the men here heart attacks." He spun me around into a strong, comforting hug. "But if you want to do some yoga when we go home, I'd be more than happy to help you out."

I swatted at him. "Stop, I was just tryin' to relax and get outta my own head. I had myself so freaked out I had to try something."

"Well, I'm here now and I'll help you focus on something other than the bad things." He leaned forward, kissed my forehead and then held me tight.

Brody got me to sit for a little while and look at the TV. I was going over all of the possible complications and outcomes of a GSW in my head when Jasper and Bobby came into the waiting room.

Jasper pulled me into a warm hug. "Hey, there's my girl. How ya holdin' up?"

I put my strong face on; I couldn't let them see me cry. "Hey Jas, I'm good. Hey Bobby, I told ya y'all didn't need to come down here, I'd call ya as soon as I heard something."

"You think we'd letcha go through this alone? You're crazy, we're family. We're supposed to stick together." He gave me a quick hug.

Brody cleared his throat and stood up. "Actually, she wasn't alone. I got here about thirty minutes ago." He shook hands with both men.

Jasper addressed Brody, "I'm glad you were able to stop by and sit with her until we got here, I appreciate it."

Oh boy, here we go. Jasper is getting ready to go into overprotective, surrogate-dad mode for sure.

"Jasper, Brody has been with me since Friday morning. He's been by my side the whole time." I reached over and took Brody's hand. "I don't know if I would've made it through the last few days with my sanity, if it wasn't for him."

Now it was Bobby's turn to put in his two cents. "Lei, I told you if you needed anything to call me. I would've taken some time off to be with you." Bobby tilted his head, signaling he wanted to speak to me alone. We walked over to the vending machines. "Listen, I know you're more than capable of making your own decisions and dating whomever you want, but do you really even know this guy?"

"Ughhhh, Bobby, I'm a big girl. I can date, fuck or talk to whoever I want. I don't know why you're making such a big deal out of this. It's not like I date often, and I am not discussing my sex life with you. Ugh, gross, you're like my brother." I punched him in the arm. "I'm a damn good judge of character. It's not like I date random guys. Now, if we are done with this, I'd like to get back to Brody before Jasper handcuffs him to a chair and starts interrogating him."

"Sorry Lei. I love ya and I don't wanna see ya get hurt or used by this guy," he said just as Brody walked over to catch the end of our conversation.

"Leila, I'm going to step outside in the hallway to make a phone call really fast, but I'll be right back." He looked at me then eyed Bobby up before turning and leaving.

"Great." I blew out an exasperated breath. "I'm sure he heard you say I love you and blah, blah, blah. He probably thinks you're IN love with me."

"So, what if he does? He'll get over it," Bobby said dryly.

"So, the point is that I really like him Bobby. I don't want to mess this up." I punched him in the shoulder.

"Fuck Leila, what is it with you and punching me lately?" He rubbed is shoulder like it was hurting, which I knew it wasn't. Bobby might not be bulky like Brody, but the guy was solid muscle.

About ten minutes later, Brody walked back in with Drake beside him.

"Hey, Lei." Drake took my hand. "Everything is fine. He came through better than ever. He had a small bleeder, but I was able to suture it off and he's all good."

I took a deep, relieving breath. "Drake, I owe you one. I'm so thankful it was you in there with him."

"Don't thank me yet, I am gonna keep him pretty well sedated for the next twelve hours. I think he's been overdoing it. No visitors until Monday morning."

I started to protest. "Seriously Drake, I don't think that's necessary. What if it was just me?"

"Leila, take the rest of the day and do something." Drake turned to Brody. "Please take her home and don't let her out of your sight. She's a sneaky little shit. OWW!"

I pinched the back of Drake's arm. "That'll teach ya to call me a sneaky little shit, won't it? Seriously Drake, if he's gonna be sedated, then what's the harm in me just sittin' with him?"

"I'm gonna check in on Drew. If anything changes I'll have one of the nurses call you. Please keep your cell on tonight, would ya?"

"So you're gonna ignore me?" And that's exactly what he did. "Guhhh, you're such an ass Drake Emery Thomas."

"Oooh, middle name." He rolled his eyes at me. "Not changin' my mind, Lei. Still love ya though twat face."

Shaking my head. "Yeah, well, I hate you."

He laughed as he turned to walk away. "No, ya don't. You love me and you know it."

"Ugh, shut up. Don't ya have someone to go cut on asshat?"

He threw his hand up over his head and flipped me off as he strolled into the corridor.

"Love you too," I hollered in response. I turned to look at the three men left in the room with me, who were repressing laughter. "I guess I'll call y'all if something changes. Y'all should head on home, that's my plan."

Bobby must have felt like being a smart-ass because he turned to Brody. "Yeah, Lei'll call ya later if anything changes." He turned back to me. "I'll drop ya at your house on my way home."

"Thanks, but I have Brody's car. I'll be drivin' it home to grab some clothes, before headin' back out to his place. Ruger is already out there with his assistant," I said, rubbing it in Bobby's face as he glared at me.

Brody gave me a sweet kiss goodbye and then stopped before he reached the doors. "Oh yeah, make sure you remember your running shoes and a pair of black heels." He winked.

I felt my face getting warm and just knew I was bright fucking red. Damn him. I wondered what he is up to.

Jasper and Bobby walked with me to the valet, who gave me the keys to the silver Mercedes that was parked exactly where I left it. I looked around for Brody or the Bentley but didn't see either. He must have taken off already. I was sure I would have to deal with Bobby's little "I love you" comment when I got back to Brody's place. I hope he doesn't go all caveman again.

"Well, that's me." I pointed to the SUV. "I will call ya tomorrow if I don't hear from anyone tonight."

"Listen baby girl, I wantcha to be careful with this Brody guy. You don't know the first thing about him," Jasper started. "How 'bout I look into him?"

"That's not a bad idea," Bobby said smugly, putting his two cents in.

"No. I appreciate y'all wantin' to look out for me. But like I told Bobby, I'm perfectly capable of takin' care of myself. Besides, he's friends with Drew. How bad can he be?"

They both were quietly brooding when Bobby spoke up. "Fine, but if you need me, don't hesitate. Money or not, I'll fuck his shit up if he hurts you."

"Got it." I pulled Jasper in for a quick hug. "I'll call ya later."

I walked over and climbed up into the SUV, turned the music up and slid back the sunroof. I started home, constructing a checklist in my mind of things I needed to get done as I drove home.

Chapter Twenty

Brody

On my way back home, I called Jane to see if she was able to find the dress I wanted to get Leila. With much luck and several hundreds of dollars later, Jane had made it happen. I told her I didn't care if it cost ten thousand dollars; I wanted Lei to have this dress for tonight, when we went to Halls. When I drove past J Crew on Friday and saw it in the window, I knew it would look phenomenal on her. I just hoped she would be up for going out tonight, given Drew's condition.

I pulled into the garage and shut the Hennessey off. When I opened the door to the house to go in I was greeted by a growling shepherd.

"Ruger, hey boy, it's just me."

I heard Jane whistle from another room and with that Ruger trotted away. What the hell was that about?

"Jane, where's the dress?" I walked into the family room and saw her sitting on the couch playing on the iPad I got her last week.

"Huh?" She looked up from the tablet. "Oh, it's upstairs in your closet, where her other clothes are hanging. It's still in the garment bag. I placed the shoes on the center island and took the necklace out of the safe. It's in the study on your desk."

She knows me too well. I went to the study to see if still looked as I remembered. I opened the large, black velvet box to see my mother's diamond and sapphire necklace. The necklace was made of princess cut sapphires, surrounded by tiny flawless diamonds with the center sapphire being the largest. Seeing it flooded my mind with memories of my mother wearing this necklace. She adored this necklace and would have loved seeing it on Leila. I was pulled from my thoughts as Jane entered the study.

"Your mom would want you to give that to the woman you intend to marry, not just someone who was keeping your bed warm for a little while." She was right. This might not have been her most expensive or extravagant piece of jewelry, but it was her favorite. "So be sure you know what you're doing Brody. It's not something that can be taken back, once you've given it."

"Thanks Jane, I appreciate your loyalty to my mother and to me. I know you only want what's best for me. And I believe, without a shadow of doubt, Leila is what's best. I know it's only been a few days, but I feel like I've known her my whole life. There is just something…I can't explain it. I'm drawn to her like she's the air I breathe," I said, trying to explain how I felt.

"Oh my boy, your parents knew each other exactly five months before they got married. They knew instantly they were it for each other." Tears came to her eyes. Jane was my mother's assistant and closest friend. "When you know, you just know. Don't let anyone else change your mind or tell you how you should feel or that it's too fast. To hell with time, tomorrow is not promised and you need to enjoy every minute you have together."

I crossed the study and pulled Jane into a tight embrace. "Thanks Jane. And not just for the advice today but for stepping in and helping raise me to be the man I am today. I know I wouldn't be where I am without you. I don't want you to think that it's unnoticed or unappreciated. I do love you."

"Oh my boy, I know. I love you too. Now stop all this, you're gonna make me cry." She fanned her face and smiled. "Go get ready, she'll probably be here any minute."

She was right. I needed to get in the shower and dressed. It was already 4:00 p.m. and we had reservations at 7:00. I wanted to have enough time to surprise her with her dress and the necklace. Plus, I had to ask her about this Bobby asshole telling her he loved her. I thought he was Drew's partner. Maybe they had a thing a while ago and she didn't bother to mention it or maybe he has a crush on her and she doesn't feel the same way.

Jesus man, get it together, you need to stop freaking the fuck out over something you don't know about yet.

*****

Leila

After grabbing some clean clothes, shoes and makeup, I hopped back in the Mercedes and started back to Johns Island. My mind had been going a hundred miles an hour, trying to figure out what Brody was up to. I prayed he didn't read too much into what Bobby had said to me at the hospital. He had nothing to worry about as far as

Bobby was concerned. Bobby had always looked after me like I was his little sister. That "I love you" was the equivalent of Drew telling me he loved me.

I really wished my mom was here. Not that I wanted her to see Drew in this condition, but I needed her loving support. Plus, I wish she could have met Brody. I wish I could talk to her about all of these feelings I was having for him. I knew it was way too soon to feel this way, but I did. Part of me wished I didn't; he had the power to hurt me like no one else. It felt like everything was happening too fast. But I couldn't go through life waiting for the other shoe to drop. I needed to enjoy life, while I could. Drew's shooting reinforced what all those years in trauma had taught me; it could all be over in the blink of an eye. I needed to live life instead of safely watching it go by from my two bedroom condo, tucked away like a hermit.

I pulled up to the gate at the entrance of the estate, put the window down and pressed the intercom button.

"Hi, Leila." Jane's voice came over the speaker, and the gates parted, allowing me access. I drove down the path, pulled into the garage and hopped down from the driver's seat. I took my bag from the backseat and locked the doors.

Wait, did I really need to lock the doors? Inside a locked garage on a gated property? No, probably not, but it was the force of habit, so I did.

I started to head up the stairs when Jane and Ruger came in from the veranda.

"Hey Leila. I just brought Ruger in and was just getting ready to feed him, unless you would like to, of course," Jane said sweetly.

"No, ma'am. You're more than welcome to. Thank you for letting me in. He seems to have taken a liking to you, huh?"

"You are quite welcome dear. And he does seem to follow me around, doesn't he?" She chuckled, as if she didn't know it was because she spoiled him rotten. "Why don't you go find Brody? I believe he's in his room."

"Okay, thanks." I started up the stairs, paused and turned back to Jane. "You'll tell me if Ruger becomes a bother, right? I can bring him upstairs with me."

"Nonsense, he's keeping me company. Plus Dave, the pool guy, is coming by later. I want to introduce them, so that way if Dave comes by to clean the pool and Ruger is out there he doesn't scare

Dave." She winked at me. "Now, get on up those stairs and find Brody." Jane smiled like she knew something I didn't.

Brody's bedroom the door was shut, but I could hear music playing. I wondered if I should knock or just go in. I settled on knocking.

"Who is it?" Brody hollered.

"Leila. Can I come in?" I asked.

The door flew open and there stood Brody with a towel wrapped around that gorgeous body of his. Hot damn, I could eat him up with a spoon. I could see a few stray droplets slipping down his picture-perfect pecs. He looked at me like I was crazy. "Why are you knocking on the door? You can just come in."

"Sorry, I wasn't sure. What if you were running around naked in here?"

He burst out laughing. "Seriously, babe? It's not like you haven't seen me naked or haven't showered with me. I've got nothing to hide from you."

He gave me a little peck and then walked into the closet. There really should be a different name for that place other than a closet. It was like its own department store in there.

"Hey babe, can you run down and ask Jane if she knows what time the staff will be here tomorrow?" he shouted out.

Staff? Holy crap he has a whole staff of people for this house? "Yeah…I'll be right back."

I ran downstairs, found Jane on the veranda sipping a glass of wine and reading on her iPad. "Uh, Brody wanted me to ask if you knew what time the staff will be here tomorrow?"

"Oh yes, of course. Let's see." She tapped and swiped on the iPad. "Mary, the chef, will be here about seven a.m. John, the landscaper, is usually here no later than ten a.m. And Andrew should be here tomorrow since he took off Friday. His schedule is always so up in the air. Andrew takes care of the horses. Well, exercising, cleaning the stables and that stuff. I usually feed them when he's not here," she said, looking up from her tablet.

"Wow, I didn't realize how many people it took to keep up this place."

"Well, I mostly keep up with the day to day and manage the estate staff. It's one less thing Brody has to worry about. He's busy enough as it is," she remarked with a proud grin.

"Okay, thanks. I'll pass along the schedule." I went back inside and upstairs. Opened the door without knocking and was shocked.

Brody stood in front of the closet doors dressed in a black custom tailored suit, charcoal shirt with the top button undone and the jacket open. I knew I needed to close my mouth and stop drooling, but I couldn't. He was utterly gorgeous and alluring with those sexy crystal blue eyes.

"Wow, you clean up nice." I wanted to kick myself. But that was the only thing that came to mind. "Do you have to leave for a meeting or did I miss something?"

"Thanks. Actually, we have plans tonight. A bit of a surprise, if you will." He took my hand and pulled me to the oversized wardrobe.

"What did you do?" Eyeing him suspiciously, I followed after a slight hesitation.

"You'll see." We rounded the corner into the closet. He walked over and took a garment bag from the selection he cleared out for me. "Here, open it."

I took the bag, looked back at him; he nodded his head. His whole face was dancing with excitement. I pulled the zipper down exposing a pale blue, silk chiffon dress with a plunging V neckline, and a knee-length A-line skirt. Gasping, I looked at the dress and then back to Brody. "Oh, Brody, it's beautiful. You shouldn't have." I was really at a loss for words. "Really, you shouldn't have done this."

"I saw it driving down King the other day and knew it was made for you. I had Jane sneak in here and check your sizes while we were out." He turned to the island. "And these are for you to wear with it. I hope you like them."

I took the box and, noting it was Jimmy Choo, and found the cutest pair of three-inch stilettos. They were silver glittery strappy sandals and they were simple and perfect.

"Brody, this is too much. These shoes alone are easily six hundred dollars." I pushed the box back toward him, but he walked away.

"Leila, you need to get used to me buying things for you and spoiling you. You deserve to be treated like a princess." He walked back to me. "Get dressed and meet me downstairs, and don't keep me waiting."

As he walked past me he smacked me on the ass. "That's for arguing with me over what I spend on you. Keep that in mind going forward, because that was just a warning. When I punish you, it'll be with your new toy and you won't be in clothes. You've got one hour to get ready."

He left me standing in the closet, mouth gaping open and panties damp. How was it he had this power over me? A quick smack to the ass and I had forgotten what I'd said to him. I shook my head and then headed for the shower.

This man was going to be the death of me.

I let the conditioner sit in my hair while I shaved, then hopped out, dried off and wrapped my hair up in a towel. I flipped the stereo on in the bathroom. Yes, there is a stereo and 42" TV in this man's bathroom. I checked my cell for the fortieth time for any update on Drew and realized it was 5:00 p.m. I had less than thirty minutes to finish getting ready. I ran haphazardly, trying to keep my towel up, to Brody's closet, pulled out the clean bra and panties from my duffle.

I grabbed my pale gray bra with pink lace trim and matching cheeky panties, because I didn't want to take a chance with black under the pale blue dress. I made the decision to do my hair and makeup before getting dressed. I crossed back over to the bathroom, took the towel off my head and grabbed a wide-tooth comb. I combed out my curly mess, added some curling lotion and scrunched it a little. Hair done. Next for makeup, just a little foundation, some eyeliner, mascara and lip gloss. I didn't like wearing makeup unless I was going somewhere nice or on a real date. Barb and Drake didn't count.

I was jumping, dancing and singing "Feel This Moment" by Pitbull and Christina Aguilera, until I caught sight of Brody standing near the bathroom door. I stopped dancing and clutched my chest. "Jesus. You're gonna give me a heart attack. Stop creepin' up on me."

"Please, don't let me stop you." He smiled and walked over as I turned the volume down. "And I wasn't creeping. I was simply enjoying the show."

"Oh no you don't. I only have fifteen minutes left. Out. Lemme finish getting ready." I started to run out of the bathroom but I didn't make it far before he caught me from behind and hoisted me over his shoulder. He carried me into the closet and placed me up on the island.

"Brody, what are you doing? Let me get down." I tried to hop down, but he blocked my way.

"Lay back," he ordered, but I just looked at him like he had lost his fucking mind. "Leila, I said lay back. Don't make me ask again."

"Ask? Don't you mean, don't make you tell me again, because that wasn't a request," I said flippantly and started to lean back on the island.

"I'm adding a spanking for every smart-ass remark." He pulled my hands above my head and walked around the island. I felt the silk tie being wrapped around my wrists. Okay, so I guess he's decided now was as good a time as any to tie me up.

"Your wrists are tied together but not tied to anything. But you will not move them. Your arms are to stay above your head until I tell you to move them, understood?"

"Yeah," I said cautiously.

"Bend your knees and put your feet flat on the counter," he directed me. I obeyed, curious as hell as to what he was up to.

He grabbed me by the tops of my thighs and slid me down until my ass was almost hanging on the edge and my heels clung to the corners. He gripped both sides of my panties and I lifted my hips slightly. He slipped my panties down my legs and dropped them on the floor at his feet. Then he knelt down, placed my feet on his shoulders and, without any warning, buried his face in my pussy, licking, teasing and sucking on my clit while plunging two fingers deep in me.

"Ahhhh, oh God, Brody, mmmmmm. Don't stop. Fuck that feels so good." I rolled my hips, trying to apply more pressure from his tongue to my swollen nub. "Mmmmm oh yeah, oh God."

He pulled back. "Don't move." He stood up with my legs stretched apart resting on his chest.

I heard his zipper and the tear of the foil wrapper. He rubbed the head of his cock back and forth over my clit a few times, then sank his cock so deep into my dripping wet sex he hit my cervix.

I tensed up and sucked in a deep breath. "Ow."

He pulled out a little. "I'm sorry babe, you okay?"

"Yeah, just go slow," I encouraged him. He dropped down, slowly thrusting at an upward angle, while teasing my clit with his thumb. Oh dear God in heaven, I was going to come in 2.7 seconds flat.

"Oh my God Brody, I'm gonna come, don't stop. Mmmm." I started to pull my hands down to pinch my nipples when he admonished me.

"Do not move your hands." He kept pumping into me, but stopped rubbing my clit. "I want you to come with me. Don't come until I tell you to."

Damn, I didn't know if I could hold this one back, my body started trembling. Brody reached forward and took my nipple between his thumb and middle finger and began to roll it between them.

Fuck, he was doing this on purpose; he was enjoying torturing me. I decided I wasn't waiting anymore. I let go and the orgasm hit me like a Mack truck.

"Oh *fuck* Brody, oh God, I'm coming. Oh God...don't stop," I screamed.

In one swift motion he pulled all the way out of me and essentially killed my climax. "What the hell, Lei? I said to wait for me."

"Me what-the-hell? How about *you* what-the-hell? I was literally a second away from comin' and you pulled out." I pushed him back with my feet, but he caught them and held my ankles at arm's length and drove into me. He started fucking me punitively. It didn't take either of us long to reach our peak. He didn't wait for me this time, rub my clit or take his time. No, he slammed into me with a string of curses. As he was still thrusting wildly, I reached down, with my hands still bound and rubbed desperately until I came.

My pussy clamped down on his cock just as he was about to pull all the way out. "Holy fuck, Leila."

My moaning and writhing on the wardrobe island must have compensated for my disobeying his order to keep my hands over my head. Oh, and for almost coming without him. He lifted me off the counter, still buried deep within me, and laid me on the thick carpet.

"You have to be the worst slave ever. Damn, you don't listen for shit," he murmured into my mouth as he started kissing me. His tongue swirled and explored my mouth like he had never kissed me before. We lay there kissing for a minute before he untied me, pulled out and excused himself to the bathroom.

I sat up and looked around. Holy crap, that was intense. Somehow or another I had a feeling that was *not* my punishment.

I hoisted myself up off the floor and grabbed my panties so I could clean myself up. As I came out of the closet, Brody was standing in the bedroom.

"Hurry up and get ready. What is taking you so long?" He smirked, like he wasn't the reason I was still naked.

"Well, stop tying me up and fucking me senseless and I will." I wiggled my head when I spoke. He just smiled and walked out.

I ran to the bathroom, cleaned up quickly and hurried back to the closet. Gently I removed the dress from the garment bag, enjoying the feel of silk against my skin as I shimmied it into place. After contorting my body I managed to get the zipper all the way up, or at least I think I did. I took the shoes out of their box and slipped them on my feet. I took a quick look in the tall mirror.

Hmm, not bad if I do say so myself.

I was grateful in that moment that I almost always wear my simple princess cut diamond studs. Not that I was surprised like this often. I ran my fingers through my curls trying to tame them from the ravaging they just withstood. I looked at myself once more and then headed downstairs to find Brody.

I didn't have to search long; I found him waiting for me at the bottom of the stairs. He looked so prestigious and seductive in his suit. I silently prayed I didn't lose my balance or trip, sending me tumbling head over feet down the open staircase, taking Brody out along the way, with all my grace.

"Leila, you're even more breathtaking than usual. You look simply radiant." He took the first two steps and held out his hand to me.

"What can I say, you have good taste in clothes. It's all the dress. You could put Ruger in this dress and he'd look amazing too. So I should thank you for the most stunning outfit and shoes." I kissed his cheek.

"I have one more surprise." He tugged me down the hall to his study. He stepped around his desk to the credenza and picked up a large square velvet box. He walked back over to me, held it out to me. "Open it."

"Wow," I breathed; shocked at what I was seeing my hand flew to my mouth. "Brody, it's beautiful, but I cannot accept this. This is way too much. It's stunning and obviously incredibly expensive."

"Leila, I want you to wear this tonight. If you are not comfortable accepting it yet, then I'll understand"—he smiled—"for now. It was my mother's, and I know she'd love to see you wearing it. You deserve to wear diamonds and priceless jewels. You can wear it tonight and leave it here in the safe, if that would make you feel better."

Brody lifted the sapphire and diamond necklace from the box and motioned for me to turn around. As I held my hair up, he closed the clasp and kissed my neck. "There's a mirror in the hall bathroom if you would like to see how it looks."

"I would like to see it." I stroked my fingers down his smoothly shaved cheek and gave him a chaste kiss before exiting the study.

After I admired myself in the mirror, we finally entered the garage. Brody walked up to the Bentley, opened the passenger door for me and helped me in. It dawned on me while I was waiting for him, that I had no clue where we were going or what we were doing.

"All set?" he asked.

"Yep, sure am. Just one question, care to share where are we going?" I might as well try, I doubted he was going to tell me, but it couldn't hurt to ask.

"All you need to know is dinner and a ride," he answered cryptically. It wasn't specific, but it was more than I thought I would get from him. "I know you love surprises, even if you aren't the most patient person."

Chapter Twenty-one

Leila

When Brody finally stopped, we were in a private parking lot on King Street. He escorted me from the car and we started down King. Unlike earlier today, the humidity was low and there was a slight breeze, making the walk enjoyable. We walked until I saw Halls Chophouse and I knew that was where he was taking me.

As we entered the restaurant I heard a loud rumbling stop just outside on the street. The hostess informed us the previous private party had just wrapped up and they were setting the room up as Brody asked. She invited us to have drinks at the bar while we waited. Brody ushered me to a pair of empty barstools near the front door and helped me up. Just as we were ordering two glasses of wine, I heard a familiar voice over the crowded restaurant. I turned to see Jaxon standing near the hostess desk talking and laughing with the manager. As I started to look away our eyes met for a brief second.

Fuck. Fuckety-fuck, fuck! This was not happening. I looked over at Brody, who apparently saw Jaxon too, because he was clenching his jaw.

"Can we please just ignore him?" I reached out and took Brody's hand in mine.

"I will unless he—"Brody was interrupted as Jaxon appeared next to us.

"Leila, you look beautiful tonight, who's your friend?" Jaxon asked, like Brody was a girlfriend I was out with for drinks. Jaxon's gaze never left mine. I couldn't help but be mesmerized by his bright jade green eyes.

"Jaxon, this Brody. Brody meet Jaxon." I made a quick introduction, while silently begging God to let the hostess call us now.

"Listen, I'm glad I ran into you. How about we get dinner one night this week? Lemme thank you properly for bandaging me up." His voice was deep and suggestive.

Brody looked like he was going to punch Jaxon in the face any second. "Dude, you've got to be fucking kidding me, right? I'm sitting right fucking here and you're seriously asking her out." Brody kept his voice quiet but stern. "I think you need to walk away."

"I think you should let the lady speak for herself, *dude*. I didn't ask you out for dinner, I asked her." Jaxon turned back to me and ran his hand down my bicep. "So, dinner? Me and you. Just friends, as a thank-you."

Brody gritted his teeth, but held it together.

"Jaxon, I appreciate the offer, but I'm dating Brody. It wouldn't be appropriate to accept your invitation, no matter the pretense." I smiled sweetly. "But thank you."

"Okay, I get it. When you're available all you have to do is call me, I'll be waiting." He took my hand and kissed my knuckles. "Have a good night baby girl."

Seriously, if Brody wasn't in the picture I *might* have taken him up on his panty-melting offer. But Brody was here. And he was seething mad.

"Leila, I swear that guy is stalking you. Every time I turn around, he's there and he's hitting on you." He looked around to see where Jaxon had gone off to.

"Oh please, he's harmless. He's not stalking me, you big baby, get a grip. He happened to be in two of the same restaurants in the same area. It's not some conspiracy." I blew out a frustrated breath. At that very moment the hostess approached us, telling us our table was ready. Way to go, lady. You couldn't have possibly been five minutes earlier? I lifted my glass of Riesling and followed Brody upstairs to the second door on the left.

He had the room lit with varying sizes of white candles; a small vase of deep red calla lilies sat on the table. The doors were all glass so we could see out, but it was relatively quiet. We didn't have to talk over anyone or listen to anyone else's conversation. I sat facing the doorway into the hall and Brody across from me. He has a full view of the larger dining room, while mine was of the smaller room on the other side of the hall.

I looked around wondering where the menus were. Brody must have read my mind. "I took the liberty and placed our orders ahead of time. I hope that's okay."

"Well, I guess it all depends on what you ordered for me"

"Petite filet mignon with a baked potato and asparagus with hollandaise."

He had me at filet. "Mmm, sounds yummy." I took a sip of wine. Deciding to focus him on something other than Jaxon, I picked a subject that was deep in his comfort zone. "So what does your week look like?"

"I have several meetings tomorrow, then I have a few contracts I need to work on. I should have one settlement this week, as long as the contractors do what they are supposed to." He paused. "Sorry, I don't want to bore you with my hectic schedule. Tell me, what's your schedule this week?"

I lifted the water goblet and took a sip. "Unless I get called in for an extra shift my schedule is pretty much the same. Tuesday, Wednesday and Thursday seven to seven."

"Do you like overnights, or is that just the shift you're stuck on?"

"I love nights. There's more action on nights for the kind of trauma I like. I won't go into detail since we're at dinner." I looked up past Brody's shoulder through the glass doors into the next room and saw Jaxon seated at a small table with another gentleman. Older than him, but not old enough to be his dad.

"I have to leave for work in the morning about seven or eight. Do you want to stay at the house and maybe take one of the horses for a ride?" That sounded interesting, but I didn't want to overstay my welcome. "Or do you want me to take you and Ruger home in the morning on my way?"

"You should probably just drop me off. I'm sure you're ready to have your home back to normal. No crazy dog barking at you as you come through your own door," I said with a laugh.

"You do know you're more than welcome to stay while I'm at work, right?" He reached across the table for my hand.

"Thank you. You've been way more than generous, but I need to get laundry done and get ready to go back to work Tuesday. I have to try to sleep some during the day tomorrow so I can stay awake for my shift," I explained.

The waitress returned with our meals and poured us another glass of wine. The steak was cooked impeccably and melted in my mouth. I finished the steak before I even tried anything else. Yes, it was that delicious. I looked over at a quiet Brody, who was slicing into his steak.

"How's your steak?" I asked and then popped another bite into my mouth.

"Incredible. It's really juicy and tender. I'd ask how yours was but since it's disappeared from your plate, I'm going to guess it was pretty good?" he teased, finishing the last of his asparagus.

"It was, without a doubt, the best steak I've ever had. Thank you for bringing me here and for such a wonderful evening," I gushed.

"The night is just getting started, I have one more surprise." He smiled cunningly. "How about dessert?"

"Oh, no way. The steak was my dinner and the baked potato was my dessert." I was stuffed. "I've wanted a steak and potato dinner for ages."

He dabbed his mouth, then placed the napkin on the table before extending his hand. "Let's get out of here, I want to take you somewhere."

"Uh, Brody, what about the check? I don't think they will let us skip out on a meal like this," I said quietly even though there was no one in the room with us.

"Why are we whispering?" he whispered back at me with a chuckle. "Relax, they have my card on file here, they'll charge whatever they need. Do you want to have the leftovers bagged for Ruger?"

"Nah, he's probably already gonna have trouble fitting in his crate," I snickered.

Brody stood, my hand in his, and escorted me down the curved staircase. We paused briefly to thank the owner and then exited out the open solid oak door. When we walked out front, waiting at the curb was a small white open carriage with a beefy, dapple gray Irish Draught horse.

"Your chariot awaits you, milady," Brody said in this totally bogus English accent, or at least I think he was going for English. He sounded English, Australian and Irish all in one sentence.

"Why thank you kind sir," I said with my best Southern belle impersonation. We both laughed and he helped me up into the carriage.

"It's such a beautiful night, I thought we might take a ride through the Battery, along the water." He closed the door and off we went.

It really was a perfect night for a carriage ride. We rode all over. The driver did his best to try to give us a tour, but we were too busy making out like two high-schoolers in their mom's backseat to notice anything he pointed out. An hour later we arrived back at the parking lot, got in the Bentley and crossed back over to Johns Island.

Chapter Twenty-two

Leila

When we returned to Brody's place, I had him take the necklace off and return it to the safe. We sat and talked with Jane for a little, then decided to turn in for the night. It was already after ten and I was exhausted. I just wanted to take off my dress, curl up in bed with Brody and watch TV. But I knew that was not going to happen.

I noticed when I hung up my dress there were more clothes in my little section of the closet than when we left. They were my clothes, but I left them in my duffle.

Jane.

Shaking my head, I walked into the bathroom and brushed my teeth. Brody did the same thing, but he watched *SportsCenter* while doing it. I was splashing water on my face when Brody started hollering at the TV and scared the living shit out of me.

WTF?

"Are you okay?" I asked, unable to see anything.

"Huh? Oh yeah, I'm just watching the recap of the Braves shitty-ass game." He started going on and on about pitchers and relief or bullpen something. Who knew, I totally zoned it out. I was too tired to understand all of that crap right now. I didn't follow baseball, too many damn rules.

I dried my face off and threw the towel at him. He was standing in the middle of the bathroom with his toothbrush hanging out his mouth, watching TV.

"I'm going to bed." I went to the closet and put on a pink silk and lace baby-doll. Maybe that would get him to turn off the TV and come to bed. I walked back into the bathroom, got a sip of water and took my birth control pill. I sauntered back out, leaving him staring, mouth hanging wide-open. Of course the toothbrush was still dangling from it.

I crawled under the covers and snuggled into the king-size, down pillows, telling myself to remember to ask Jane where she got these pillows. I felt the bed dip and a warm pair of arms yanked me backward.

"And just what do you think you're doin', sweetheart?" he asked, like he was planning something.

I yawned loudly and stretched. "I'm going to sleep honey. I'm exhausted. Plus, we have to get up early so you can drop me off at home."

"You're right, we should get some sleep. There will be plenty of time to punish you later," he quipped.

I snuggled into his arms. "Punish me? For what, exactly, do I need to be punished?"

"Hmm, where do I start? Several smart-ass comments, trying to come without me, putting your hands down without permission," he rattled off. "See, three, right off the top of my head."

"Well, I'll be sure to come over tomorrow evening so you can have your way with me." I yawned again.

"Promise?" he asked like I was going to leave tomorrow and never come back. He stroked his hand up and down my hip and side so gently it almost put me to sleep immediately.

"I promise." I turned my head and kissed him. "You can't get rid of me that easily."

"Good to know. Night babe, sleep well."

"You"—I started to doze off—"too."

*****

Brody

I brushed aside her unruly curls exposing the tan curve of her slender neck as it met her delicate collarbone, leaned forward and trailed kisses from her earlobe down her soft neck. Even though she was sound asleep, she smiled and cooed a little. It brought forth emotions I had tried to keep buried since my parents died. No matter how hard I pressed them down or how much I tried to ignore them, they kept surfacing. Leila gave me hope that I might be able to find the same kind of undying love my mom and dad had. The kind of love that would transcend earthly bounds and overcome all odds.

I whispered, "Night honey, thank you for being here with me. For just me."

As I drifted off to sleep, I reminded myself to ask her about the charity dinner in September for wounded soldiers. I couldn't wait to see her in an evening gown, as my mother would call them, all dressed up.

My cell phone started blaring Buckcherry's "Crazy Bitch" at 2:38 in the morning. I snatched it off the nightstand, hit silent and snuck from the bed to answer it.

"Jenifer, do you have any fucking clue what time it is? What the fuck do you want at two fucking thirty in the morning?" I whisper-yelled.

"Oh Brody, is that any way to answer your phone darling," she simpered. "I just called to say I'm back in New York from Paris. We should get together, maybe have dinner and then we can go back to your penthouse. I've missed you. You must have missed me too, haven't you baby?"

"No, not in the least. You have to stop calling me. I've told you we are not together. We'll never be together again. Yes, we fucked from time to time, but that was a year ago. After everything you did, do you really think I'd ever be with you again? You need to move on." I tried not to sound like too much of an asshole but the woman wasn't getting it.

"Why? Why do we have to move on? Don't you remember how great the sex was? Come on, let's just have dinner and see what happens?" she said, pleading.

"Jenifer, I am with someone. So no, we are not having dinner or fucking or even having a phone conversation." I sighed. "I want you to be happy, but that will not be with me. I have to go."

"Please, Brody, just give us another chance," she begged in her pathetic, whiny voice.

"Begging is beneath you Jenifer. Show a little class." With that I hung up. I went to her listing and marked her number as blocked. She can still call, but it will always send her to voicemail. I don't want her calling and Leila hearing her or, God forbid, answering my phone.

I quietly crept back into the bedroom from the balcony. I stood by the bed for a minute watching Leila sleep, her chest rose and fell slowly. She looked so tranquil and beautiful. I opened the camera app on my phone and snapped a quick picture for later. I decide to have it printed so I could put it on my desk.

Yeah, yeah, yeah. I know. It was a little creepy. But I wanted to capture this moment and cement it in sand.

Chapter Twenty-three

Leila

I woke before Brody, quickly ran to the bathroom, peed, brushed my teeth and pulled my hair back. Unlike his bedhead, mine was not sexy. No way did any man want to wake up next to that horror scene.

Walking back into the bedroom, I found Brody asleep on his back, sprawled out in the middle of the bed. Hmm, I thought of a creative way to wake him up and make up for falling asleep last night. I shimmied my panties down, leaving my baby-doll nightie on, and crawled under the sheet.

Thankfully, Brody slept in the nude, making my goal much more attainable. Carefully, I nestled myself between his legs, took his semi-erect cock in my hand and slowly ran my tongue around the head, making it jerk to life. He tightened and flexed in my grip, encouraging me to continue. Not stopping, I traced the thick head in circles then licked all the way down his swelling dick to his smooth sack. Using my nails, I gently scratched and teased them while I continued to lick all the way back up before taking his now stiff cock into my mouth and swirling my tongue around him.

"Mmmm babe. Damn. Your mouth feels so fuckin' good."

Brody was awake. I grinned with a mouthful of cock.

I started sucking up and down while stroking him with my right hand and teasing his balls with my left. Brody gripped my hair with one hand and my right breast with the other. He pinched and rolled my nipple causing me to moan while I was going down on him.

"Fuck, Leila. That's it, baby, suck my dick. Oh God, you're gonna make me come. You want me to come in your mouth or in that sweet tight pussy?" he asked.

Pulling him out of my mouth. "I want your cock in me, now."

Brody sat up, grabbed me under my arms and flung me onto the pillows. Before I could blink, he shoved his cock into my awaiting wet cunt and started pounding into me. Holy shit it was amazing. Better than anything I had ever felt in my entire life. Electricity shot out of every nerve end, setting me a flame.

"Oh God. Mmmm," I screamed and my body shook. "Fuck me Brody, oh fuck, don't stop. Oh yeah, I'm coming."

My orgasm crashed into me like waves slamming into a cliff. Brody gave me no reprieve, he kept fucking me. Hard and fast until I felt his body tighten and his climax wrack his body. "Oh fuuuuck."

He slowed his rhythm and suddenly I felt a burst of wetness. Oh shit! That's not good. Oh God, please tell me that he did not just come inside me. This cannot be happening. Brody collapsed on top of me.

"Brody get up." I planted my hands on his shoulders trying to push him but he barely budged.

"Relax, I don't care if I'm late for work today. Not after a wake up like that." He was completely at ease and unmoving.

"Brody, get off. I have to go to the bathroom. You didn't use a condom. Move." I squirmed out from underneath of him.

"Oh fuck, Lei. Shit babe, I'm sorry. I was just so caught up and only half awake." He scrubbed his hands down his face.

I ran to the bathroom, sat on the toilet and prayed I didn't get pregnant. I decided to take a quick shower to clean myself up. I got as far as shampooing my hair when I heard Brody open the glass door. He slipped his hand into my hair with mine and starting massaging my scalp.

"Let me." He pushed my hands out of the way, giving himself full access. "Leila, I swear to you I did not intend for that to happen. I'm so sorry."

I wasn't sure what to say so I just stood there facing away from him. How could I be so careless? I had never had unprotected sex, with anyone. My plan was to wait until I met the man I intended to marry. I rinsed my hair while Brody washed himself.

"Lei, say something, anything. Call me names, cuss me or yell at me. Just say something. Please."

I stood there under the cascading water until he finally spun me around to look at him.

Finally, I said, "I don't know what to say Brody. I told you we had to be extra careful because I was on antibiotics. But this isn't all your fault, I'm just as much to blame. I should've grabbed a condom before I started going down on you, I just didn't think. I saw you lying there and I wanted you. Oh God, I can't get pregnant Brody."

"Babe, it was one time. You ran to the bathroom right away, you probably got everything out before anything could happen. It will be fine. Besides, your birth control is probably still effective," he tried to rationalize. "I thought it only lessened the effectiveness not negates it all together."

"Yeah." I tried to understand his thought process, but I was too wrapped up in my own shit.

He picked me up and squeezed me in a tight bear hug. "It will all be fine. Don't worry."

Laying my head on his shoulder, I was determined not to cry. I had to stay positive and not worry until I had a reason to worry. We dried off and got dressed. Brody in his charcoal gray suit, and me in my navy blue shorts and buttercup yellow cowl-neck sleeveless shirt from Target. We were total opposites in some ways and so much alike in others.

We grabbed a quick breakfast together and then got into the Hennessey. He drove me to my place and made it in record time. He drove that thing so damn fast, I thought I left my stomach at his driveway gate when he floored it for the first time.

As I got out of the car he gave me a long, passionate kiss like he wasn't going to see me for weeks.

"You do know I'm gonna come over later, right?" I teased him.

"I know. I just don't want to leave. I wish I could take the day off and take you down to the beach."

"Oh, that's a great idea. I'm gonna call Barb and Drake and see if they wanna hit the beach with me. Drake and I were talkin' about gettin' together the other day and this would be perfect." I gave him a little peck on his cheek. "Thanks for the great idea. See you tonight at your place." I turned and reached over to open the door. "Oh wait, what time should I come over?"

"You're welcome to come over any time, but I'll be home about six or so." He pulled my hand to his lips.

"Okay, I'll see ya tonight. And I'm bringing my dog home tonight, so be sure to tell Jane," I gave him fair warning.

"Yeah, okay, I'll call her later. How are you getting out to the house? I can pick you up on my way home," he offered.

"Well, since my flying carpet is at the dry cleaners and my helicopter is out for repairs," I mocked, tapping my finger over my lips like I was in deep thought. "In my car, how else would I get there?"

"Oh that smart mouth is writing a check I hope your ass can cash Miss Matthews," he said brazenly.

"Oh, just try and keep up." I smiled, stuck my tongue out at him and leapt from the car.

When I shut the door all I could see was Brody shaking his head and laughing.

Chapter Twenty-four

Leila

"Yo, hooker, wake up and come get me. It's a beach day, baby."

"Ugh, Lei, what time is it?" Barb groaned; obviously I woke her up.

"It's almost ten. Get your lazy ass outta the bed and get over here. I've yummy details to share," I tried for enticement.

"You big whore, you didn't? Please tell me you did. Brody?"

"Yep, and let's just say the man is well endowed in more ways than one," I said with a giggle.

"Shut the front door. Now I'm awake. I'll be there in an hour. Call Drake." With that, she hung up.

I sent a text to Drake telling him to meet us at Sullivan's Island at Station 26 at noon and that I'd pack us a lunch. I set out for the kitchen and packed us some sandwiches and snacks.

About ten till eleven Barb waltzed through the front door.

"Tell me everything," she ordered, wide-eyed.

"Jesus, did you look in the mirror before you left?" I asked, taking in her appearance. Her oversized Corona shirt, that had the neck cut out of it, was inside out. Her hair looked like she had licked a light socket and her lime green string bikini was in the process of untying itself. Any second she'd be flashing her ginormous boobs at me.

"What?"

"Uh, your top's gettin' ready to fall off, your shirt's on inside out and what the fuck is up with your hair?"

She looked over at the mirror in the foyer and laughed. "Damn, I do look a hot mess, huh?"

She spun back to me with a chuckle, reached back and secured the strings around her neck, then fixed her shirt. "What can I say…you said you were sharin' juicy details so I came flyin' over here. Speakin' of flyin', the top's down on the Jeep, so bring a hair tie and a hat. Otherwise, you're gonna look like Magenta from *Rocky Horror Picture Show*."

"Oh, you got jokes, huh?" I glared then decided to taunt her instead. "Hmph, see if I share my good sex stories now?"

"What? You know it's true. Besides, you know you're dyin' to tell me all about the kinky sex you're havin'. Get your shit and let's roll. I wanna get a good spot before all of the high school brats get outta bed."

"Yeah, yeah, yeah, hold your horses. I need to grab the cooler and set the alarm. I'll meetcha out there."

"Uh, Lei, where's your dog?" She looked around the lofty condo.

"Oh, he's at Brody's with Jane. I'm startin' to worry she's gonna try and steal him. She's constantly givin' him treats and takin' him out to play." I laughed. "He's not gonna wanna come home."

Twenty minutes later, we were trudging through the white-hot sand out past the tidal pools in search of a place to set up camp. It was a quarter till noon, so Drake would be here soon.

Barb and I spread out the king-size white fitted sheet. Putting shoes, clothes, cooler and bag in each of the corners, essentially we created a shallow box. This way the sand wouldn't blow onto the sheet. We put a towel next to it to clean our feet off before stepping in.

Yep, thank you, Lifehack.

After shellacking ourselves in SPF 30 suntan oil, we got comfy and settled in for a little tête-à-tête.

"So, that good, huh?" She beamed after I told her about the crazy hedonistic filled days I spent with Brody.

"Yeah, really, *really* amazing. He's quite enthusiastic." I burst out laughing.

"Who's quite enthusiastic?" Drake asked as he crashed our giggle fit.

"Brody, Drew's friend," Barb squealed.

"Oh, he's a fuckin' hottie all right. Man's got an ass you could bounce quarters off of. You should've seen the death glare he gave me before he found out I'd rather be doin' him than Lei."

"Drake."

"What? It's the truth. That guy looked like he was gonna club you and drag you back to a cave somewhere."

"Okay, enough about me. What's up with you?" I asked Barb, who woefully rolled her eyes.

"Skip me and ask Doctor Hornypants over there. My sex life is nonexistent right now."

"Shiiiit. I've been playin' doctor so much I've barely had time to go to the gym, let alone find anyone to fuck." He pulled a bottle of water out of the cooler. "The only decent-lookin' man I've seen in a month is Drew. As much as I'd love that, he's not a willing participant."

"Gross douche bag. That's my brother."

"Seriously, Lei? Have you looked at him? He's fuckin' gorgeous. Bangin' body, killer smile and great sense of humor. What's not to like?" Barb rolled onto her stomach and set up on her elbows.

"Oh God, not you too?"

"Oh hell yeah. I'd fuck him in a heartbeat, if he wasn't your brother and if I hadn't known him for years. It'd be too weird now. So…" I sensed a change of subject coming. "What's up with Brody? You serious about him?"

"I don't know. I mean, I think I want it to be, but I'm not sure. He's got quite the reputation, from what Drew says. We've agreed to take things slow and just see where they go," I answered as blasé as I could to discourage any further questions.

You think it worked? Nope. Not even close. They pestered me for another hour before I got up, mid conversation, and walked into the lukewarm water. Seriously, it wasn't even refreshing when it was that warm.

We packed up around 3:30 and drove back over the bridge before traffic got too insane.

Once home, I did laundry, cleaned the house, then went to the gym. After the gym, I went back home, showered, got ready and then hopped into my baby, a Dodge Challenger Hellcat with a supercharged 6.2 liter Hemi, 707 horsepower, Tremec six-speed manual transmission and high capacity cooling system. She didn't purr like a kitten. No, my girl roared like a lioness and she could do a quarter mile in 10.8. Well, at least that was what was advertised; it's not like I was down at the drag strip testing her out.

I couldn't wait for Brody to get an eyeful of my baby. His cars may cost a million dollars more than mine, but she was all-American muscle, baby. I kept her in the garage at the back of the building since I didn't drive her as much as I would like, but I worked within walking distance and refuse to pay for parking when I can walk for free.

I made my way out of the city and finally hit the highway. She growled as I accelerated, weaving in and out of cars. In no time at all I pulled up to the gate and suddenly realized I couldn't get in. Stopping at the intercom, I pressed the button and the gates magically opened without as much as a word. I looked at the clock, 6:18 p.m. Hmm, Brody must be home already. The thought had me smiling stupidly.

I emerged from the grove of trees to see a familiar Aston Martin and an unfamiliar yellow Hummer parked in front of the attached garage. On the front porch, I could see Brody, Damon and I think Sean. They all looked a little shocked to see me. Putting the car in park, I got out and leaned on the front quarter panel.

Brody was the first to speak. "Hey babe. Whose car did you borrow? I thought you said you had a car. I would've let you take one of mine home this morning if I would've known."

Oh dear sweet, naïve Brody. I laughed and shook my head.

"What're you laughin' 'bout?" Damon asked, looking as confused as Sean.

"I'm laughin' at you guys. What? Because I have boobs I couldn't possibly own a car like this?" I cocked my head to the side waiting for an answer.

Sean was the first one brave enough to chime in. "Well, yeah, sorta. Girls don't know anything about cars, let alone a sports car. So why would we think you owned this one?"

Oh, poor unsuspecting Sean. He was about to have his ass served to him and he didn't even know it.

"First of all, she's not a"—I tilted my head being overly dramatic—"sports car. This car is a muscle car. You're right, *most* girls don't know shit about cars, but let me take you to school little boy. My Hellcat here has a supercharged and intercooled pushrod sixteen-valve V-eight, iron block and aluminum heads, port fuel injection that puts out about seven hundred horses and six hundred and fifty pounds of torque. She has Tremec six-speed manual and will do a quarter mile in ten point eight seconds, and zero to sixty in three point six. Oh, and she has gas charged adjustable shock absorbers."

Put that in your pipe and smoke it boys. They all looked dumbfounded.

"Babe, that was seriously the hottest thing that has come out of any woman's mouth, ever." Brody jumped off the porch and wrapped me up in his strong arms. He whispered in my ear, "Good God, I want to take you right here, right now on the hood of your car."

I swatted at him. "No way. You're not scratching my car."

"I have to agree with Brody here Lei. It's really fuckin' sexy that you know all that about your car." Damon walked around my car, looking her over. Sean was still astonished. "Okay, I stand corrected, *most* girls. Start 'er up and let's hear this thing."

The guys congregated around the Dodge in the sweltering heat for more than an hour, fascinated by the shiny new toy. They begged, pleaded and tried to trade their first born for a chance to drive it. I shook my head at each and every offer.

After collective begging, we went inside and had dinner. Damon and Sean hit the road around 8:30 or so. Brody and I wound up in the shower together, which turned into wall sex. Followed by bathroom floor sex and then over the back of the couch sex. He was insatiable. When I told him I needed to stay up all night, I really didn't think we would fuck on every surface in the house. But we came pretty damn close.

Finally, around 2:30 a.m., I was too sore to walk, let alone have sex for the fifth time. I'd lost count of my orgasms after the fifth or sixth one. Just wanting to sleep, I conceded and flopped down on the bed. I swear that man is part rabbit.

Waking up in the middle of the night, I reached out and found the bed empty. I got up quietly and went in search of Brody. I didn't have to look far, I saw him on the balcony, staring out over the river. The night sky this far out of the city was astonishing. It was so dark you could see thousands of stars. The full moon shone brightly, mirroring itself off the calm waters of the Stono.

"Hey, what're you doin' out here?" I asked, quietly padding toward him.

Brody jumped and spun around, unaware I was there. "Jesus Christ Leila, you scared me. Why are you up? You should go back to bed."

He sounded agitated and I was really not in the mood for the Dr. Jekyll–Mr. Hide thing tonight.

"I woke up and you weren't there. Why are you out here? Come back to bed."

"I've got a lot on my mind right now. Please just go back to sleep." He turned back, facing the railing.

"Brody, it's four in the morning. I didn't come over to sleep alone in your bed," I said trying to be enticing, but apparently that was not a good move.

"Leila, just go back to bed, I don't want to talk right now. Just leave me alone." He gritted his teeth. "Please, just go sleep."

"Ya know what…whatever Brody, good night." I rolled my eyes and closed the large glass doors behind me.

I went to the bathroom, got dressed, called Ruger and walked right out the front door with Brody none the wiser. Well, at least not until I started the car and took off. As loud as the Hellcat engine roared, I was sure he heard us leave. Thankfully, the front gate exit was on a motion sensor and I didn't have to stop.

I got about a mile from the house when my cell started ringing. I didn't need to look at it to know it was him. "Brody, I don't want to talk, just leave me alone."

Before I could hang up, he said. "Always throwing my words back in my face."

It was 4:16 a.m., I was exhausted, emotionally drained and driving down a road I didn't know. I said a quick prayer and pressed on. I made it home in about thirty minutes, crawled into my bed, turned my phone to vibrate and set my alarm for 3 p.m. I woke up a couple of times to the sound of buzzing, but refused to look at the phone or answer it.

At 12:42, the shrill noise of my doorbell jarred me from my slumber. I rolled over and looked up at the tray ceiling, resolute in my decision not to answer it. The bell stopped for a split second, but was replaced with someone's fist, or possibly boot, on my solid wood front door.

"Ugh! I am gonna cut whoever it is." I slung the covers back and stomped down the steps, gripped the door handle and flinging it open, I almost got punched in the face.

"Go away Brody!" I tried to slam the door in his face, but his hand stopped the momentum.

"Not a chance." He pushed his way in. "What the hell Lei? Why did you just fucking take off last night? I've been calling you all morning."

"Hmm and I didn't answer or call you back? I wonder what that could've meant?" Sarcasm dripped like water from my voice. "Uhh, maybe it means I don't want to talk to you." I tried to shut the front door because it was apparent he wasn't going to leave until I spoke to him.

Again, he pushed the door open. "You can't just up and leave and not tell me you're leaving or why. I've been freaking the fuck out all damn day," he shouted.

"Really? Because I'm pretty sure that's exactly what I did," I yelled right back. "You don't like being ignored and dismissed, do you Brody?"

"No and it would be wise of you to remember that." He was seething mad.

"Then it would be wise of you to not do it first, huh?" I hollered, flailing my hands like a mad woman. I was ready to break down.

Brody stopped, eyebrows knitted and just stood there.

"Look Brody, I'm really tired and I have to be at work in six hours and I want to see Drew before I start my shift. I just want to go back to sleep. Can we not do this?"

"No Leila, we are talking about this. I pushed off two meetings to come over here and straighten this out."

"I didn't tell you to do that," I rebutted.

"No, I wanted to be here. I couldn't concentrate at work. I had to see you, know you were okay and figure this out." He huffed. "Lei, I'm sorry I was an asshole last night, I shouldn't have taken it out on you."

"I don't even know why you were so cold and harsh last night, but I didn't deserve it." I sat down on the couch and pulled my chenille throw over my bare legs. "You were a total asshole. So what the hell?"

"You're right. You didn't deserve it and I wish I could explain, but I can't." He unbuttoned his suit and sat with me.

"Can't or won't?" I pulled my knees up and wrapped my arms around them.

"Does it matter?" he asked.

"If that is really your answer, then no, it doesn't." I stood abruptly and started for the stairs before he grabbed my hand.

"Wait, please." His blue eyes clouded over. "It's not that I don't want to tell you, I do, I'm just not ready to. I'm sorry I fucked up last night. But just give me a little time. I want to be able to explain, but I…I can't."

I sat there, waging war inside my own head. On the one hand, I was still pissed about everything that went down at 4:00 in the morning, and after such an amazing night. But on the other hand, I wanted to give him the benefit of the doubt and be understanding. I was sure there were plenty of things I wasn't ready to share with him yet.

"That is an answer I can accept. Doesn't mean I like it, but I can be understanding—for now." I turned to the kitchen and blew out a frustrated breath. "Do you want something to drink?"

"No, I can't stay. I was supposed to be at a lunch meeting with a potential investor at Hymans fifteen minutes ago." He stood and strode toward me. I met him halfway.

"Then you should go." I tried not to sound too disappointed.

"No, I can cancel. Let me take you upstairs and hold you while you sleep, like I should've done last night."

"No, you should go to your meeting. Investors are important to your business and you don't want the reputation for just blowing off meetings," I tried to convince him.

"Are you sure?"

"Yeah. Go. Call me later."

"Can we at least have dinner before your shift tonight?" he asked as he walked to the front door.

"Yeah, just pick me up here about five."

"Get some sleep, babe, I'll see you in a little while." He slid his hand along my jaw and pulled me into a slow, deep, soul penetrating kiss.

"Oh my God," I moaned. "You should really go, now."

"Bye babe." He shut the door behind him. I turned the dead bolt and folded my head forward until it rested on the doorframe. I took a deep breath, trying to regain my composure. Finally, I returned to bed and took the time to look at my phone. Thirteen missed calls and eight text messages and all but one were from Brody. I had one text from Barb asking me to call her later. I started to read through the texts and decided to wait until I woke up. I pulled the covers over my head and fell back to sleep.

*****

Brody
I made it to Hymans Seafood just in time. Luckily, Sara was able to reach the investor and tell him I was stuck in traffic on 26. The meeting went according to plan and before I knew it, I was out of there and on my way back to the office. I had a 3:00 staff meeting and then a 3:45 with a decorator for the New York penthouse I was having redesigned and remodeled. I hoped to have it ready by the end of September when Leila would join me for a charity dinner for Semper Fi Fund. Shit, I meant to ask her about that last night.

Sara buzzed my phone, reminding me I had to head to the conference room for the staff meeting. I really wished that Human Resources could handle that shit without me, but my father attended all of the meetings and the employees liked feeling they knew who they worked for.

I asked Sara to come in. "I need you to order flowers and have them sent to Leila's. I'll email you the address. Oh, and send two dozen long stem red roses and green calla lilies. On the card, have them put 'I'm sorry I messed up. I promise to make it up to you. XOXO B.'"

"I'll take care of it boss," she said pleasantly before cutting her eyes to me. "What'd ya do? Because if *you* are sending a woman flowers and admitting you messed up, it must be big."

"You know, if I didn't need you like a blind man needs a cane and you hadn't worked for me for almost a decade, I'd fire you for asking me that."

Sara silently laughed. "No you wouldn't, ya big softie. Out there with those fools, you might be ruthless and scary. But in here"—she pointed back and forth between us—"you're a big teddy bear that likes puppies and unicorns. Besides, I know where all your bodies are buried." With a quick smirk and a cunning laugh she walked out the office. "Don't forget the address, busman."

I shook my head as Sara walked away while muttering under my breath, "Yeah, yeah, yeah."

Hmph, I was not a teddy bear. She just knew where everything was in this office. She could recite my appointments, date, time and with whom for the next week, if not two. She was the controller and organizer of my chaos. Truly, she was invaluable.

And damn if she didn't know it.

The staff meeting only lasted thirty minutes, which gave me plenty of time to get back to my office. I called and made a reservation at California Dreamin'; I wanted to make up for our first dinner catastrophe. The rest of the day went by without incident and 4:45 was here before I knew it.

"Sara." I waited for her to come into the office. "I'm heading out for the day. I need these contracts sent over to legal, those notes typed up and sent to the designer and for you to take the rest of the day off. This stuff will wait until tomorrow. Have a good night, and thanks for all of your hard work."

"Of course, thank you. See ya in the morning." She beamed with excitement. Probably because she worked as many, if not more, hours than I did. She was richly compensated and not just salary. Sara had a company Mercedes, monthly bonus and an apartment that the company paid for. But she earned every bit of it. I wouldn't be able to function without her.

I raced across town to Leila's place, parked and rang the doorbell. She answered the door in a sage fluffy towel.

"Jesus Leila, you can't answer the door in just a damn towel. What would've happened if it wasn't me?" I'm pissed she put herself at risk.

"Oh, stop. I checked the peephole and saw it was you," she said with a smirk. "Besides, if it was someone else all I would have to do is say Ruger *pass auf.*"

With those two small words, Ruger put himself between us, started snarling and baring his teeth. Leila just laughed as I took a step back.

"Lass es," she said sternly and Ruger turned around and walked back over to his bed and lay down.

"Okay, point taken. Just please be careful."

"Don't worry, I will be. Thank you for the beautiful roses and callas, that was very sweet of you." She gave me a quick kiss. "I need to go get dressed and I'll be ready. Gimme a minute, okay?" She sprinted up the stairs. Most of me wanted to tackle her, rip her towel off and fuck her right there on the stairs, but I needed to make up for last night and dinner was a good start.

She was back down in no time at all, dressed in light blue scrubs and shiny opal colored Danskos, or at least that's what I think she called them. We locked up and hopped in the Hennessey.

"Where are we going?" She placed her purse on the floor and secured her seat belt.

"California Dreamin'. I thought I owed you a do-over there." I shifted into second gear as I pulled onto East Bay.

"Sounds perfect," she said with a smile.

"And no business calls. I gave Sara the evening off," I explained.

She just smiled and stared out the window.

We made it to the restaurant in about fifteen minutes. Downtown was a mess this time of day, but Lei was worth all the traffic. We had a great meal and even better conversation. Finally, I asked her to accompany me to New York for the charity function. I promised to take her shopping this weekend to find a dress. The date was going perfect, and then it went to hell in a handbasket.

As we were leaving I heard the roar of a Harley and then that fucker was there at the bottom of the steps as we were leaving. What in the fucking hell? This asshole couldn't be serious.

"Hey, he's not stalking you or anything," I muttered cynically to Leila as we descended the steps.

"Brody, please. Can we just get in the car without a scene? Just be polite please," she begged. "I'll just say hi quickly, besides my shift starts in forty-five minutes."

"Fine."

Jaxon approached us with a cagey look on his face, but smiled when Leila greeted him.

"Hey Jaxon. How are ya?" She kept her arm looped through mine.

"Good, and you? Have a better dinner this time?" He cut his eyes in my direction.

Fucker.

"Yes, we did. Are you here to have dinner?" she asked, making small talk.

"Nope, you could say I have an interest in the place. Need to check in then I might have a drink. Care to join me?" he asked boldly as if I wasn't right fucking there. Seriously, this shit's going to stop. And now.

"Jaxon, I told you, I'm with Brody. Plus my shift starts in forty-five minutes, so we need to get going. It was nice running into you, see ya around." She was too fucking nice and that shit had to stop. He clearly wanted her and she had to stop leading him on.

"Yeah, baby girl you will. Have a real good night at work." Baby girl, my ass. Last straw.

"Stay the fuck away from her. She's told you more than once that she's with me." Leila started to pull on my arm. "No, Lei, enough already. We are together and that's not changing." To Jaxon I added, "Back off or next time I say this I won't be so nice."

Jaxon stepped forward, stabbing his finger in my direction. "And just what the fuck are you gonna do about it pretty boy?"

Leila stepped between us. "Enough, both of you. Y'all are acting like jerks; stop it. Brody, let's go. Jaxon, leave it alone and go inside."

I grabbed Leila by the elbow and practically dragged her to the car. I didn't mean to but I was so pissed I couldn't see straight. We didn't talk for a few minutes. She could see I needed to cool off.

"You know he's just pushing your buttons, right?" she asked.

"This guy just keeps fucking popping up everywhere you are Leila and you aren't the slightest bit concerned?" I stared at her, shocked by how naïve she was being.

"He is harmless. You need to relax. You have no reason to be so jealous. I've told him, in front of you no less, that we are together and I'm not interested."

She didn't have any idea how fucking gorgeous she was. Of course I had reason to be worried. She was mine. And he'd get to her over my cold, dead body.

When we pulled up at the hospital, she leaned over and gave me an unforgettable kiss. "I'll call you tomorrow sometime. 'Night."

"Have a good night at work babe." I tried to sound like I meant it but I didn't. I wanted her in my bed, under my sheets, next to my body.

Chapter Twenty-five

Leila

Over the next three days I went to work and didn't see Brody. I talked to him in the mornings after I got off shift and then before I went in, but he was so busy we couldn't get a minute alone; we resorted to text messages to communicate.

Drew was released Wednesday. I took him home and checked in on him every couple of hours since he flat-out refused to let me stay with him.

I got a voicemail Wednesday night that Brody was leaving for New York City. From what I could gather, one of the businesses he invested in was having some problems. He said he'd call Friday and to plan on spending the weekend with him.

As I walked home on Thursday, I ran into Jaxon on East Bay. Now I was starting to wonder if he was stalking me. He was in his white tee, black leather vest—*hello it's summer*—and tattered, faded blue jeans. If his shirt could speak, it would be screaming for reprieve. The shirt was taut over his flawless chest. I couldn't help but look over the full sleeve tattoos that covered both of his thick arms. Mostly tribal, but a few Marine references.

"Leila, what the hell are ya doin' walkin' around at eight in the mornin'?" He seemed irritated.

"Uh, not that it's any of your business, but I just got off work and I'm goin' home."

"Wait, you live around here?"

"Yeah. What's your excuse?"

"I live over on Laurens near East Bay." He nodded to his left.

"Really? How long have you lived there?" I asked, surprised by his answer. I didn't remember seeing him around.

"I don't know, bought the place a while ago and had some work done. Moved my stuff in about two months ago. I don't stay there often. I usually stay at the clubhouse. How 'bout you? Where do you live?" he asked, seemingly innocently as we walked down the street.

"Honestly, about a block and a half from you...which is silly, because I don't ever remember seeing you around here." I tried not to sound skeptical. My phone started ringing in my bag. I pulled it out and saw Brody was calling.

"Ah, callin' to check up on ya already?" Jaxon asked, a bit sanctimoniously.

"I've gotta go." I walked ahead and answered the call. "Hey, honey, I'm just walkin' home from work. Can I call ya in a few minutes? I'm almost home."

"Nah. I can't, babe. I'm sorry. I'm getting ready to go into a meeting. I just had a minute and I wanted to hear your sweet voice. Did you have a good night?" he asked.

"Yeah, busy as shit. Made the night fly by, so that was good. How about you? How was your flight?" I asked, trying to forget Jaxon was following me.

"Uneventful. Listen babe, I have to run. I just wanted to make sure you got home okay." He seemed preoccupied.

"Yeah, I'm just down the block. Talk to you later I guess." I continued walking, looking back to see Jaxon still right behind me.

"See ya babe." He hung up.

"That wasn't a long conversation. You suppose I can walk next to you again?" Jaxon hollered from behind me.

I stopped and turned my attention to him. "Listen Jaxon, I don't want to be rude, but like I said before, I'm with Brody. As in, I'm dating him, and only him."

"And like I told you before, I'll be waiting." He stopped next to me. His green eyes raked over my body. "Pretty boy doesn't deserve you. If he did, he'd make sure you weren't walkin' home alone."

"Bye Jaxon." I had my keys out and stopped on my stoop. It didn't escape me that he now knew where I lived.

"See ya later baby girl." He kept walking without so much as a look back.

I let myself in the house, locked the door, then let Ruger out of his crate.

"Hey, boy, you need ta go outside?" I scratched his neck just behind his ear where he loved it. After opening the back door to the small courtyard, I went to the kitchen and opened a bottle of water, taking a long pull. After letting Ruger back in, I jumped into the shower to wash the germs and grime off.

I threw on PJs and fell face-first into my fresh sheets. It didn't take long to succumb to sleep.

I woke at 5:15 p.m., and it was like *Groundhog Day*: Go to work, talk and text with Brody a few times, then run into Jaxon on my way home. He walked me to the front door then continued along.

I got a text from Barb on the walk home to tell me to be ready at 7:00 p.m., that she and Drake were picking me up and we were going to Jake's for a few drinks.

I woke up about 5:30 p.m. and saw I had three text messages and one missed phone call from Brody.

Have fun, b safe. Where r u going? What time do u think u'll b home?

U there? U must've fallen asleep. Sleep well babe. See ya tonight.

Hey almost 6 & I haven't heard from u. I tried 2 call no ans. What time r u gonna b home? My flight gets in @10p call me

I tried to return his call, but it went straight to voicemail so I sent a text.

Going to Jakes @ 7, shld b home by 9 or 10. Call when u land. I'll meet u @my place.

Barb honked from the street. I grabbed my small wristlet and was out the door.

"What up, chick? You ready? Drake is meetin' us there in a few." Barb was dressed damn near identical to me. Skirt, T-shirt and cowboy boots.

"I swear we do this every time we go out. People are gonna start to think we're sisters," I said with a smirk.

"Ha, we must have been twins in another life." She pulled back onto East Bay.

"Ya know we could've walked. It's only a few blocks." I hate looking for a parking spot near Jake's. The parking lot out back was always fun.

"No way in hell. Not in boots." She turned into the parking lot and miraculously found an empty space.

"Well, I'll be damned, must be our lucky night." I hopped out of the Jeep.

"I'll settle for *getting* lucky tonight." Barb checked her lipstick and then followed me around to the front door.

Jake's is a smaller bar in downtown that had a long bar down one side, a stage opposite and high-top tables and barstools scattered between and near the back. There were three pool tables and a dart board by the bathrooms. Barb, Drake and I have closed this place down on more than one occasion. We were all thankful on those occasions that I lived within walking distance, and crawling distance once or twice.

We got there before they started cover charge, but the atmosphere was already abuzz. We found two empty spots at the corner of the bar and sidled up. Barb flagged Bobbi, the bartender, and ordered our usual Captain and Sprite for me, Jack and Coke for her.

"So, I was hoping you might be able to cover a couple of shifts for me in October. I'm gonna go see my parents in Maryland." She swirled the straw in her drink.

"As if you have to ask. Of course I will. Just remind me when it gets closer. Do you know the exact dates yet?" I sipped my cocktail.

"Yeah, from the second to the third Saturday of the month." She yelled the last part as Adam Levine's sexy voice started coming through the speakers.

My cell started vibrating and flashing on the bar. Brody.

Hey babe, won't be home tonight, last minute dinner meeting. Sorry, have fun tonight. xo B

"Okayyyy, well, looks like you got me all to yourself tonight; Brody is stuck in a dinner meeting and won't be home until tomorrow," I said as I sent a quick reply letting him know I got his text.

K. I'll call ya tomorrow…

I was disappointed. But he said from the beginning he worked crazy hours and had to travel. I knew this going in, so I had to deal.

Barb and I were chatting when all of a sudden her eyes lit up and her jaw went slack.

"Holy fucking shit, look at that guy that just walked in. Good God all mighty, he's sexy as sin and has the boots to match," she shrieked.

I turned to nonchalantly check out the hottie she was admiring; then I whipped my head around not so casually.

Of all of the bars, he had to walk into this one tonight.

I glanced around my shoulder out of the corner of my eye to see another large surly man walk in behind him, and I recognized him from the restaurant last week. I watched him, in his tattered jeans and leather vest, as he shook hands with several customers. Out of nowhere a skanky blonde launched herself at him, shoving her tongue down his throat. He certainly didn't seem to mind, but it didn't last long as he shrugged her off. I turned back to the bar and prayed that he would not notice me.

"Oh fuck, Lei, he's comin' over here." She hushed abruptly.

Why me? Just shoot me now.

"Well, look who we have here. If I didn't know better I would say you're followin' me." His voice oozed sex.

"If anyone is following someone, it would be you. We've been here for almost a half hour." I spun around to face him.

"Leila, who's your friend here?" Barb inquired with a shit-eating grin plastered across her face.

"Barb, this is Jaxon. Jaxon this is my best friend and partner in crime Barb." I grabbed my drink and all but slammed it.

"Nice to meet you, Jaxon." She looked him up and down like he was a prized pig at the county fair.

"Friends call me Remi." He turned his attention back to me. "Since I don't see your boy, does this mean I can buy ya a drink?"

"If I say yes will you stop askin' me out?" I said plainly.

"Maybe, maybe not." He whistled at the bartender. "Aye, get another round over here, on me."

"Thanks Jaxon. Now, if you don't mind we are having a girl's night out. That means no men. Besides, your little blonde is looking mighty impatient." I nodded toward the pool tables. "Every time she looks over here, she stomps her foot and makes a face."

His lips twitched. "I *will* see you later baby girl." He strolled back to the tall biker and skanky blonde.

"Oh. My. God. You better start talking," Barb demanded.

I explained the whole Jaxon thing in great detail. I stopped to look at the time, realizing we had been there for a while and had way too much to drink.

"Where the fuck is Drake? Bastard's always late. Check your phone. Did he call you?" I asked Barb.

"No, but he texted"—Barb hiccupped—"me. He's in surgery. He's not coming." Katy Perry's "Dark Horse" started playing.

"Oh hell yeah, I love this song, let's dance." Barb yanked me off my stool with such force it almost fell over.

We hit the dance floor in front of the stage and stayed there for three more songs. We had to push a couple of overly flirtatious guys off of us, but nothing too demoralizing. That is until I tried to go back to my barstool. This young blond frat boy, who clearly had too much to drink and reeked of booze, grabbed me by my hips and pulled me back against him. He tried to wrap his arms around my waist as I pushed at them. I spun around and planted my hands firmly against his chest and tried shoving him away, but he grabbed the sides of my face and started to kiss me until a mammoth hand covered his entire face and sent him flying backward into a mess of people.

"Keep your fuckin' hands off her. You hear me preppy?" Jaxon stood over the guy pointing in his face. "Next time I break both of your hands and anything else that might have touched her."

"Jaxon, it's okay. I can handle myself."

He snatched hold of my wrist and dragged me from the dance floor. "You mean before or after that fuckin' douche shoved his tongue in your mouth?"

"I was just about to knee him in the balls when your massive paw hurled him across the room," I pointed out.

He released me when we reached the bar. I looked back to see Barb dancing with a guy who was built like a tank. No neck, just muscles. But damn, he had some moves for a white boy; he salsa-ed Barb all over that floor. She might have met her match with that one.

"Who's the guy Barb is dancing with?" I looked back at Jaxon.

"Viper, he's a brother of Marines MC." He ordered another beer. "Good guy, but he hops from bed to bed. Hope she ain't lookin' for anything serious."

I burst out laughing. "Ha. Not Barb. She's the life of the party and is always looking for the next one. You might wanna warn him."

"What about you? What are you lookin' for?"

"Jaxon, please." I looked down and picked at my fingernails not wanting to answer that question.

"What? It's a simple question. What. Do. You. Want?" He leaned his face closer with each word.

I knew I should have said Brody, but I couldn't say anything.

"I think you're not sure what you want. Am I right?" he probed.

"I just want to finish my drink and go home." I threw back the last few swallows. "Bye, Jaxon."

Finding Barb, I told her I was walking home, hugged her and exited the same way we came in. I made it about a block before I heard the rumbling of a motorcycle. It got louder until it idled next to me. There on an all black Rough Crafts' Shadow Rocket sat Jaxon.

"Hop on Leila." He nodded back to the tail.

Not, "Hey would you like a ride home?" or "Can I take you home?" Nope. Like a caveman grunting, he ordered me to get on.

"Bwahaha." I kept walking as he walked the idling bike next to me.

"I'm not lettin' you walk home in the dark, regardless of how close you live. Now, get on the bike," he commanded while I laughed.

"Let's get a few things straight right here, right now buddy. One, I don't do orders." I shook my head with all kinds of attitude. "Two, I am perfectly capable of walkin' a few blocks to my home. Three, I have a CWP and am an excellent shot. I think I'll be fine. But thanks."

Shaking his head, Jaxon kept following me. "So, where's your friend? What's his name? Brady."

"You know damn well it's Brody and he's traveling on business." I was trying not to let Jaxon get under my skin. That's what he wanted and I'd be damned if I was giving him that satisfaction.

"Sorry, Brody. He know you're traipsing all over downtown in the dark by yourself?" He shot me a look out of the corner of his eye.

"Yes, he knows I went out tonight with Barb, not that I answer to him or anyone else since..." Shit. I didn't mean for that to come out. "So I will be fine. Good night Jaxon."

"Whoa, I think you forgot a few words in there." He stopped the bike and looked at me with knowing eyes.

"Nope, you must be hearing things."

"Oh no, sweet cheeks, you said you didn't answer to him or anyone *since*. So, since when?" He was not letting this go.

"Just drop it, 'kay?"

"Since when?" he kept on. "You started it, you need to finish it."

"Ugh, since my mother died. Okay, since my mom died. I only ever answered to her." I spun around and started heading for my house, resolved not to let him see me upset. Damn you Captain Morgan for lowering my walls. Talking about my mom was still hard. I didn't think it would ever not be.

"Leila, I'm sorry. I shouldn't have pried." He started walking the bike again. "Will you please let me just see you home? I promise I won't make you get on the bike."

"Fine." I had to admit, I did appreciate his concern. It was sweet, even though if Brody found out it would definitely be World War III in the making.

Jaxon swung his thick, jean-clad leg over the tail of the bike and joined me on the sidewalk.

"Don't you want to ride, so you don't have to come back here to get your bike?" I stopped to wait for his answer.

"Nah, it's not far. Besides, I like walking with you. I've gotten pretty accustom to our morning walks. But something tells me when Brady..."

"Brody," I corrected.

"Yeah, when he comes home, I won't have the pleasure of seeing you in the mornings anymore. Right?" He was insinuating Brody dictated who I could and couldn't see.

"Maybe. I'll still walk home some. But occasionally he picks me up and takes me to breakfast, depends on his schedule," I explained.

We approached my house and Jaxon took my hand in his, brought it to his lips and placed a delicate, yet oddly sensual kiss to the back of my hand.

"Thanks for walking me home. Even though I'm quite capable of making it myself, it was sweet of you." I took my keys out and unlocked my dead bolt.

"Anything for you baby girl. Anything." He returned to the direction from where we came.

Chapter Twenty-six

Leila

The doorbell roused me from an erotic, highly inappropriate dream about Jaxon. What the hell? Who was waking my ass up this early on a Saturday? Someone better be bleeding, dying or on fire, otherwise they were going to need a doctor when I finished with them.

The asshole on the other side of the door rang the bell incessantly as I stumbled down the stairs, trying to tie my silk robe around my body. I snatched open the door in the middle of yelling out, "If you press that freakin' button one more time, I'm breakin' your finger."

"Well, good morning to you too, sweetheart." Brody stood there in a snug white crew neck tee, khaki cargo shorts and running shoes, holding a coffee and a bag for East Bay Deli.

"Oh shit, I'm sorry honey. I had a late night. Come in." I instantly felt like an asshole.

"I brought sustenance." He sat the bag on the granite bar and started pulling stuff out. "Coffee for me and Mountain Dew for my princess."

He brought it over to me and scooped me up in a whirlwind, sweep you off your feet kind of kiss.

"Whoa." I tried to catch my breath. "Good morning to you too."

"What can I say, I missed you." He walked back into the kitchen. "I brought breakfast."

"How thoughtful. I need to brush my teeth and use the bathroom. Be right back." I rushed upstairs before my bladder exploded.

I hollered down that I was going to take a quick shower and for him to make himself at home, secretly hoping he'd join me in the shower. I didn't hold my breath; I saw the way he was eyeing that bacon, egg and cheese.

Both hands were in my hair lathering it up when a cool draft caused my nipples to tighten and peak. I smiled, knowing Brody had opened the glass door and he'd missed me as much as I had missed him.

"Can I help you with that?" He slid his fingers into my soapy hair and massaged.

"Mmm, by all means, please do."

Brody finished washing my hair and rinsed it with the handheld showerhead. I conditioned my hair while he shampooed his. I was rinsing as he was scrubbing his body. Our shower was intimate and relaxing. Yes, the sexual chemistry was bubbling over, but he showed me that he could be loving and attentive without groping or fucking me. It made me realize that perhaps we have a chance. It wasn't just sex; there was a real connection. This awareness heightened my need for him.

We toweled off and started to go back to the bedroom when I grabbed him and pinned him to the wall. I launched myself at him, wrapped my arms around his neck to steady myself since I was on my tippy toes. I kissed him with the passion of a thousand suns. Our tongues slipped and slid around each other, caressing and exploring. Brody lifted me by the waist to rest on the vanity and I tangled my legs around him.

"Wait," he groaned and pulled back. "Condom. We need a condom."

He released me and I dragged him to the bed. "I bought some the other day for here, top drawer on your side of the bed."

Whoa, your side of the bed. I totally freaked myself out, but if I corrected it then I would look like an ass. *Exhale Leila, it's a figure of speech.* Thank God Brody was none the wiser to my anxiety.

He grabbed a condom and tossed it on the pillow, then pulled me up until I was kneeling on the bed just as he was. He kissed and sucked in my bottom lip, then moved to my chin, my throat, my sternum and my navel. He pushed me back onto my elbows and continued. When he stopped just above my labia, I groaned.

"Wow, are we impatient or what? What do you want me to do? Tell me," he said, his voice deep and sultry.

"Mmm, lick me," I whispered, feeling the heat in my cheeks.

"Damn, I love when you blush. Where do you want me to lick you?" He licked along the outline of my hip bone.

"You're really gonna make me say it, aren't you?" I have no idea why it embarrassed me to tell him but I was mortified.

He nodded his head, kissing and lightly dragging his tongue over the sensitive area.

"I want you to lick my pussy. Make me come, Brody." Saying it actually turned me on, once it was out. It was freeing, strangely enough. And dear God, did he ever lick my pussy. He licked, sucked and rubbed it in just the right spot. He reached up and grabbed the condom. With magic and probably lots of practice, he sheathed himself while still going down on me.

Just as I was about to come, he sat up, positioned his throbbing dick at my opening and rammed in, balls deep. He pumped in and out a few times while massaging my clit. As my walls began to contract and squeeze him, he stilled. With his free hand, he reached up pinched my nipple roughly. With the pain came my climax.

"Fuck babe, I could come just feeling you pulsing all over my cock, you're so tight," he said still rubbing my clit.

"Oh God Brody, move, I need for you to move. Ahhh, fuck me hard, Brody, oh yeah," I screamed out, begging him to fuck me and not stop.

He rolled me over so I was on top. "Ride me babe, take control and fuck me."

Oh hell yeah. I had been looking forward to this since I first dreamed of Brody. I rolled my hips, bouncing fast and then slowing down to tease him. I rose up until only the tip was inside me, then I rolled my hips to slide him in just an inch, then back out. Just as he got used to that I slammed down, impaling myself on him. Each and every time, he would gasp and groan. I wasn't sure how long I could continue to tease him before he shattered or reclaimed control. Controlling the depth and exact position made reaching my boiling point that much easier. I was there and I needed him to get there with me. I wanted to feel him come at the same time I did.

I jumped off the bed and positioned myself at the bottom, bent over the edge. I propped one foot up on the bed, opening myself up to him. I didn't have a chance to explain before he was thrusting himself into my hot, wet cunt. He grabbed a handful of now dry, unruly curls to hold me in place. I knew he was close because he started pumping into me faster and faster. Each thrust had more force behind it than the last. He hammered away and just before he came, he slipped his hand around my leg and found my clit. All I needed was a graze and I burst. White pings of light danced behind my tightly closed eyes. We both yelled each other's name and finally sagged against the bed.

"Holy shit Brody. If that is what sex is like when we haven't seen each other in four days, imagine what's gonna happen when we have to wait six or seven days." My body still quivered.

"Uh, why would we wait six or seven days? Hell, I don't want to wait six or seven hours." He disappeared into the bathroom.

"There will be times when we can't. Ya know," I hinted, but didn't want to say it.

"Oh." it finally dawned on him what I was referring to. "You think that's going to stop me?" With a wicked smile he pulled me to him and kissed me senseless.

We spent the day walking around downtown and wandering in the open air market. We held hands and snuck kisses like teenagers. About 3 p.m. Brody got a call and had to go to the office for a while. But he promised to be back before dinner.

I decided to take Ruger out for a run along the Battery. On the way home we walked past Jaxon's house. As we passed I heard the low, heavy rolling hum of a bike in the distance and knew it was him. His Shadow Rocket had a distinct deep growl that only a custom Harley can achieve. As he approached, I saw he was not alone. Another custom chopper trailed a few yards behind him carrying the guy, Viper, who was all over Barb last night.

Jaxon pulled over after I caught his eye. Ruger immediately went into protective mode, putting himself between the large burly men and me. He never growled or barked; he just kept them at a distance.

"And here I had you pegged as a little foo-foo dog type." Jaxon walked right up to Ruger before I could warn him. Ruger didn't take too kindly to his cavalier approach and snarled, barking and lunging at Jaxon like he was trying to smuggle drugs on a plane.

"Whoa, what the fuck?" Both Jaxon and Viper stumbled backward in retreat.

"Ruger, *fuss, platz*." I gripped the leather lead. "Sorry you were too fast, I didn't get a chance to warn you. Ruger is a retired K-nine officer and maybe slightly protective."

"Yeah, slightly," Viper chuckled.

"I'm glad you have him. You can't be too careful walkin' 'round here." Jaxon held his hand out, palm up, allowing Ruger to check him out. After a quick sniff, his tail started swinging wildly in circles. "See bud, I'm a good guy. I'm not gonna hurt her. *Braver hund.*"

I relaxed the leash in my hand, surprised at Jaxon's words. Ruger was now letting Jaxon scratch behind his ears.

"Didn't know you speak German," I stated as I watched Ruger notice a squirrel across the street.

"Not a whole lot, just a few words. I worked with bomb dogs on a couple of tours, so you pick up things." He stood.

"Oh, wow, that's cool. Ruger was trained for drug detection for NCPD. They retired him a year or so ago, but he doesn't seem to understand that."

The three of us stood on the corner chatting. Viper excused himself and went into Jaxon's house. Briefly we discussed his time in the Marines and my brother Drew's shooting came up. Before I knew it, an hour had passed in the blink of an eye. I wouldn't have realized the time if I didn't see Brody's Hennessey drive past.

Fuck. That was so not good.

I know he saw me and he definitely saw Jaxon. It wasn't like you can miss his 6'4" thick frame. The man could have been a linebacker for the Dallas Cowboys.

"Shit. I gotta go. Sorry, I lost track of the time. Brody is meetin' me at my place. I'm supposed to be cooking dinner. Ruger *fuss*. Bye Jaxon." I hurried south down the sidewalk. I could see Brody leaning on the Venom and he did not look the least bit happy.

"Hey baby, I'm sorry. I took Ruger for a walk and ran into Jaxon. We started talking and I lost track of the time," I explained as I unlocked the door.

"How the fuck does he know where you live?" Brody was fuming. He might as well have had steam coming from his ears.

Oh shit, shit, shit. I completely forgot to tell him Jaxon lived around the corner, and hadn't gotten around to telling him about last night at the bar. In my defense, I was a little overwhelmed this morning and nearly forgot my name after the morning of mind-blowing sex.

"Uh, well he lives down the street and a few blocks over," I mumbled.

"Wait, what did you say?" Brody carried his bag in and set in down by the stairs.

"He lives on Laurens. I run into him from time to time when I walk Ruger."

"So he is stalking you. That's just fuckin' great." Brody clenched his fists at his side.

"Stop it. He's not stalking me. How many times do I need to say that? Jesus do you hear yourself? You have *nothing* to worry about. Why can't you see he is harmless? Yes, he flirts with me, but so does almost every dirty ol' man that comes through the ER. You need to trust me and know that I am with *you*. If you stress about every man, and yes woman too, that flirts with me or asks me out, then you're gonna have a heart attack. People flirt with nurses, it just happens." I took a deep breath, pushed him down on the couch and straddled his lap. "If I wanted to be with him I would be honest with you and tell you. But I'm here with you, where I want to be, I might add."

I laced my hands together behind his neck and kissed his nose, then his cheeks. I made a point to wiggle my hips just enough to elicit a groan from deep in his chest.

"How about we order in? That way I can spend the entire evening proving to you just how much I really want you." I stood facing away from him, unbuttoned my shorts and slid them down my legs to my ankles, putting my ass on display in my skimpy thong panties.

Without warning or explanation Brody's palm collided with my butt cheek. Holy fuck that hurt. I lurched forward fleeing his reach. That was definitely going to leave a mark. "Ow!"

"Do women really flirt with you?" He waggled his eyebrows.

"Out of everything I said that's what you honed in on?" I walked to the kitchen shaking my head. "Why am not I surprised?"

"What can I say babe? It's every man's fantasy, two chicks."

"Well, that won't ever happen, so put it out of your mind, perv."

"Oh, I'm going to enjoy making that ass all kinds of pink." He ran for me.

"Ahhh." I slammed the refrigerator door shut and looked around for a weapon, finding only a plastic spatula in the sink. I grabbed it and raised it, but it was quickly snatched from my hands. He scooped me up and threw me over his shoulder. "Put me down."

He trudged up the stairs to the master bedroom and threw me on the bed. "You are so lucky that your toys aren't here, because I would love to flog that sexy little ass of yours. Guess I will have to settle for using my hand." He stripped, throwing his clothes carelessly behind him.

I knew being a smart-ass would only add fuel to the fire, but I couldn't help myself. I loved messing with him. "If you're gonna put on a strip show at least let me put some music on for ya." I laughed trying to get down from the large bed.

"Oh, I don't think so. You're not getting away that easy. Nice try babe, but you're mine. Strip...now!"

Ooh, Mr. Bossy is back. I love Mr. Bossy. The second Mr. Bossy showed up I needed a new pair of panties. I loved when he went all alpha during sex. Manhandling me and taking what he wanted. God, it was so fuckin' hot.

"You want it off, then you're gonna have to do it yourself."

"Suit yourself. Hope you don't have any attachment to your clothes." He had this look of pure mischief in his beautiful blue eyes.

Before I could reply, he gripped my thong on both sides of my hips and ripped it off of me. Next was my shirt. The four small buttons flew all over the comforter. Then my bra sailed across the room. He lunged forward, pinning my back to the mattress and capturing my mouth. He was rough and forceful as he assaulted my mouth, grasping a handful of hair and forcing my head back. His mouth nipped and licked at my throat before sucking in my nipple, palming my breasts together, squeezing them. He pinched my other nipple between his fingers and was rewarded with a long whimper. I could feel him grinning against my breast.

"I wonder if you're ready for me. Should we check?" He trailed his tongue down my body, finding that sensitive spot that made me shatter beneath him. "Mmm, you are. You're so wet baby. God, you're so fuckin' gorgeous."

He pushed two fingers in and out of me as he worked his tongue around my hardened nub. It didn't take long for my body to tighten and explode. As soon as I came, he tore open a condom and was in me before by body stopped spasming. He was slow and hard in his movements. Pushing all the way in and stopping briefly to roll his hips. He'd pull all the way out then slam back into me.

"Mine. You're mine. Tell me." He looked deeply into my eyes. I wanted to deny that I was his because it was too fast, but the fact was, I was his. I felt like I was in the ocean being pulled out in a rip current. The harder I fought against the attraction the more I was pulled under.

"Say it Lei. I know you feel it too." He stopped moving. "You do feel this between us, right? The electricity that dances along all of my nerve endings, the all-consuming need to be near you, touching you, feeling you. I know you feel it. I can see it in your eyes and feel it in your touch."

"I do feel it Brody. I'm just scared." I was honest in how I felt. "You have the power to shatter me and that terrifies me to no end. Don't hurt me, please."

He didn't say anything; he just kissed me. It was a kiss that said what he couldn't. It was warm, soft and attentive. He slipped his arm underneath me to hold me tight as he rocked into my body, finding his release.

He pulled out of me, gently brushed the hair from my eyes and just stared at me. He looked at me like he was searching for something, but it was only for a split second. Then he was gone and in the bathroom.

I pulled the comforter over my chilled skin and stared at the ceiling fan spinning around. Why was I over-thinking this? Why couldn't I tell him I was his? I wanted to be his, but he was so far out of my league. I didn't own multiple homes or cars. I didn't have a staff to wait on my every need. But he was good to me and genuinely seemed to want to be with me. But why? Why me? I was nothing special.

Stop Leila, a voice inside finally spoke up. *You're amazing and he'd be fucking lucky to have you, whether it's for a minute or for the rest of his life. You deserve to be treated like a princess.*

"Babe, did you hear me?" Brody stood by the bed, pulling me out of my thoughts.

Looking up at him, I shook my head. "No, sorry. What?"

"I'm going to hop in the shower, then order some pizza. Or if you would rather order, my wallet is in my pants. Just grab the all-white Visa and pay with that."

"I'll pay. It was my idea to order in," I offered, even though I knew he wouldn't let me pay.

"Babe, not happening. I'll order first, because knowing your sneaky ass, you'll order and pay while I'm in the shower." He pulled his phone and wallet out of his pants. "What do you want on the pizza?"

"Uh, I'll eat just about anything, except olives, peppers, anchovies or red onions. I'm not a fan of lots of veggies on a pizza. In a salad I love them, but not on pizza."

"So, then, pepperoni, sausage and mushroom. Okay?"

He dialed the Pizzeria di Giovanni just down the street and ordered, then took a shower. I stayed in the bed, thinking. This time my thoughts were how abruptly I ran away from Jaxon. It was quite rude actually. We were having a great conversation. Brody was so wrong about him. Yes, Jaxon was forward and self-assured, but he was sweet and genuine. He wasn't stalking me like Brody insisted.

Once Brody finished up in the shower, I went in the bathroom and closed the door. I had to pee and I wasn't ready to do all that in front of him. I popped in the shower quickly, got dressed in a cotton T-shirt and a pair of boy shorts and went downstairs to find the sexy man who wanted to claim me.

We picked out a movie to watch, ate pizza on the couch and laughed at Harry and Lloyd. Of course, I fell asleep on Brody before the end of the movie.

I woke up in the middle of the night and we were tangled around each other on the couch. "Brody, hey, let's go up to bed." He blinked a few times, stretched, then followed behind.

Chapter Twenty-seven

Leila

The next few weeks were pretty much the same. Brody traveled a few days a week, mostly when I was working, and he was home on the weekends. I walked home from work every morning, stopping to say hi to Jaxon. Some mornings he walked me to my front door, others he rode off on his Harley in the other direction. He tried a few times to get me on the back of his bike, but I declined. That was the last thing I wanted Brody to see. I knew he wasn't happy with me talking with Jaxon, but he was trying to be tolerant.

Last weekend we stayed at Brody's place and took Ruger. We spent most of it riding the horses and having sex in the barn. I was shocked I didn't have splinters in my ass the way he fucked me against the barn wall. When we got back to the house, Jane's face clued me into the fact I had pieces of hay still in my hair. Mortified, I ran to the master bath as Brody snickered.

Sunday, he had racks of formal dresses brought out to the house for me to choose from. We had that charity dinner in two weeks in New York City. I chose a gown covered in hand beaded, daintily scrolling vines. It was a dark, shadowy gray, sleeveless silhouette gown with an open back and a V neckline. I knew as soon as I saw it; I fell in love. Putting it on was like a dream come true. The new sandals Brody had given me were a perfect match.

Since last weekend, Brody had been acting off. He was sneaking phone calls and being really secretive. I started to think he was second-guessing our relationship. We had been seeing each other for about six weeks. Maybe he wasn't as invested as he said.

Thursday's shift blew by and Friday morning Jaxon met me in front of his house, like normal. He walked me to my house as he had done so many times over the few weeks. Except, this morning there was a silver Mercedes SUV parked in front of my house.

"Maybe you should head home from here. He knows we're friends and that you walk me home occasionally, but I don't want to rub it in his face Remi."

"I told you to call me Jaxon. Why are you so afraid of him? He doesn't—" His eyes were dark as I cut him off.

"No. Brody is a perfect gentleman. He has never and would never hurt me. I'm not afraid of him, I just care about him and I don't want to upset him. I can't say I'd be as understanding if he walked home with some woman who wanted him. And you said your friends call you Remi, why can't I call you that?"

"Whoa baby girl." He refused to stop calling me that. "Why are you so pissed at me? I haven't asked you out in over a month. I just don't understand why the fuck you placate him. And I've told you why I don't want you callin' me that."

"Jax, put yourself in his shoes. If I were dating you and he walked me home every day, how would you feel?" I ignored the fact that he refused to let me call him by his nickname because I was *different*.

"Fuck that, you wouldn't walk home without me. Ever. I'd meet you every morning and drop you off every night. No way in fuckin' hell I'd let you walk these streets without me, especially with another man who wants to fuck you."

"See. I'm going now. See ya later *Jaxon*."

Brody opened the door, exited the vehicle and watched Jax as I approached the back of the Mercedes.

"Hey honey. I didn't expect you this morning. I love when you surprise me." I wrapped my arms around his waist, trying to get him to focus on me and not the massive biker lurking nearby. I popped up on my tippy toes and captured his lips in a quick kiss before going to unlock the door. As I turned, I saw Jaxon still watching me, so I waved and entered the house, letting Ruger out.

"I don't understand why you feel the need to be friends with that prick."

"Brody, don't call him that. He's not a prick and he's done nothing to warrant you callin' him that. He walks me home to make sure I'm safe and that is it. He hasn't asked me out in weeks and promised he was done askin'. He wants to be friends. That's it."

"Okay, whatever. I'm not having this argument again. Besides, I didn't come here to fight with you. I came to surprise you and that's what I intend to do."

I was confused. "Wait, you already surprised me. What are you up to?"

He grinned mischievously. "Sit down on the couch. I'm going to pack you a bag and I will tell you once we're in the air."

Air? What? Oh no. He was really up to something. "Where are you taking me? Just tell me so I can pack my own stuff. You won't know what I will need."

"Trust me."

That's all he said as he bounded up the stairs to my room. Crap, I need my birth control pills and tampons. I was due to start any day now. Great, I was sure I would start in the next twenty-four hours since Brody was whisking me away somewhere. Just my luck.

I started up the stairs when he appeared at the top. "No. I got everything. Yes, before you ask, I got your pills."

"Tampons?"

"What? You started?" He looked like someone kicked his puppy.

"No, not yet, but I should be any day now. I'm supposed to start a new pack of pills Sunday, did you get those?"

"Yes, dear, I did."

"So, where are you taking me? I'm assuming you're taking me somewhere special because I have some clothes at your house." I was fishing for hints.

"I told you I'd fill you in once we got in the air. No more questions or I will have to punish you for not listening."

"Hmm, maybe I want to be punished." I waggled my eyebrows at him.

"Let's go." He tugged me down the stairs to the front door.

"Wait, what about Ruger? I can't just leave him here." I looked over at my furry baby all cuddled in his bed.

"Jane should be here any second to pick him up. He's going to stay with her while we are away." He dropped my duffle on a dining room chair and walked to the kitchen. He grabbed Ruger's lead and jingled it, getting Ruger's attention. "Let's go boy, want to go for a ride?" That got his attention; he loved rides, especially in the last couple of months because Jane spoiled that dog rotten. He was up and at the front door waiting for us. Jane was pulling up and I locked the front door while Brody threw my bag in the car. Sara hopped out of the passenger door. Before I could ask why she was here Brody opened both passenger doors. Uh, WTF is she going with us?

"Hi Leila! How are ya?" She smiled politely.

"Good, and you?" I tried to remind myself she was only his assistant.

"I'm wonderful, thanks."

I didn't know why she rubbed me the wrong way, but she did. She wasn't drop-dead gorgeous, but she was pretty and intelligent. If I had to guess, I would say she was about thirty-five, 5'6", with long, board-straight brunette hair, and she was no bigger than a toothpick. I had no reason to think she was after Brody, but I did. She was always dressed in short skirts or dresses or her shirts were low-cut. Why she wore anything to show off her boobs—or rather lack thereof—was beyond me. But I trusted him, so whether she wanted him or not didn't matter.

We drove north to Charleston International Airport and I never bothered to ask if she was coming with us, but during the drive I received my answer.

"While we are away, please try to keep an eye on the New York project and make sure that it's on time and under budget. I have a feeling that the designer is going to try to slip charges in under the radar, so be diligent."

"Yes sir. If anything should come up I'll do my best to handle without disturbing you." She clicked away on her phone. "Don't forget you have a meeting on Tuesday at nine a.m. That's the one I moved from Monday. Speaking of Monday, I'll be here to pick y'all up at three p.m. unless there is a change of plans."

"No, I've already filed the flight plans, Monday at three is fine." He put the SUV in park and I realize we were not at the airport but at Atlantic Aviation. He got out, grabbed our bags and opened my door.

"Seriously, Brody, a private plane? You didn't have to rent a plane. We could have flown commercial."

He stifled a laugh. "Lei, it's not rented. It's mine."

"Oh." For the first time ever, I didn't know what to say.

He owns a plane. What do you say to that?

"Come on honey, let's get out of here." He held out his hand to me.

"Have a nice vacation," Sara said graciously.

"Thank you Sara. See you Monday." I was genuine in my reply. I turned and put my hand in Brody's and let him spirit me away to parts unknown.

We were on a large private jet that probably had the capacity to seat twenty to thirty people. Contemporary in design, it had several reclining seats scattered about, a galley kitchen near the front, a large table surrounded by six chairs and a serpentine couch in the middle.

During the flight Brody got up, unbuckled my seat belt and pulled me to the back of the jet. He opened a door, which I thought was the bathroom, to reveal a bedroom with a TV and en-suite bathroom.

In his sexy I'm-going-to-eat-you-alive voice he said "How you doin'?"

I burst out laughing. I couldn't help it and I couldn't stop. Tears ran down my face as he tackled me to the bed.

"You're laughin' at me. Oh, you're in so much trouble little slave girl." He pinned my wrists above my head and consumed me like I was his last meal. We were literally in the middle of having sex when there was a knock at the door.

"Mr. Davis we will be making our descent momentarily, you may want to return to your seats," the stewardess advised.

"Oh my God, I was so loud, I know she heard me." I felt the heat rushing to my face.

"Who cares, I'm sure it's not the first time she's heard people having sex on a plane." He started sliding in and out of me again, driving me closer and closer to my release.

"Oh God Brody, don't stop. Aww yeah, oh my God," I screamed as I came. I could see the muscles in the side of his neck strain as he began thrusting aggressively, fucking me across the bed as he exploded inside of me.

"Fuck," he panted. "I will never get tired of fucking you. You're amazing, you know that."

"What can I say, I do what I can." I would never get tired of teasing him. He made this adorable scowl and rolled his eyes. It always made me smile.

We got cleaned up and returned to the couch to enjoy a flute of Veuve Clicquot, which happened to be my favorite champagne. Not that I had a huge familiarity with different champagnes, but it was what Barb and I always drank. The stewardess, Nicole, took her seat in the front cabin and told us we would be landing in just a few minutes. I noted she didn't once say where we were landing. Weren't they supposed to say where we were landing or something? Geez-pete, why wouldn't he tell me already?

Suddenly the plane hit a pocket of air and plummeted downward, shooting my stomach into my throat. I gripped Brody's strong forearm in a panic.

"It's okay, babe, just a little turbulence."

I threw my hand over my mouth, feeling sick. I flung my seat belt off and ran for the bathroom, making it just in time. I felt Brody's warm hand running up and down my spine and I realized I didn't lock the door.

"I'm fine, please go. You don't want to be in here for this." I started dry heaving again.

"Babe, why don't you let me decide what I want to be here for?" He pulled my hair back. "Feel a little better now? Want some ginger ale or a Sprite?"

"No, I'm okay. Can you please get me a wet washcloth?" I wanted to make sure I didn't have any vomit on my face before he looked at me. I sat on my feet in front of the toilet, still not sure if I was done. Brody handed me a white washcloth with an embroidered "D" in the corner. I almost felt bad using it to wipe my face. Almost.

"Babe, if you're okay, we need to sit back down." He brushed my hair from my face.

"Okay. I'm okay."

We landed and taxied to the hanger. The air was warm and sticky with humidity. We had to be on some tropical island. That's when it dawned on me, his parents place in the Caribbean. The place they were traveling to when they died. Brody had not been down here since they died. The gravity of him bringing me here hit me like a ton of bricks. Suddenly, I felt nauseous again. I threw my hand over my mouth and my body convulsed. I tried to hold it back, but there was no use. Thankfully, there was a trash can in the hanger. I stood with my head in it retching over and over again.

"Babe." Brody, who was talking with the flight crew, ran over to me. "Leila, are you okay? Your stomach still queasy from the turbulence?"

"Oh God. I'm so embarrassed, Brody." I refused to look at him. "I probably should have told you I've never flown before."

"Aw sweetie, I'm sorry. I should have asked if you get motion sickness. Fuck. I feel like such an idiot."

"I wouldn't have known. I don't get sick in the car or on boats. I don't know why the plane affected me like this." Above being embarrassed, I was dumbfounded why turbulence in a plane made me sick and choppy waters on a boat didn't. As I was pondering that thought, a wave of nausea wracked me again. This time I was able to ride it out without vomiting. Thank God for small miracles.

A small helicopter roared to life out on the tarmac. "Babe, I hate to do this, but that's our next ride. It's the only way out to the house."

"I think I'm okay now." Actually, I did feel better after fighting back the last bout. I took a sip of the ginger ale Nicole had brought me on the plane, took a deep breath and told Brody I was ready.

The ride to the house was magnificent. We flew over the tiny islands, crystal clear waters and landed on a helipad next to a massive compound. This place was a mansion, easily more than ten thousand square feet, complete with pool, helipad, tennis court, beach access, pool house and outdoor kitchen.

"Wow, Brody, this is…it's incredible."

He laughed. "You…at a loss for words? I have to write this down, so I don't forget the day."

I nudged him with my shoulder. He threw his arm over my shoulder and gave me the tour. I was lost on the first floor, forget the second or third.

We spent the first day lying around the pool, drinking margaritas and listening to music. Brody danced me all over the terrace. We walked down to the beach after dinner where we could hear music in the distance. He held me and we swayed in the moonlight down on the beach. When we returned from our walk there were candles lining the path. As we climbed the stairs up to the house I saw hundreds of candles spread over the expansive patio, even floating in the pool.

"Oh, Brody it's beautiful." I stopped walking to take it all in.

"It has nothing on you, sweetheart." He pulled me along to the outdoor canopied bed. It had long, flowing white sheets draping the sides not overlooking the ocean.

We made love under the stars with the waves crashing in the background. Brody was tender and loving. He was slow, deliberate and methodical in his rhythm. He held me in his arms and never took his eyes from mine. I knew at that very moment I had fallen deeply and irrevocably in love with him. I was no longer scared to tell him how I felt. I needed him to know. He had always been honest with me; it was my turn.

I took his face in my hands and he stilled. "Are you okay babe?"

"Yeah, I am." I pressed my lips to his, kissing him ever so gently, then pulled back and gazed into his eyes. "Brody Davis, I love you. I'm terrified you will destroy me, but I can't fight it anymore. I have probably loved you for a while, but I was too scared to admit it to myself, let alone to you. I don't need you to say it back, but I had to admit to both of us how I feel."

He slipped both hands under my shoulders and buried himself to the hilt. "Leila, you have to know I love you. I knew I was in trouble from the first moment I saw you. You captured my heart in that waiting room." He thrust in and out, hard and slow. "You're mine and I'll never let you go. No matter how far you run or no matter how many times you try to flee, I'll hold on to you forever."

I yanked his face back to mine and kissed him until I could no longer hold my breath. He drove into me sending us both over the edge. I screamed out his name as we both came together.

We stayed right there and slept tangled and snaked around each other.

The next two days flew by way too quickly. We spent most of our time having sex in random crazy places like the deck of his 103' Italian-built yacht and on the Jet Ski, after I accidently flipped him off. I didn't think he would ever let me drive again. I laughed so hard I cried and Brody just cussed me. The more he scolded me, the harder I laughed. The harder I cackled, the more he yelled at me for laughing. It ended up with us making up on the back of the Jet Ski, which he promptly pushed me off of as soon as he pulled out.

I blinked and it was Monday and we were on the plane to go home. Brody got me Dramamine for the plane ride and we made it home with no issues.

Monday night we stayed at Brody's since Ruger was there and Brody had to be at work the next morning. Tuesday morning about 5:30 I woke up, ripped the blankets back and sprinted for the bathroom like someone lit my ass on fire. This time I made it with enough time to spare to shut the door before puking up my guts. As I sat on the cold tile floor, I heard a soft knock on the door.

"Leila, are you okay? I thought I heard you running from the bed." He sounded half awake.

"Yeah, sorry. I'm fine."

"Are you throwing up again? Babe, can I come in?"

"No. Really, I'm fine. I will be out in just a—" I was cut short by my stomach's next round of heaves.

Brody opened the door and was by my side, holding my hair back. "I don't think this constitutes being fine Leila."

"Oh God this sucks. I must have eaten something last night that didn't agree with me." I wiped my mouth with a wad of toilet paper. "I think I'm done now." I stood up and immediately threw my hand up to the wall and caught myself from falling over.

"Jesus babe, come here, let me carry you back to bed." He tried to cradle me.

"No, I'm okay. I just stood up too fast. That's all. I'm gonna throw some water on my face, brush my teeth and then I will come back to bed." I walked over to the double vanity.

"I think I'll wait right here to make sure you don't pass out again."

"Brody just go to bed. I didn't pass out, I just got light-headed. Which is really quite normal when you're puking your guts up like I just did." I turned the cold water on and dowsed my clammy face. Maybe I was coming down with something, or maybe I really did just eat something bad. Either way I felt better now getting it all out of my system. I looked up in the mirror to see that he was still standing behind me, although now he was holding a hand towel for me to dry my face off.

"Come on, let's go back to bed," he yawned.

"I'm right behind ya." I brushed my teeth trying to get rid of the putrid taste in my mouth. By the time I got back to bed Brody was already fast asleep. I settled under the fluffy duvet and tried to shake the uneasy feeling that had taken over my entire body.

Chapter Twenty-eight

Leila

I woke to an empty bed. I sat up and looked around the room for Brody, until I saw the clock on the bedside table that read 11:09 a.m. Holy shit, why did he let me sleep so late? I had to get home. I had to work tonight and I needed to check in with Drew. I hadn't talked to him since we left for Caicos on Friday.

I pulled the duvet back and found a note from Brody. I must have knocked it off when I was sleeping.

Had to get to the office early. I hope you got some sleep and feel better. I will call you at the normal time before you go to work.

I love you.

B

Hearing it was one thing, but to see it there in front of me in black and white made the butterflies in my belly flutter to life. Or wait, was that..."Uh, no, not again." I made a break for the toilet. This time I wasn't so lucky. Brody and his princely etiquette put the toilet seat down so I threw up in the trash can. As if things couldn't possibly get any worse, I heard the bathroom door open.

"Leila, are you in here love?" It was Jane. Brody must have told her I wasn't feeling well.

Before I could answer her I started heaving again. Jane appeared in the door with a clear, bubbly drink. "Oh heavens."

"I'm sorry Jane. I'll clean up the trash can myself." I was so embarrassed. I was pretty sure I made it all in the bag, but I didn't even want to look.

"Here you drink this and give me that trash can, I'll take care of that. Brody gave me plenty of opportunities to take care of him when he was sick. Granted, he was hung over, but I still am quite capable." She took the trash can out and lifted the toilet seat for me.

"Thank you Jane, you're a lifesaver." I was becoming really attached to this woman. She was so sweet and loving. And damn could she cook. *Oh God, food...*

Jane returned to catch yet another round of my stunning digestive pyrotechnics. She kneeled down on the floor next to me and rubbed my back.

"Ugh, what in the world is wrong with me? I ate the same thing
Brody did and he's fine. Well, I did eat the scallops. He said he
didn't really like them." I turned to her. "You don't think that I could
have picked up something in Parrot Cay, do you?"

"No, Brody would have gotten sick by now too if it was viral.
Could've been the scallops though." She handed me a wet washcloth.

"I have to work tonight, I don't have time to be sick." I stood
and flushed the toilet.

"Well, let's get you an antiemetic. I'll take you and Ruger to
your house and get you settled." She smiled. "I'll meet you down
there."

I grabbed a few things and threw them in duffle that Brody had
packed for our getaway. I left my fancy clothes in the closet for this
coming weekend, but grabbed most of the other stuff. I needed to
wash clothes and it was starting to get cooler; tank tops and shorts
could get left at my place. I would bring back clothes more
appropriate for the middle of September.

I met Jane downstairs and we took her dark gray Range Rover
to my home. She stayed with me until I woke later that evening
before my shift. Thankfully, all of my praying to the porcelain God
paid off. I woke up and felt much better. I was even hungry.

Jane insisted she drop me off at work on her way home. I made
it through the first ten hours of work with no problem. But at 5:30
a.m. Wednesday I got violently ill in the middle of a trauma. I damn
near threw up on a patient.

Barb came down the hall as I exited trauma room two. "Hey girl,
I heard you got sick. You feelin' okay?"

"Ugh, I don't even want to think about it." I pulled her into a
cubicle and whispered, "I've been throwing up since last Friday
when we hit turbulence on the way to the island."

"Holy shit." Barb's eyes were popping out of her head. "Holy
fuckin' shit. You're pregnant, aren't you?"

"No. Why the fuck would you say something like that?" I
swatted at her without actually making contact.

"When was your last period?" As soon as she uttered those
dreaded words I ran to the trash can.

"Oh, this is *so* not happening. I should have started last week.
I'm only a few days late. Barb, I can't be pregnant. I'm on birth
control and we always use—" I just remembered the one time we

didn't use a condom. But that was two months ago and I had a period after that.

"Always use what?" Barb looked at me waiting for an answer.

"Okay, so, one time we didn't use a condom, but that was two months ago and I've had a period since then." I was trying to remember my last period. It wasn't long, but I definitely had one.

Barb grabbed a cup and threw it at me. "Go pee and we will do a rapid hCG."

"No, I'm not pregnant." I tried to walk out to the hallway, but Barb grabbed my arm before I could get far.

"Okay, so, then there is no harm in checking."

She was not going to let this go. "Fine. Give me the damn cup, but I am telling you, it's gonna be negative. Meet me in the locker room." I shoved the cup in the front pocket of my scrubs and went to the locker room bathroom.

After I peed, I let Barb in with the test. I let her do the honors so she could see she was dead wrong. The sixty second wait felt like two hours.

"Holy motherfucking shitball. You're pregnant! I was right." Barb jumped around the small bathroom like this was a good thing.

"No, it's a false positive." I was in total denial.

"I knew you'd say that. That's why I brought two. Ha!" She pulled another test out of her scrubs and put a few drops of urine on it.

"See. I told you. You. Are. Pregnant." She handed me the second test.

"No fuckin' way. This can't be happening. I'm not ready for a child." I stood there staring at the tests and the tears just poured down my face.

"Lei, it'll be okay. I'll be right here for you the entire time. You'll see it will be fine." She hugged me trying to reassure me.

I finished my shift and walked home. I passed Jaxon's but he wasn't there today. I got home, took a shower and climbed into bed. I had to figure out how I was going to tell Brody. I knew he didn't want kids right now. Neither of us did, but that was before we knew we loved each other. Sure, the timing sucked and I still had a million and one more things I wanted to do before I had babies, but God works in mysterious ways. I fell asleep before I heard from Brody. I made the decision to tell him when we came back from New York.

Chapter Twenty-nine

Leila

The week passed by with only a few more bouts of what I now knew was morning sickness. I made an appointment with my OBGYN and she confirmed I was pregnant, nine weeks approximately. Apparently the period I thought I had last month was just the baby implanting and that's why it was only a few days long. I kept the one picture of the sonogram in my wallet, where no one would see it.

Saturday, we left for New York City. We were staying at Brody's penthouse, even though it was still going through a redesign. The bedrooms, living room and bathrooms were done. The kitchen was still in midproject.

Brody had a limo pick us up. He looked so damn sexy in his tuxedo. His hair still unruly and his face still had a little scruff, just the way I liked it. I stood at the top of the open staircase watching him fidget with his phone until I cleared my throat, garnering his attention.

"Wow, Leila. I'm at a loss for words. You are breathtakingly beautiful baby. I'm not going to be able to leave you alone for a minute." He pulled me into a tight embrace, dipped me backward and kissed me breathless.

"Not tonight honey. We have to be there in five minutes." I patted his chest.

"We aren't staying long. I can't wait to get you back here and fuck you on every available flat surface I can find." He smacked my ass.

*****

Brody

I heard her clear her throat from the top of the stairs. I spun around and was in awe of just how gorgeous she was. There were no words to explain. The dress she picked out looked like it was made for her and her alone. The V neckline showed off her ample cleavage in a tasteful, appropriate way. Without a shadow of a doubt, my favorite part of the dress was the back. It was open and showcased her sexy, lean shoulders and neck. I had to adjust myself at just the sight of her. I checked my watch, five minutes. Damn. Maybe we could be just a little late. With that thought, I pulled her to me and kissed her.

Unfortunately, she knew me too well and stopped me before I had a chance. But she was right; we needed to get to this event. The sooner we got there, the sooner we could leave. I didn't want to stay long. I knew Jenifer would be there and I wanted to keep her away from Leila. Jenifer was a vindictive, conniving bitch and I wouldn't put it past her to say something just to upset Leila.

The limo was waiting in front of the building and took us to the Surrey. I escorted Leila to the ballroom and headed straight for the bar.

"So you never did tell me what tonight's charity was," Leila said while I tried to get the bartender's attention.

"Oh, it's the Semper Fi Fund, to help Marines."

"Oh how awesome. That's a wonderful thing to donate to Brody." She leaned in and gave me a quick approving peck.

"You have got to be fucking shitting me right now," I growled, staring at the man across the room. "Did you know he would be here?"

"Huh? Who? I don't know anyone in New York. You just told me about the charity when we got here like two point seven seconds ago." She turned to look around the room.

"Your buddy Jaxon is here," I said seething.

"Are you sure you're not seeing things honey?" She tried to calm me.

"Nope and here he comes. I swear the man follows you."

*****

Leila

"Jaxon. What are you doing here?" I asked as he approached. "I'm surprised to see you. And in a tux, no less." I stayed at Brody's side but welcomed Jaxon over.

"If you will excuse me, I see some friends of my parents I need to say hello to. Jaxon." Brody nodded curtly in his direction.

"Brody, wait. I'll come with you. I'd like to meet them—" He cut me off before I could finish.

"No darling. Please stay and talk with your friend. I'll only be a minute." He leaned down and gave me a gentle kiss, sucking in my bottom lip just long enough to trace it with the tip of his tongue.

I turned to Jaxon. "Well, don't you clean up nice. Hot damn. So what brings you up here to New York?" I knew Jaxon was a Marine and tried to help other Marines when he could.

"I'm on the Board of Directors of the charity. What are you doing here?" He turned his attention to the bar. "I'll have a beer. Leila, what do you want to drink?"

Oh shit. I hadn't thought about how to avoid alcohol yet. *Think Lei, quick.* "Uh, just a bottle of water. I don't want to drink quite yet, I haven't eaten in a while."

Wheeeew. That was a close one.

Jaxon ordered a drink and handed me a bottle of water. I looked around to see if I could find Brody. I found him all right, with a tall, fake-breasted blonde bombshell hanging on his shoulder.

"Your boyfriend looks a little preoccupied. Wanna have a seat?" Jaxon nodded to an open table.

"Yeah, my feet are killing me anyway, thanks." I sat down and positioned myself so I could see Brody.

Jaxon and I discussed the charity and I learned that he donated and helped raise over a million dollars a year for the Semper Fi Fund, SFF as he called it.

Occasionally I glanced at Brody. His body language was casual with this woman, who was now trying to wrap herself around him. He finally freed himself and started to look around for me. Hmph, well, I wasn't getting up. He would just have to fucking look for me. Jaxon excused himself to the bar.

"Babe, there you are. I want you to meet some friends." He extended his hand to assist me in standing. "Leila, please meet Robert and Whitney Vanderbilt and their daughter Jenifer. They were friends of my parents. This is Leila Matthews, the woman I've told you about." He leaned in and gave me a chaste kiss.

"It's very nice to meet you all." Robert and Whitney smiled warmly and shook my hand, while Jenifer just glared at me.

"Jenifer, say hello. Don't be rude, dear." Whitney gave her a nudge.

"Of course. Hello, Leila. Brody's told me all about you." She plastered a fake, patronizing smile across her perfectly sculpted face. I guessed she had her nose, lips and cheeks done.

"Funny, he's never mentioned you before." My lioness purred in victory.

"Sweetheart, we should take our seats. We are all seated together over at table twelve." Brody ushered me to the table. *Awesome.* We ate dinner and made polite conversation until the band began to play. Whitney and Robert excused themselves for a dance and Jenifer had the nerve to ask Brody to join her. He didn't even answer, just stood and held his hand out to me.

We waltzed around the room for a song or two before I needed to use the restroom. "I'll be back shortly, just need to visit the restroom."

"Certainly, I will meet you back at the bar. Do you want a drink?" he asked.

"No, I'm fine for now." I made my way off the dance floor to the hallway where the bathrooms were located. I entered a stall and shut the white louver floor-to-ceiling door. As I was peeing I could hear two ladies come in.

"Mother, he may be here with *her*, but he will be mine again."

Oh, fuck no. That's that bitch Jenifer I-can't-keep-my-hands-to-myself Vanderbilt.

The other voice chimed in, "Honey, he is taken. You need to move on. He certainly has."

"He didn't seem to mention her when we had dinner here last month. And yes, he might have turned me down but he's never been able to turn down sex with me for too long. You watch, he will come back, he always does."

"Jenifer, must you be so crass?"

"Sorry Mother, but he is mine. He will always be mine. Just because he thinks he wants to be with her, doesn't change that," she huffed and stomped out.

I sat on the toilet, tears streaming down my face. Dinner? He had dinner with her when he was in New York. I wondered what else had happened while he'd been traveling. Oh my God, I felt like a fool. He told me he loved me. I finished my business, wiped my eyes and went to confront him.

Only when I made it back out to the ballroom, he was otherwise engaged.

With. Her.

Dancing.

Slut.

I found Jaxon at the bar and asked to borrow his cell. I had to get the fuck out of here.

"Leila, what's wrong? Why are you crying? What did that fuckin' asshole do?" he asked, the questions coming one right after another.

"I just need to call a cab, I can't be here." I grabbed a bar napkin and blotted my eyes.

Jaxon looked around and found Brody with Jenifer swaying in his arms. I sat his cell down and disappeared in the crowd of people as Jaxon stalked over to Brody. I didn't wait around to see what happened. I walked briskly through the ballroom, down the hall to the lobby and out the front door. I almost made it to the doorman out by the street before I heard Brody and Jaxon hollering after me.

"Leila, stop. Where are you going?" Brody acted surprised I was running away.

"Brody, leave me the hell alone, go back inside. I'm sure Jenifer will be wondering where you are. Maybe you can take her to dinner again and this time maybe you can fuck her since I won't be in your way." I tried my best to hold back the tears.

"Leila, why don't you let me take—?"

"You aren't taking her anywhere. Go the fuck away and let us talk." Brody turned back to me. "Babe, let me take you home so we can talk. I don't know what you think is going on with Jenifer but I can promise you it's not at all what you think. Please." He reached for my hand, but I snatched it away. "Let me take you to the penthouse so we can talk. I will explain and answer any and all questions you have. I have never lied to you and I won't start now."

I realized as I was standing on the dark, damp streets of New York City that the temperature had fallen since our arrival. I was shivering and I just wanted to go home. Knowing I had to go to the penthouse and at least get my things, I realized I had no choice, I had to go with him.

"Fine, but I'm only going because I'm cold and I need my things." I turned to Jaxon. "Will you have your cell on, in case I need a ride to the airport?"

"You won't," Brody said before Jaxon replied.

"Of course. Call if you need anything baby girl." Jaxon hesitated and then walked back into the lobby of the Surrey.

The limo pulled up seconds later and Brody opened the door and held out his hand to help me.

"I'm fine." I didn't want him to touch me. Not until he explained what the fuck she was talking about.

"Do you want to explain why you are running away from me in the middle of New York City?" He looked completely at a loss.

"I happened to hear a conversation between your *friend* Jenifer and her mother in which she recounted your wonderful dinner together last month and that you didn't so much as mention having a girlfriend. Then she discussed throwing herself at you." My voice dripped with disdain. "Apparently, you are hers, no matter what you or I may think. So I came to find you, and you were wrapped around her skanky body on the dance floor. That is when I had enough and left. Not ran, Brody, but left."

"Jesus Christ, she is a fucking psycho bitch. I had dinner with all of them. Robert, Whitney and Jenifer. I didn't even know she would be there. You have to believe me. And yes, she did ask me to go home with her, but I said no." He took a deep breath. "She and I were two people who fucked every once in a while. I swear to you I have no feelings for her other than being a longtime family friend."

A wave of nausea rolled through me. Fuck. Really? Right now? "Stop the car. Stop now."

The limo screeched to a halt on the damp roadway. I shoved the car door open and threw up all over the sidewalk.

"Baby, you're still sick? Why didn't you say something? We need to get you to a doctor."

"I've been to a doctor Brody, I'm not sick. Can you please just take us home?"

"If you're not sick then what the hell?" He ran his hand through his hair messing it up further.

"I'll tell you what's going on once we get back to the penthouse. I just want to get out of this dress, please." I closed my eyes and tilted my head back.

We rode in silence the rest of the way, all the way up the private elevator and through the foyer. I went straight to the bedroom to change. I returned in sweats and a tank to find him in the living room drinking a beer.

"You wanna beer or glass of wine?" he offered, walking toward the refrigerator that was in the middle of the war zone he called a kitchen.

"No, I want answers, Brody," I said quietly as I sat down on the large leather sofa.

"What do you want to know? I already told you I had dinner with all of them, not just her." He sat down on the couch a little ways away. "I won't deny that I've had sex with her, but it's been over a year. Despite what she might have said, I did tell her about you."

He stared straight ahead, taking his eyes off me. "She did call a couple of times, but after the second time I blocked her number. I've explained to her in no uncertain terms that I am with you and that I have no interest in her, whatsoever. You have to believe me. I didn't tell you about dinner because I honestly didn't think it was a big deal."

"I believe you." A tear slipped from the corner of my eye. I quickly wiped it away in the hope he didn't see it.

"Please don't cry. It kills me when you cry babe." He turned back to me and took my hand. "Tell me what to do, and I will. How can I make this right? You know I love you and want only you, right?"

"I think I do. I just lost it, sitting there listening to her talk about getting you back. She's your equal. She comes from wealth and from an aristocratic family. She's who you should be with. Not me. I'm an RN who doesn't come from money and works every day. It doesn't make sense for you to want me or love me." I looked down at my hands, where I was picking at my cuticles.

"I wouldn't care if you were from homeless people. You work hard for what you have and I love that about you. You make me smile and laugh. I love you because you never make it easy, you always give me a hard time." He lifted my chin, in his cupped hand. "I love you because you are you. You are honest, wholesome, beautiful, loyal and vivacious. Although, I am a little concerned about why you've been so sick lately."

Damn, I guess it was time to come clean. I took a deep breath. "Listen, there's something I need to tell you." I got up and went for my wallet in my handbag.

"You are sick, aren't you? Why didn't you tell me? What's wrong?"

After another deep breath, I took the sonogram picture out of the wallet and held it to my chest as I walked back over to him.

"I'm not sick like you think... Oh God, I didn't think this would be so hard." I started to panic, rethinking whether I should tell him now. I could feel the pit growing in my stomach.

"Whatever it is, you can tell me Leila."

"So remember last weekend I told you to grab the tampons because I would be starting my period anytime." I looked at him and he started leaning back into the couch. I think he knew what I was getting ready to say, which totally freaked me out even more.

"I still hadn't started on Wednesday and I got sick at work a couple of times. Barb, of course, saw me and made me take a test." The awkward silence was deafening. I sat up and pulled the picture from my chest and held it out to him.

"I'm pregnant Brody."

He took the sonogram picture and looked at it, but said nothing. He was dead silent.

"The doctor estimates I'm about nine weeks, maybe closer to ten."

"You've already been to a doctor, but you're just now telling me?" He did not look pleased. Anger was radiating off of him in waves. "What the fuck Leila? When were you going to tell me?"

"This weekend. I wanted to tell you tonight, once we were home." I took the ultrasound back from him. I was scared he was going to rip it up, he was so upset.

"It's not like I planned to get pregnant Brody. For Christ's sake, I even warned you we needed to be careful. Now you're pissed that I'm pregnant."

He stood and paced around the room, stopping to ask, "And just what do you plan on doing?"

Come again? What? What in the fuck did he just ask me? Lioness's hair stood up from hackles to haunches. "What do you mean, what am I gonna do? Please don't tell me you're asking if I'm gonna have an abortion." I narrowed my eyes at him.

"I'm asking what you are planning on doing. Having this kid, aborting, giving it up for adoption?" He stopped in front of me.

I had never been on the receiving end of a heated conversation with Brody. Sure, I had heard them when he was discussing business, but never directed at me. I still was dumbfounded by the fact he actually didn't know me well enough to know what I was going to do. I was shocked I didn't know him well enough to know his reaction would be so livid.

"Answer me goddamn it," he yelled, almost directly in my face, and threw his bottle of beer at the wall. It shattered and sent shards of brown glass flying all around us.

On sheer instincts, I raised my hand and slapped him across his right cheek, as the tears poured down my face. "Fuck you, Brody."

Before he could respond, I ran from the living room to the bedroom, locked the door and started gathering all of my stuff. I laid the expensive dress out on the bed along with the gorgeous shoes beside it. I took his mother's priceless sapphire and diamond necklace off and placed it on the dresser in the closet. My sobs racked my body and my vision blurred. I had to stop several times to wipe my eyes so I could see.

I pulled out my phone and sent Jaxon a text message. I had no other choice. There was no chance on God's green earth I was staying in this house with Brody. Not acting like the fucking asshat he was.

Jax, can u pls pick me up? I need a ride to JFK.

I sent the text and started looking for a flight home. Before I could even get my browser to US Airways's webpage my phone chimed.

Tell me where ur @ baby girl & I'll b there in mins. R u ok?

I sent him the address and told him I was okay, that I'd explain once he was here. He replied he'd be here in four to five minutes and to wait with the doorman. I grabbed a handful of tissues, shoved them in my duffle and unlocked the door to go downstairs.

I reached the living room and it was eerily quiet. I looked around, but Brody was nowhere to be found. I took a piece of paper off the printer in the study and left him a note, telling him I was going home. Earlier, I had hoped maybe he would come around once he settled down and let it sink in. Apparently not.

I set the sonogram picture on top of the note on the coffee table. I thought maybe if he kept looking at it he would realize that it was our baby. The baby we made together, even though it wasn't planned. Maybe he would remember we loved each other and that babies were miracles. But, until he calmed down I didn't want to see him. I had never been afraid of him before but in that moment when he lost it, I was.

He screamed in my face, knowing I was carrying his son or daughter inside of me. He was cold and cruel and I wanted no part of that.

I grabbed my purse and overnight bag, took one last look around. Seeing the broken glass still littering the living room solidified my decision to leave. I walked over to the foyer and pressed the button for the elevator. I had to wait a few minutes for it to ascend from the lower floors.

My heart was annihilated just like the broken beer bottle. He shattered me just the same. The worst part was I still loved him. I just stood there and stared at the beautiful penthouse until I heard the ding of the elevator.

"Goodbye Brody. I love you," I whispered to no one as the elevator doors closed in front of me.

As I walked through the lobby of the building, I looked to my left and saw him sitting at the bar. He seemed to sense me and looked up from his glass of scotch. Our eyes met and I could still see the anger, but for a split second I could see something else. Maybe sadness or guilt.

I wasn't sure and I certainly wasn't going to ask him. I stood there looking at him, red faced and crying. He had to have seen my bags, but he never moved. I knew right then I had made my decision and he had made his.

I only hoped he would change his mind and remember that we loved each other. I didn't want to raise our baby alone.

LEI AND BRODY'S STORY

CONTINUES IN

PULLED,

COMING IN FALL 2015!

ABOUT THE AUTHOR

A.F. Crowell's love of books did not start until her husband forced her to watch *Twilight* one weekend when they were snowed in. From there her love only grew. Contemporary romance, paranormal, YA, and dystopian are her preferred reads, but she also loves Patricia Cornwell novels. *Pushed* is her debut and the first book in the Torn Series. It will be followed by *Pulled*, book two, and *Torn*, book three.

Crowell lives in Charleston, SC, with her husband and also her two boys, who at seven and eleven share her love of reading. The family has two dogs, Diesel, a German Shepherd rescue, and Dez, a black Labrador Retriever.

200

Did you enjoy this book? Drop us a line and say so! We love to hear from readers, and so do our authors. To connect, visit www.boroughspublishinggroup.com online, send comments directly to info@boroughspublishinggroup.com, or friend us on Facebook and Twitter. And be sure to check back regularly for contests and new releases in your favorite subgenres of romance!

Are you an aspiring writer? Check out www.boroughspublishinggroup.com/submit and see if we can help you make your dreams come true.

Made in the USA
San Bernardino, CA
25 June 2016